Hopatcong
Vision Quest

Steve Lindahl

Solstice Publishing - www.solsticepublishing.com

Hopatcong Vision Quest
Steve Lindahl

Dedication

I dedicate this novel to its setting, Lake Hopatcong—the magical place where I spent the summers of my youth with my family, my lifelong friends, and the love of my life, my wife, Toni.

Chapter One
Lori

Time slowed while the overturned tractor-trailer spun toward Gary's car. The trailer slid on its side, wheels spinning in the air, soaring straight at him, skidding across the pavement like a rolling boulder. Gary's eyes froze on the huge, steel load until the mass hit, startling Lori from her nightmare.

She sat up in bed, inhaled a deep breath, then stood, her nightgown so drenched in sweat she needed to change. She stretched, paced for a few minutes, then moved to her bathroom where she swallowed an Ambien. Whenever Lori dreamed of the accident, her dream was always a nightmare and always the same graphic, painful experience.

But each time Lori imagined the accident while she was awake, she didn't think of the pain. Instead, she wondered what went through her husband's mind. Did her image come to him just before he died, perhaps in the light spring nightgown that had once been his favorite? Did he picture her holding Diane when their child was a newborn? Were his wife and daughter in his heart, thought of as two gifts from God fixed in time? Or were Gary's last thoughts of that other woman?

***

Lori found it easier to cope when her twenty-seven year old daughter, Diane, was with her. But today Diane was at her apartment in Caldwell and Lori was turning to wine to help her forget. She was sipping her fourth glass of

Cabernet Sauvignon, which had as much to do with the way her world was spinning as the grief did.

It was a cool day in late September. Lori wore a flannel shirt and an old pair of jeans, work clothes once belonging to her husband. She intended to restart her garden. The good days had passed for the peppers, eggplants, and tomatoes, so now it was time to make a fall planting. She would put in radishes, cabbage, and broccoli, vegetables that thrived in the cooler weather.

Her home was on the shore of Lake Hopatcong in New Jersey on a peninsula named Prospect Point and her garden was a small plot beside the seawall. The New Jersey soil and abundant water from the lake provided a perfect place to plant. The garden was generally productive and she was sure it would be again, even if planted while she was dizzy.

Lori swallowed a mouthful of wine then got down on her knees. At fifty-six years old, standing and bending flared her arthritis and reminded her she was aging like her withered plants. The world was more stable when she was on all fours. She laughed at that, although she wasn't sure why.

She wrapped her fingers around the stalk of a tomato plant that had been good to her for the last couple of months. She pulled and the stalk broke off. She knew from experience that the plant's roots were at least a foot deep, and would best be dug up with a shovel. She dug with her fingers anyway, because she liked the feel of topsoil on her bare hands.

She wished she, like this garden, could get a fresh start. She sniffed then wiped her wet eyes and nose on the sleeve of her shirt, or rather Gary's shirt. She held her face against her arm and breathed in the damp flannel odor that smelled like her husband. Four months had passed since the accident. She should have learned to deal with those emotions by now, but here she was, crying again.

Lori felt a hand on her shoulder, then another grabbing the cloth of her shirt. She turned to see who was holding her, but her eyes couldn't focus. They were filled with tears and the world was still spinning.

Whoever had grabbed her was pushing now, to the seawall and over into the lake.

The cold water brought Lori back to her senses. She hadn't caught a breath. The water was only four feet deep. She struggled to stand, but someone was holding her down, keeping her head underwater. Her eyes were open and the lake was clear. She saw the lower part of the seawall and rocks, waterlogged sticks, and mucky leaves on the bottom.

Her lungs hurt too much. She couldn't hold her breath even a minute. She gasped and choked. The world swirled then went dark.

***

Beth

Beth Jensen read about the death of Lori Larimer two days after it happened. She didn't know the woman, but took note of a drowning the way all lake people do. The Jensen home was across the lake from Prospect Point, yet she couldn't see the Larimer house from her dock. It was on the opposite side of the point near the little community beach. The article in *The Daily Record* said Ms. Larimer's body had washed up near a dock on Raccoon Island. Martha Getty, a close friend of the victim, owned the island property. Beth realized she had met Martha, who worked at the vitamin store on Route 15.

She put down the paper when she finished her coffee and went to the hamper in the bathroom to collect the laundry. There were plenty of opportunities to get chores done now that Maya had returned to school. Beth had appreciated the time alone for a few days, but the school year had begun more than two weeks earlier. She was happy that afternoon when her daughter's bus arrived.

"Hi," Maya yelled as she closed the door. Beth came into the living room to see her daughter. Maya was nine, in fourth grade, and nearly five feet tall. She had a broad, playful smile with a crooked tooth on the right side of her mouth. Her shoulder length, straight hair was light blond, but would darken when the weather turned cold. Beth was still having trouble thinking of her child as old enough to ride the bus to school, yet Ryan insisted driving her would be overprotective.

"You hungry?" Beth asked.

"Sure." Maya dropped her backpack on the floor rather than carrying it upstairs to her room, but Beth didn't scold her.

"We've got muffins if you want one, blueberry or apple, and a glass of milk. Sound good?"

"I like blueberry."

While they enjoyed their snack, Maya explained the memory jar project her class was working on. The children were supposed to bring in jars containing small items they'd collected from places they'd visited over the summer. It would have been helpful to know about the project before the summer began, but if a note had been sent home, Beth hadn't seen it. Still, having a home on the lake would make it easier. Most of their memories had come from their own yard, dock, and boats. They could collect pebbles from the lake bottom or take the bobber off the floating keychain they used for the boat key. They could also scavenge the yard for duck feathers, a bird's nest, or something else of interest.

"Can we play outside?" Maya asked.

Beth was in the mood for one of Maya's games and decided they could collect memory items on the weekend. "Do you want to play hide and seek?" she asked.

"Oh yes, Mommy."

Beth had wondered when Maya would outgrow hide and seek. They'd been sharing the activity since she was in preschool, but even in fourth grade, Maya still loved finding places to hide from her mother.

Once they were outside, Maya declared she would hide and her mom would seek, so Beth stayed on the patio, sat in a chair, and began counting to one hundred.

The house had two yards, one on the lakeside and one on the roadside. The game was starting near the lake, but the rules allowed them to circle the house. The dock and the boats had been off limits when Maya was very young, but at nine, she swam well enough to risk falling in the water.

Beth generally approached the game with enthusiasm, often getting dirty as she lay on her belly behind their shrubs or covered herself with leaves near the shed. She tried to win. The game wouldn't have been fun for either of them if she hadn't. Besides, part of the charm of hide and seek was that Maya's size gave her an advantage.

This time, however, Beth's mind was on the memory jar project. After she stopped counting and started looking for her daughter, she kept an eye open for interesting objects that might fit. She could clip leaves or blossoms from the plants around the house, then press them and iron them into wax paper. Of course, the project was supposed to be Maya's and her teacher would know Beth had helped with the ironing. Maybe a bad idea.

There were plenty of interesting things in Ryan's boat; items like tie ropes and life preservers, but none were small enough to fit in a jar. She looked down at the dock and noticed the boat's cover was loose on the dock side.

Maya wasn't supposed to play in the boat. Ryan had said he was concerned about her safety, but Beth thought it had more to do with the possibility Maya could damage something. The bass boat was Ryan's toy and he could be possessive about it. Beth sighed. Sometimes he acted more like Maya's brother than her father. Still, playing in the boat was against the rules.

Beth walked in the direction of the dock until she heard something behind her. She spun around, but didn't see anyone. Perhaps Maya wasn't in the boat. Maybe she had just undone a few snaps along the side of the cover to throw Beth off her trail. Beth turned back toward the lake and stepped onto the dock.

She moved as softly as she could, but one of the wood planks creaked. When Beth reached the boat, she got down on her knees and lifted the cover. The top half of her daughter's body was positioned under the steering column with her little legs sticking out like two angled flagpoles flying Mary Jane shoes. Hiding like an ostrich, Beth thought.

This was too sweet for Beth to bring to a close, so instead of telling Maya she'd been found, Beth continued the search. She let the side of the cover fall down and poked at the cover on either side of the windshield.

She wanted to get close to her daughter, but not close enough to touch her. Ryan would be so irritated if he saw her doing this. He'd say she was encouraging Maya's misbehavior. But she didn't see any harm, as long as they didn't hurt anything in the boat or damage the cover. She crawled backwards a foot or so, then started to stand when she heard the dock board creak again.

Beth tried to turn, but before she could move, someone jumped at her and pushed her head down between the dock and the boat. What the Hell? she thought. Who? The boat banged against the dock, smashing her skull. She felt intense pain and started to scream, but muffled her cry, thinking of Maya hiding under the boat cover, hoping her daughter would stay out of sight. They'd taught her to stay hidden if someone broke into their house. Maybe she would...

The boat bashed her head against the dock again, causing more sharp pain. Someone was holding her down, but there was someone else there, pulling the boat back each time, forcing it against her head like a massive sledgehammer.

Beth's life flashed in her head: memories of Maya as a two year old splashing about in a plastic pool on the yard in front of the lake, Ryan kissing her gently when she lay in the hospital bed hours after Maya's birth, and the first night she'd spent with her husband in their Lake Hopatcong home.

The boat rammed against her a third time, then she was pushed head first into the water between the boat and the dock. Her lungs filled with liquid and she choked until everything stopped.

***

Ryan

On the day of his wife's death, Ryan had been installing kitchen cabinets in a small home in Sparta. After he finished, he called his shop to speak with Heather Cox, the drafter who had been working for him for more than five years. He heard enough rings to know his call had forwarded to her cell, which generally meant she was in the shop with Martin Malek, a cabinetmaker and Ryan's only other employee. When she picked up, he told her he planned to take the rest of the day off. She said she would see him tomorrow and promised to lock up at five. He drove home, but Beth and Maya weren't in the house when he arrived.

Ryan looked out back, hoping to find his wife and child and was irritated when he noticed the cover on his boat flapping in the light breeze. He had told Beth to keep their hide and seek games away from his fishing boat. He kept stuff in it, stuff he wouldn't want damaged. Maya was a good girl, but she could break the rules when she wanted to. He stepped toward the dock.

It seemed strange they were both missing. One could be hiding under the cover, but the other had to be searching. His stomach tightened. Something might be wrong. He picked up the pace, not running, but walking faster.

Ryan froze as soon as he saw Beth's leg. His wife was face down in the water with her left tennis shoe caught between two ropes attached to one of the boat bumpers, her foot still in the shoe.

All of her body except for her left leg was under water with her head straight down. He untied the back rope, freed her foot from the bumper, then held her body up while he pushed the boat away to gain space. The dock seemed to swirl as he worked. He could feel his heart pumping, yet didn't stop to regain his senses. Any hope he had of saving Beth depended on how quickly he could work. When he pulled her up on the dock, he scraped her body against the edge of the wood. His instinct told him not to hurt her, but he knew to ignore the feeling. Only time mattered now.

Beth wore one of his oversized white T-shirts, which stuck to her bra and body like a second skin. She also wore denim shorts and her tennis shoes, one wet and one dry.

He rolled her to her back, then straightened her legs and arms. There were wounds on her face bleeding the color of dark wine, but only slightly. They were mostly clean from the lake water. He opened her mouth and reached in with his fingers to be certain her tongue hadn't slipped down her throat. When he could tell her air passage was clear, he leaned in and blew into her mouth. He pulled away, sucked in another deep breath, then blew again. He repeated this action five times then sat up and pressed both hands against Beth's chest five times. She didn't respond, so he started the mouth to mouth again. He kept repeating his attempts.

Too exhausted to go on, he sat up, leaned back, and stared at his wife's body. Ryan's spirit had been sucked clean the way a beach is emptied of water in the moments before a tsunami. Then the wave hit. He gasped for air in spurts. His voice finally came out in short high-pitched moans, like the squeal of an injured animal.

He reached in his pocket for his phone, dialed 911, and let it drop to the dock. He heard a woman answer. He heard her call out, asking the nature of the emergency, but he couldn't speak. He leaned forward and shook his wife's wet, bloody body as he cried and begged her to be alive. He could smell her damp hair. Her wet skin seemed to shine.

Maya? Ryan thought as he looked at the boat, still attached to the dock by a single rope. He scrambled to the edge and pulled the boat in. He lifted the cover and saw her on the floor, shaking like a dog in a thunderstorm.

Ryan picked up his phone. When he tried to speak, he choked on his words, but sucked in a deep breath and tried again. "My wife and daughter have been hurt! My wife, I think she's…." His voice trailed off. He couldn't say the word *dead*, but again he forced the important words out. "We need an ambulance. Please help us! Please!"

***

Maya stayed at Dover General for two days. The doctors couldn't find anything wrong with her physically, but Dr. Kari Montero, a child psychiatrist, spoke with her three separate times. She told Ryan his daughter had dissociative disorder, a fancy way of saying she'd forgotten the entire day of her mother's death.

The memory lapse didn't help when the police interviewed the child, but after they spoke with Ryan, they declared the event an accident. They theorized that Beth had slipped while looking for Maya, trapping Beth between the dock and the boat. They said a wave must have jammed the boat against her, knocking her unconscious and causing her to slip into the lake headfirst. She didn't die from the injury to her head. She drowned.

Ryan stayed with his daughter, sleeping sporadically in a chair beside her bed. He stepped out of the hospital only once, when he arranged for a funeral home to pick up Beth's body.

Beth's parents came to the room to see their granddaughter. Her mother, normally a self-confident, friendly, and talkative woman, trembled and barely spoke. Ryan convinced Beth's father that Maya would be all right and he should take Beth's mother home to rest. They didn't return the next day.

Heather came by to let him know she had taken care of his work obligations by calling people and explaining the situation. She had also checked on his house, closing the windows and locking the doors. She offered to help in any other way she could.

Although Heather and Ryan's in-laws were the only visitors, there were more than a dozen calls from friends. These included his own parents who were in Florida for a couple of weeks, visiting his younger brother's family. His mom told him they would change their flight schedule and be home for Beth's service.

The house felt empty when Ryan brought Maya home. Everything inside from the throw rugs on the tile floors to the wood grain walls reminded him of Beth. He had done the work himself, but Beth had made the choices. She fell in love with the house when they first saw it, the open interior, and the huge windows that blurred the edge between inside and outside. She convinced him the house, with work, would be perfect.

Ryan crossed immediately to the patio door and looked out at the lake. He had come home often to find her standing there, staring out at the water. He shook his head and looked up at the ceiling, trying to keep the tears from flowing. He had to be strong for Maya, who walked straight through the great room and headed up the stairs. He couldn't blame her for wanting to be alone with her emotions. He did as well.

The house felt stuffy. He opened the patio door, leaving the screen door closed, then moved to the kitchen to open a window. When Ryan passed the kitchen table, he noticed the paper Beth had been reading the day she died, open to a story about another woman's death. The subject surprised him. In such a small community, two drownings so close to each other were unusual.

Ryan put the newspaper down and headed toward the stairs and Maya's room. He'd given his daughter a few minutes to settle, but he didn't want to leave her alone too long. Maya had to feel the same wrenching sadness he felt knowing Beth would never be in the house again.

Ryan knocked on Maya's door. "Are you OK in there?"

"I'm all right." Her words were good, but her voice shaky. He could hear her trying to convince herself.

"What would you like for dinner?" he asked. Ryan wanted to get back into a routine, to let Maya know life would be going on. "I can fix your favorite—hot dogs with macaroni and cheese. Does that sound good?"

"Sounds all right."

Maya spoke so softly Ryan almost couldn't hear her reply. He needed to carry her through her depression even though he felt incapacitated by his own grief. He went into his daughter's room and put his arms around her. She returned the hug.

"I'll do the cooking if you make the salad. Is that a deal?" he asked.

She answered by holding him tighter.

"We can work as a team and get things done. Your mom would want that."

By this time, Maya was crying hard enough for him to feel her shaking. He stroked her hair while she buried her face in his neck. She said, "I miss Mommy."

"I know you do, honey. I do, too."

The dinner preparations started well. Ryan put a couple of pots on the stove, one for the macaroni and a smaller one for the hot dogs. He turned on the burners to boil the water. While he waited, he took lettuce, a tomato, and a carrot out of the refrigerator and placed them on the counter. Maya had the difficult task of cutting up the vegetables. Perhaps too much for a nine year old child? But Beth had always let their daughter do this job and he wasn't about to change the routine.

Everything went well until Maya took the tomato to the sink to wash it. She started to stare at the water rushing over the red object in her hand and seemed to freeze in that position.

"What's wrong?" Ryan asked. He looked at her fingers to see if she'd cut herself. There was no blood.

"I had dreams," Maya said, still staring at the water.

"Of course you did," he told her. "So do I, sometimes. But Mommy's in heaven. That's a beautiful place. We'll see Mommy someday and we should dream of that wonderful time when we're all together again."

Dr. Montero expressed concern about her memory loss, but Ryan worried more about the memories returning. He would give anything to forget, even for a brief moment.

"I didn't dream about Mommy," Maya told him. "I dreamed about a waterfall with a lady standing in the water at the bottom."

Her father put his hands on her shoulders and turned her, so she could see him. He asked, "What did she look like?"

"She had long black hair. I remember she was wearing something that looked like a white robe."

"Like Mommy's"

"No."

"Can you tell me anything else?"

"She had a band on her head with a red jewel that hung down over her nose. She also had another little necklace in her hand. She was holding it out—like she was handing it to me." Maya hesitated. "I didn't take it."

Ryan worried about any dream of a woman in water, but he tried to hide what he felt by saying, "When you lie in bed at night think of good things. Think of peaceful things." He wanted to say: *Try not to think of your mother*, but he couldn't get the words out right.

Chapter Two
Diane

$\mathcal{D}$iane waited for the sun to set before she left the house. She walked down to the water's edge, sat on the seawall beside her mother's garden, and looked out over the lake. The calm of the water during the twilight hour helped her deal with the constant sadness she'd felt since her mother's death.

She wore an oversized blue blouse and a pair of short denim cutoffs, cut high enough for the white pockets to hang out at the bottom. She had tied her blond hair in a ponytail that reached below her shoulders. Her feet and legs were bare. She shifted out of her cross-legged position and dipped them in the water, high for this late in the season and warm. She swirled her right leg in a small circular motion, creating tiny spreading waves. Some ripples touched the seawall while others headed out toward the center of the lake. The further they traveled from her the more they diminished. Like the ripples, Diane believed she would become less and less alive as she pushed through life without the person she loved most.

What really happened with Mom? she asked herself. Was her death another accident like Dad's? Or did she kill herself? The police tested her blood and said the alcohol content was high. Could her weakness for alcohol have led to her death? Or was her drinking the first step toward suicide?

The setting sun left the island across the lake in shadow, making the homes and docks indistinguishable from the trees. The sky was a darker blue than it had been ten minutes earlier and its color reflected throughout the water. The few boats on the lake had their lights turned on. They moved slowly because lake laws allowed no wake after dark. It was a peaceful, mellow time of the day, but peace was not coming to Diane. She pulled her legs out of the water and turned back to look at the garden in the light of the moon.

Her mother, Lori, had been pulling tomato plants, breaking their stalks and tossing them to the side of the garden. Diane wondered what she had been up to. Perhaps she was depressed and taking her feelings out on the plants. But she hadn't stomped on them or tore at them randomly. What she'd done seemed organized. She'd piled the stalks neatly beside the garden. It seemed early for the end of the season clearing, but not unreasonably so. In any case, the way she had been working seemed to conflict with the idea she might have killed herself intentionally.

The police believed Diane's mother had fallen in the lake and drowned because she was drunk. Yet the water at the seawall wasn't deep. If she wasn't able to swim, she could have just stood. The argument she was too drunk to stand didn't make sense. Diane had never known her mother to drink enough to be incapacitated and falling in the water should have sobered her enough to survive.

Lori had worked the same small square of land for years, replenishing the nutrients annually with compost. She had started with flowers, impatiens, and begonias among others. After a couple of seasons, she had switched to vegetables. She often said she expressed her love through the entire process of feeding her family: planting, tending the garden, harvesting, cooking, and serving meals everyone could enjoy.

My family is gone forever, Diane told herself. She used the back of her wrist to rub away the tears starting to run down her cheeks and stared at the dirt in the garden.

A thumb size stone lay in the garden, large enough to see in the moon light. She had to shift her head back and forth to see it through the vines. Diane's mother had been a meticulous gardener and had carefully removed any stone larger than a pencil eraser from the topsoil, so someone or some animal must have knocked this one into the garden after she had died.

Although parts of the plot had been cleared, thick vines were still growing in this section. Diane would need to get dirty to look any closer. She stepped into the garden, bent down, and tried to pick up the small stone, larger than it had first appeared, but not by much. She had just dug her fingers into the rich top soil surrounding the rock when she heard a voice. She jumped, breathing heavily.

Her mom's best friend, Martha, stood beside the garden. "You startled me," Diane said.

"I'm sorry. I was hoping you would be here—to find out if there's anything I can do to help."

"Thanks, Martha. I've gone through most of Mom's stuff. She was good about throwing things away she didn't need, but there's still work to do." Martha had always seemed much older than Diane's mom, although their actual difference was only five years and a few months. The thick, gray hair Martha kept in a long braid aged her and her skin hung loose on her neck. It was clear she had spent much of her life outdoors.

"You're working in the garden at this hour?" Martha asked.

Diane looked down. Her hands were filthy, but she had the stone. She tossed it in the lake. "I saw that rock and thought how Mom wouldn't have wanted it there. She was a fanatic when it came to this garden."

"It's good you remember her, but you don't have to do everything you think she would have done."

"I don't. It just bothered me to see something in the soil that wouldn't have been there if she was alive."

"Bothered you?"

"Yeah. Maybe it's because I believe there was more to her death than what the police say." Diane stood, then stepped out of the garden. "The medical examiner said her body had bruises. They didn't occur after she died, so the theory is they happened when she fell into the water. I don't believe that—maybe one or two, but she had lots of bruises. I think someone else was involved."

"Did you mention your ideas to the police?"

"I called them and talked it over with the man who answered the phone, whoever he was. Then an officer came out here. I showed him how shallow the water is where Mom fell in and told him she never drank more than she could handle. He looked at me as if he thought I was too emotional, like I was someone he should pity, but *never* listen to. He said he knew I wanted to blame someone, but sometimes accidents happen. He'd seen cases like this before and wished there was something he could say to make them easier to understand. But he couldn't. Then he said, life can be horrible. I suppose he was trying to be nice, but he just seemed condescending, which annoyed me more than if he'd yelled at me." She paused for a moment, then added, "I don't believe he would have treated a man that way."

"And that surprised you?" Martha said, as they walked toward the house.

***

Ryan

Maya didn't mention any more nightmares—with or without water. Ryan, however, had a dream every night, a brutal, repeating image of Beth's foot tangled in the bumper rope.

He tried to deal with his problem by concentrating on good moments he'd shared with his wife. He hoped pleasant thoughts would sweeten his nights. Eventually they did, but not in the way he had expected. Winter came and went. When a new spring arrived, he began to dream of touching a hand, or burying his face in thick, sweet smelling hair, or listening to the lilt of a woman's voice. The problem was the woman wasn't Beth and he didn't want to think about someone else. He still loved his wife.

Ryan started to believe he needed help more than his daughter did, but he couldn't afford two psychiatrists. Instead, he tried to deal with his problem on his own. He kept reminding himself of Beth by putting pictures of her near his bed. He picked the best old shots and had prints made. He also bought a digital frame so he could load a sequence to carry him through memories while he drifted to sleep.

Nothing worked. The dream woman had dark hair, like Beth's, but much longer, reaching five inches below her shoulder. Beth's hair had been short, almost as short as his. Both women had dark eyes, but the other lady's eyes were more oval than Beth's and gave her a dark, worried appearance, worlds apart from Beth's hopeful gaze. In one dream the woman was dressed in a long, tan skirt, a loose top decorated with beads, and a multicolored, woven shawl. She walked away from him and Ryan learned he didn't want her to go any more than he had wanted Beth to go.

One night in July, more than eleven months after the tragedy had changed his life so radically, Ryan dreamed of the woman again. For the first time they had been naked, in a wooded area by a pond. Ryan and the woman had been swimming and were now warming themselves by a fire they'd built.

She came up behind him while he was feeding the fire with pieces of a branch he had cut. She wrapped her arms around his waist, leaned in, and kissed his neck. Her body felt warm against his, like the flames. She whispered, "Ehoalan," a word he understood to mean "beloved," then pushed against his body with her hips. His mind began to swirl so violently he awoke.

Ryan shook and breathed hard. He sat up on the bed, trying to collect his thoughts. He recognized the word she had spoken as a language he shouldn't have been able to understand. Yet he had known its meaning while dreaming. And although it had seemed natural she would call him beloved while he was dreaming, once awake he couldn't understand their intimacy. He didn't remember ever meeting anyone who looked like her. Where had she come from and why wasn't she in his dreams before his wife died? Had she been waiting? He felt drawn to her the way he had once been drawn to Beth. There had been guilt in the feeling, but it had faded when the dreams persisted over the winter.

If he stayed in bed, he knew he would be awake for hours. Instead, he went to the kitchen for an Advil. The pain pill would help him relax and, hopefully, get back to sleep. When he left his room, he glanced at Maya's door and saw it was open. That's odd, he thought.

A feeling of déjà vu swept over Ryan, almost causing him to stumble. He stopped for a moment and breathed. He knew the horrible sensation before he had any inclination of what he was reliving. He recognized the unease he had felt while walking to the boat on the day Beth died, a tightening in his stomach that told him something was wrong. "Oh my God!" he cried out, running down the hall to Maya's room. He swung the door open and stared at his daughter's bed. The sheets and blankets were thrown back in a pile. She was not on the bed or anywhere else in the room.

He ran out of the room toward the bathroom. The open door revealed an empty room, but he went inside. He turned around after a quick glance and headed for the stairs. Maya might have gone to the kitchen to grab a snack, although it would be totally out of character for her to do so. Disappearing in the middle of the night was also out of character, he thought, and she'd done that.

Ryan saw the open front door as soon as he reached the bottom of the stairs. A full moon provided plenty of light as he ran across his yard toward the waterfront. It also provided enough light for him to see a pile of clothes before he stepped on the dock. The green nightgown Maya had worn to bed lay in front of him, crumpled on one of the dock chairs with a pair of white and blue, flowered panties.

"God!" he yelled. At first, he thought Maya had fallen in, but the idea didn't make sense. People who fell into the lake didn't stop to take off their clothes.

He looked at his black fishing boat, tied beside the dock, uncovered. She wasn't in it this time, so he turned his attention to the lake. He saw a dark spot on the water more than twenty yards out. If Ryan hadn't known his daughter was missing, he might have thought her small head was a muskrat. She was swimming, gliding through the water like a tiny boat.

"Get back here now!" Ryan shouted. Maya didn't answer or even turn in his direction. He started to pull his shirt off, then stopped.

It's faster in the boat, he thought.

Ryan untied the ropes and jumped in. The engine started with the first turn. He had to back up slowly, but hit the throttle and spun the boat when he was clear of the dock. It took seconds to reach Maya, who was swimming toward the middle of the lake.

"Maya! What are you doing?"

His daughter kept swimming without turning her head.

Ryan circled the girl and approached slowly. He shut the engine and coasted by her while holding out the paddle, but since Maya didn't grab it, he couldn't pull her in.

Ryan tried a second time, steering closer. As the boat coasted again, he jumped away from the wheel. This time he grabbed her arm, but Maya squirmed and kept swimming. Her wet skin was slippery.

Ryan circled for a third try and grabbed a handful of Maya's hair. She gasped, sucked in water, and started to choke. "Daddy!" she shouted when she caught her breath. "What are you doing?"

"I'm saving you from drowning!" he yelled back.

"How did I get here?" She was treading water, trying to keep her head up.

"I have no idea, but I'm pulling you out!"

Ryan grabbed Maya's arms. He pulled her up the side and into the boat head-first. She ended up on the floor, naked and shivering. She'd grown taller recently, but still had a thin, child's body. Ryan grabbed a towel and wrapped it around her.

"What were you thinking?" he asked.

"I was in the house, lying in bed," she sobbed, "then all at once I was out here and you were pulling me into the boat. My hair hurts." She pulled the towel tight around her and stared at the floor of the boat.

"You have no idea how you ended up in the middle of the lake?"

"Nooo," she wailed. She gulped in air before adding, "I was in bed then I was here. What's happening to me?"

When they pulled toward the dock, Ryan cut the engine. He grabbed hold as the boat coasted into place then hopped out. He tied the boat in the front and back while Maya sat there. She was shivering, tears running down her cheeks. He went to the chair for her clothes and handed them to her. He helped her stand, hugged her briefly, then kissed her forehead and helped her out of the boat.

"Everything is all right now," he said. "You're safe. I won't let anything hurt you."

***

When Maya was back in her room, Ryan became concerned she would sleepwalk again. He secured the deadlocks on the doors to the front yard, to the back yard, and to the garage, taking the keys with him. He went to his own room, but instead of lying down, he sat on his bed, listening for sounds from his daughter. He stayed there for more than an hour until exhaustion got the better of him.

He wasn't sure how long he slept when he woke from another vivid dream. The dark haired woman had returned. This time he had greeted her with a name, Oota Dabun, which he knew meant Day Star. Her hair was braided, and she was again dressed in a two-piece buckskin dress with tassels on the hems of the skirt and the top. She used a strange word, Wtschitschank, and he had understood it as if she spoke his native language. It meant spirit.

He went to the hall to check on Maya and found her door closed. He opened it, went inside, and put two fingers by her face so he could feel her breath. Maya was fine. She was where she belonged and sleeping soundly. The peaceful scene reminded him of the years when Beth used to rock her in her arms at night. Just to be certain, he took his pillow and a blanket out of his bedroom and spent the rest of the night on the hall floor.

***

Maya

The room was too bright when Maya woke and glanced at her clock. It read ten after nine. "I slept late," she told herself. "That's nice." She rolled over to her belly, deciding to stay in bed as long as possible, but couldn't stop thinking about the afternoon games she used to play with her mom before everything became so bad. She rolled over again, then shifted her legs off the bed and sat up.

Memories of the weird night came rushing back. She'd been in the middle of the lake in the middle of the night with nothing on. Her dad had picked her out of the water, so embarrassing, she didn't see how she could face him again. Maybe she could sneak out and run away. Or maybe not. She had no idea where she would go. She fell back on the bed and covered her face with her pillow.

She figured she'd been sleepwalking, or maybe sleep-swimming was the right word. Normal kids didn't do those things. Dr. Kari could tell her if she was crazy, but she wasn't supposed to see the lady until Thursday, which seemed almost forever.

She had to pee, so she tossed the pillow and got up. There was no putting off this horrible day. When she was done in the bathroom, she went downstairs to face her father and the day got worse. Heather from her dad's work was sitting at the kitchen table like she belonged.

"Here's the little girl now," Heather told Maya's dad in her stupid singsong voice.

"Hi," Maya said, thinking how Heather had dull, zombie eyes.

"I heard you had quite an adventure last night."

He told her? Maya thought, looking at her dad. Why would he do that? She could feel her cheeks redden.

"Yes ma'am," she said aloud, not knowing what else to say. She stared at her bare feet.

Her dad reached out and took Maya's hand. "I called Dr. Montero. She wants to talk to you about last night. Heather came by to pick up some papers, so I can drive you to her office. Wasn't that nice of her?"

Maya nodded her head, but nice was not the word for Heather. Fake was a better term.

Heather was always popping up at strange times. Once she brought her ugly bathing suit, a pink thing she must have picked out of some garbage can. That day Maya and her dad had to sit on the dock watching her do stupid shallow dives, climbing back out time after time to do another. Her bathing suit bottom slid down so much her butt crack showed. Maya had thought she was funny, but her dad didn't laugh. He didn't even seem to notice. Then she cringed, because the memory of Heather's swim reminded her of her own the night before. At least Heather had something on, Maya thought.

"When do we go to Dr. Kari?" The doctor liked Maya using her first name, so that's what she did.

"You should eat breakfast first," Heather told her.

"I'm not hungry."

"Breakfast is the most important meal of the day. We've got Cheerios. Should I pour a bowl for you?"

Maya hated when Heather said things like we've, as if this was her house.

"I'll get my own," Maya told her, listening for Heather's reaction as she reached for the Lucky Charms. After she poured the cereal, Maya turned around to see the expression on Heather's face. As she spun about, something sharp cut her cheek.

"Ouch. You cut me!"

"Sorry," Heather said in a voice that sounded strained. "You moved faster than I expected."

"Why were you holding the knife up like that?" Maya's dad sounded more confused than angry. He held a napkin up to his daughter's cheek.

"I was reaching. It was an accident."

"It was careless. You could have put her eye out."

"You're right. I should have held it in my other hand. It won't happen again."

Maya's dad lifted the napkin to look at the wound. "It's just a scratch," he told his daughter. "It shouldn't scar.

I'll put a Band-Aid on it. Meanwhile, you have to get ready. Your appointment with Dr. Montero is at 11:00. Finish your breakfast quickly so we have time to get ready."

Chapter Three
Diane

"It's been a long time. You need to move on," Martha said one evening when Diane had come to her house for dinner. "Your mother would want you to. You shouldn't forget her, but you don't need to mourn forever. You're a young woman. You need to get out of the house and meet people."

"I'm not in mourning, I'm trying to get the justice Mom deserves. And I'll keep trying until I succeed."

"I know," Martha told her. "I wish I could help."

"We need to talk to Ryan Jensen. Maybe there was something odd about his wife's death, something that doesn't add up, like with my mom."

"What will you say?" Martha asked. "We need to come up with a way to approach him or he's going to think we're crazy."

Diane and Martha were at the dining room table in Martha's island home. Despite the numerous dings and scratches, and perhaps because of them, the table suited the small cabin. The house had a central room surrounded by three bedrooms, a bathroom, a kitchen, and a screened porch. The walls were knotty pine that had been stained cherry at least fifty years earlier. The mismatched furniture had all been purchased at yard sales, giving the place a warm and comfortable, rustic feel. The way Martha dressed, always in long skirts and peasant blouses, also seemed suited to the cabin.

"We'll say we're sorry for your loss," Diane replied.

"His wife died over a year ago."

"And that means we can't be sorry?"

"He'll want to know why we're contacting him now. We can't just jump in and start talking about murder. We need an excuse, so we can have time to bring the conversation around."

"His wife drowned, like Mom. If he shares any of my suspicions, he'll want to solve the crimes."

Diane looked out the open front door, through the porch, and across the lake at the place she now called home. She couldn't see details from such a distance, but she knew the spot where her mother had gone into the lake on the last day she was alive. After Martha had started coming around the house, Diane decided to give up the apartment in Caldwell and her job at Ann Taylor. She moved to the lake house and began to live off her inheritance. She had more time to think about the unanswered questions.

Martha touched Diane's hand, causing the younger woman to turn away from the view. "Ryan and his wife used to shop at the store. I haven't seen him since his wife died. Maybe that would be a reason to contact him."

"To sell him vitamins?"

"I can say I'm concerned because it's been so long since he was in the store. Then we could invite him and his daughter to dinner. It can be at your house, so he won't have to come to the island."

Diane rolled her eyes. "You don't think a dinner invitation from two women he barely knows will seem strange?"

Martha looked down and started to fiddle with a bear claw attached to a leather thong around her neck. The claw was half the size of her thumb and had a small hole bored in the root through which she had strung the leather. She claimed the claw had belonged to her great grandmother, her good luck charm. She also claimed it helped her think. Martha's ancestors were full-blooded Lenapes who had lived on the shores of Hopatcong.

"Have it your way. Dinner is out. But maybe the vitamin angle is not so bad. I can show up at his door and tell him I'm visiting customers I haven't seen for a while. If he thinks that's strange, it won't matter because we'll already be there. Hopefully, we can get a conversation rolling. Let's go now before we change our minds."

***

Martha rang the bell before Diane had climbed the porch steps. She had always been forceful once she made her mind up to do something, a trait Diane admired.

Ryan opened the door.

Diane recognized Ryan as someone she'd seen around the lake, although she couldn't remember where. He was an attractive man in his early to mid-thirties, a few inches taller than she was. He had thick, dark hair, cropped short, as well as kind, but tired, brown eyes.

"Martha?" he said, sounding surprised.

"You recognized me. I'm impressed. This is Diane, a friend of mine." Martha turned toward Diane as she made the introduction. "I'm visiting some of the customers I haven't seen in months. She offered to drive. I wanted to bring samples, to thank you for being a good customer in the past and to let you know we miss you at the store."

Ryan took the samples, saying, "I would invite you in, but it isn't a good time. I've got to get Maya to an appointment."

Diane felt a wave of panic. If they lost this opportunity, they might never talk to him about his wife's death. She made an impulsive decision to go back to plan B.

"How about dinner?" Diane blurted out. "Martha could talk to you then. I live across the lake on Prospect Point."

He paused for a moment as if he didn't know how to respond. "I have Maya with me."

"Bring her along. I can cook for four and Martha has really missed you. She told me so."

"Really?" Ryan asked, turning to Martha. "I always enjoyed chatting with you. But I thought I was just one of your customers."

"No such thing as *just* a customer."

A young woman appeared behind Ryan, tapping her foot and shaking her head like a horse at feeding time. The short woman had thin, blond hair hanging loosely over her shoulders, the way Diane wore her own. She had a strong, straight nose, but her most prominent feature was her frown. She didn't seem very happy with the unexpected visit.

Ryan looked over his shoulder at the woman. "We'll just be a moment, Heather." He turned his gaze to someone else inside the house as he opened the door wide. Diane could see his daughter. "Would you like to have dinner at Diane's? She lives across Brady's Bridge."

"You're asking a ten year old?" Heather said, rolling her eyes.

Diane noticed Maya's expression. She was staring at Martha's bear claw necklace and seemed surprised.

"Maya's old enough to know her own mind," Ryan told Heather.

"I want to go," Maya answered, smiling, as the small, blond woman kept shaking her head.

"Will tonight work for you?" Diane asked. "We could make it early, so it will still be light enough for a boat ride—if you want one." She wondered if Ryan's surprising openness to the dinner invitation had something to do with Heather's annoying behavior.

"Tonight's good."

"We'll eat around 5:00," Martha told him. "Try to come early. And keep those samples. I'll have more at Diane's.

**

Ryan

"What did you and Dr. Kari talk about?" Ryan asked. He and Maya were in his van, driving out of Dr. Montero's driveway onto Route 10. The doctor had a ranch style home with the section that had once been a garage converted into an office. There was a green waiting room, and a pink room where she held her sessions. Ryan had just spent an hour in the waiting area while Dr. Montero and Maya talked. After the session, he spoke briefly with the doctor. She handed him a prescription to renew Maya's medication.

When she had first prescribed the Valium, Dr. Montero had said to Ryan, "Sleepwalking occurs during the deepest stage of sleep. It's generally associated with other sleep issues and can often be treated with sleep aids."

His daughter's night swim had occurred months earlier and there hadn't been any similar incidents. Ryan wasn't certain he liked the doctor's decision to prescribe medication for something that could have been an isolated event. He wondered if he should get a second opinion.

"She was talking about the night I went swimming," Maya said. "Then she asked me if we were fighting, you and me."

"Did she?"

"I said things were good. I hope that was right."

"Honey, it's always right to tell her the truth. We weren't fighting, so that was good. But if there's anything that's bothering you, Dr. Kari needs to know about it."

Dr. Montero's question about fighting irritated Ryan, but he understood why she asked it. Maya had been dealing well with her mother's death, then the setback came out of nowhere. She seemed all right now, but was on drugs. The doctor had an obligation to look into the possibility Ryan had done something wrong.

"I haven't told her everything," Maya said.

"Oh?"

"I don't want her to think I'm crazy."

"Nobody thinks you're crazy. Lots of people sleepwalk and you had plenty of reasons, given all the bad things that have happened."

"Most kids don't wake up in the middle of the lake, even if they walk in their sleep."

"It doesn't mean you're crazy. What were the things you didn't tell her?"

Maya paused for a moment before saying, "I told her I didn't remember anything from the night I went swimming, but there was a dream I kinda remember. There was this lady calling to me. I tried not to listen, but she kept calling my name and telling me I needed to go to her. Was it bad not to tell Dr. Kari that?"

"It's good you told me now. Is this the woman you told me about before, the one who was standing under a waterfall?"

Maya twisted in her seat to look at her dad as he drove. "Yes, but this was a different dream. This time she was standing near the waterfall, but not in it. She was wearing a bear claw on a leather string like the old lady with the woman who invited us to dinner."

"Is she the reason you went in the lake?" Ryan asked.

"I don't know why I ended up in the water. I don't remember. But I was dreaming about that lady and she was calling me without speaking, like I could read her mind or something. See what I mean about this stuff sounding crazy. I'm scared."

"There's no reason to be afraid. If Dr. Montero can't help you, I'll find someone who can. No matter what we'll keep you safe. Remember that."

"I love you, Daddy."

Maya didn't toss the love word around often, so when she said it, Ryan's heart melted. But this time his thoughts were on another part of her story. Why had the woman in Maya's dream worn a necklace like the one Martha had been wearing?

He strained to think of Oota Dabun in his own dreams. In the one dream, she wasn't wearing anything, not even jewelry. But she might have had something around her neck in others. Unlike most dreams, the memories of her had stayed with him, but even with those lasting memories, he couldn't remember every detail.

Ryan gazed at the buildings they passed as they drove through Dover. There were old two-story homes mixed with small stores and other businesses: a tax preparer, a picture frame store and an auto body shop, all on their left. They passed a headquarters for the Army National Guard on their right.

He thought how Martha and her friend had arranged this dinner so Martha could talk about health supplements, but he was already planning to turn the conversation to the claw on her necklace. It's not going to be the night they're expecting, he told himself, glancing again at his daughter who was staring out the side window.

***

Diane

Two cooks working in the same kitchen would normally get in each other's way, but Martha and Diane didn't. The menu helped. Diane had exclusive use of the stove for the eggplant and spaghetti while Martha worked on the kitchen table, putting together the antipasto. They had to step around each other to reach the refrigerator and the utensil drawer, but they managed fine.

Ryan and Maya arrived ten minutes before five o'clock.

Martha was still dressed in her long skirt, peasant blouse, and bear claw on a leather necklace, the outfit she'd been wearing earlier, when they had knocked on Ryan's door.

Diane had changed her own outfit to a green sundress with a leaf pattern, thin and light enough to be halfway between a dress and a swimwear cover-up. It had an elegant feel to it. The dress had been a gift from her mom, too girly for Diane's taste. She had worn it only once and chose it this time because she wanted to impress Ryan. She thought the soft, feminine quality would do the trick. She was disappointed when he seemed more interested in what Martha was wearing.

"Is there something special about that necklace?" Ryan asked Martha after Diane had led them into her living room. "I first noticed it when I used to shop at your store, but never asked you about it. It's very unique."

"Bear claw jewelry is not unique among citizens of the tribe," she told him. "Modern generations tend to bring out their traditional jewelry once a year at the annual pow-wow. I'm more receptive to the old ways than others, so I wear it all the time. This claw has helped me through 62 years of life and I'm still going strong.

"I hope it doesn't bother you. A young woman at the store once chewed me out for over an hour, saying it was worse than wearing leather. I don't see it that way. This claw is about tradition and old ways that respect nature. Killing a bear was once a rite of passage for people who hunted to live."

"You have me intrigued."

"I'd like to show Maya the boathouse before we eat," Diane told Ryan and Martha. "Care to join us?"

"Sure," Martha answered. Ryan nodded in agreement.

Diane opened the lakeside door and nodded toward the patio. "There's wine on the table and a cooler with beer and soda beside it. You're welcome to grab a drink."

Maya ran toward the dock, while Ryan stopped to pour a glass of the Cabernet. Diane kept going so she could keep an eye on the young girl.

The sun hung low on the horizon and a cool breeze provided perfect weather for sitting on the dock.

"Can I go in?" Maya asked. She had hold of the door to the boathouse.

"Of course, but watch your step by the water. I don't want to have to pull you out."

The boathouse had a wonderful smell from the unique combination of wood and water under a roof. Sometimes the odor of gasoline from the boat's tank would mix in as well, but this day that smell was imperceptible. Small waves could still come in through the wide lake door, but since they were limited by the structure on all sides, the water was peaceful inside. And only indirect sunlight shone through the windows.

"Your boat is awesome," Maya said, looking at the red and white Bowrider.

"Thanks. It was my dad's. He enjoyed it for only two years. Before that we had a little aluminum rowboat with a small outboard motor. It got us where we needed to go, but wasn't comfortable."

"We have a boat, too, but it isn't red and you can't ride up front. I always wanted to ride up front."

"Well that's easy enough to arrange. We'll check with your dad. If it's OK with him, I'll take you out after dinner. There should be plenty of time before it's too dark. What color is your boat?"

"Black."

"Black's a wonderful color."

"I don't like it."

"But you should. Black goes with all other colors: green, blue, red, orange, pink, purple—any color at all. That makes it friendly, don't you think?"

"I guess so."

"You never told me you don't like black," Ryan said. He and Martha were standing in the doorway, looking in. Diane heard an element of surprise in his voice causing her to think he was upset. She wondered if his inflection was caused by the realization that he didn't know something as basic as his daughter's least favorite color or a sign of something more serious. His wife had died beside his boat. Diane knew from her own experience how the grief would always be brought back by certain places or objects. The triggers were different for everyone who had lost someone they loved.

"Black is a strong color," Diane told Maya, diverting her focus from Ryan's reaction. "I didn't like it when I was young, but I do now."

Martha leaned around Ryan, who was still standing in the doorway. "We should head back up to the house. The eggplant will be ready to pull out of the oven soon."

"Eggplant?" Maya groaned, wrinkling her brow and looking at her father.

Diane leaned over, touching the girl's shoulder. "You want to be strong like your dad, don't you? Eggplant will help."

Martha and Diane led the way out of the boathouse to the patio where the table was set. They left Ryan and Maya outside while they went in to get the food, providing Diane the opportunity to whisper, "I need to have time alone with Ryan. I'll put off dessert until we get back from the boat ride. Then I'll get Ryan to help me tie up while you and Maya go to the house to dish out the ice cream. We'll be down by my mom's garden, so it will be easy to talk about her death. Bringing up his wife will be harder, but I'll figure it out."

Martha nodded. "I'll put on a pot of coffee while talking to Maya, to stall longer."

"Thanks."

**

Ryan

Ryan watched his daughter skip the olives, carrots, and peppers on the antipasto plate, but grab the cheese, pickles, and salami. She passed on the eggplant, but when the spaghetti came out, she filled her dish. After her morning with the therapist, he was glad she was getting a chance to relax.

Meanwhile, he and Martha each had a couple of glasses of wine to wash the food down, but Diane begged off the alcohol, saying she was going to be driving the boat.

Dinner conversation centered on Martha's bear claw necklace. Maya brought the subject up, asking the older woman if she wore it every day. When she said she did, Ryan jumped in the conversation to ask if people other than the woman she'd mentioned earlier ever objected to jewelry made from animals.

"That woman talked the longest by far, but others mentioned it. Every once in a while, someone would ask how I'd feel if my own fingers were cut off and strung on a necklace. But the most offensive comment came from someone who compared it to a fox stole her grandmother had worn in the thirties."

"That comment offended you?"

"Fox skins were worn by vain women who only cared about fashion. I care about tradition."

Martha's pride in her heritage seemed sincere and even admirable, but Ryan had always thought people who paid too much attention to their bloodlines were focused in the wrong direction. "You're proud of who you are. That's good. But I believe what we achieve is related more to how hard we work than what we're born with."

Diane laughed. "Nurture verses nature, right?"

"There's another layer," Martha said as she sipped her Chablis. "You know those Russian dolls, the wooden ones that unscrew and have another, identical, but smaller doll inside? It's like those. The way you're raised, the friends and family you have, the money and security you're blessed with, and everything else you experience while you're alive, that's the outside layer. The second layer is your gene pool. I don't think it matters so much if your ancestors were Native Americans, like mine, or from Europe, Africa, or Asia. What's important is the physical and mental gifts you inherit: how fast you can figure things out, how much you can carry, how far you can run, and how healthy you are. Then there's a third layer—the human soul. It's the source of your strength, your kindness, and your empathy. It's your core. If your core's weak, nothing else matters."

"Interesting," Ryan said.

Diane smiled. "You think so? Let her keep talking. I've heard this before."

Martha shook her head at Diane. "She's right. Here's the kicker. I believe, like billions of other people around the world, that your soul has many opportunities to live a good life."

"Reincarnation?" Ryan asked as he reached for the basket of French bread. "Could you pass the butter?" he asked Diane.

"Yes, reincarnation," Martha told him. "And think of what that means. Who knows where your soul was? Yours might have been the core of one of my ancestors, while mine might have been the soul of someone who never even saw this continent. We can't know."

"Some people can," Diane said.

"Why do you say that?" Martha asked.

"I was reading an article about a hypnotist who solves crimes by bringing out memories from the past lives of victims."

"Really?"

"The article said this man can do all that, but you can't always believe what's on the Internet." Diane smiled, then pushed her chair back and stood. "Leave the dishes where they are. I promised you a ride in my boat. We need to get to it while there's still enough light. I'll meet you in the boathouse in a minute. I've got to change first."

Martha brought bread to the dock, so she and Maya could feed the ducks while they waited for Diane. Martha led the girl to the steps leading down into water. Ryan stood beside the boathouse and watched his daughter. The way Maya seemed to get along with both Martha and Diane pleased and surprised Ryan. He wondered if the place was the reason. They were still by the lake she loved, but not at the house where the memories of her mom were so strong. Maybe this house was the right mixture of new and old. Or maybe it had nothing to do with the house. Perhaps both Diane and Martha were genuine enough to impress a ten-year-old girl.

Maya had broken half of her slices of bread into small pieces for duck feeding when Diane came walking down the path to join them. She was dressed in a white tank top, black athletic shorts, and a pair of running sneakers. Ryan missed the pretty sundress, but thought she looked nice in this outfit, as well.

Diane stood next to Ryan, but spoke to Maya. "We can go as soon as you're ready."

Maya smiled, then tore up the rest of the bread and tossed it to the ducks. "Let's go!" she shouted as she led Diane into the boathouse.

Diane opened the overhead door with a push of a button while Ryan set his empty wine glass on a shelf, untied the ropes, then got in the boat. Diane backed out and turned to head south toward Halsey Island. She cut to the left, toward Ryan's home, but when they rounded the point, Diane turned to the right, away from his house.

It was before 6:00. Many of the people had left the lake to eat dinner, but this area was still crowded. There was a cluster of restaurants on their left with plenty of dock space for diners to arrive by water. The traffic to those establishments was noticeable. Two sets of waves from a couple of decent sized speedboats crossed in front of Diane. Her boat bounced, causing a spray to hit her passengers. Ryan shook his head, but up front, Maya was laughing out loud.

They reached a smooth section of water and Diane upped the throttle. Her blond hair was flying, like a boat flag. He thought she was as beautiful as any woman since Beth and Oota Dabun.

She spun around the widest part of the lake until they were near Bertrand Island, then turned back, took a small detour to see the River Styx Bridge, and finished with a straight ride home.

After they stepped out of the boathouse, Martha and Maya went to the house to get the ice cream, while Diane and Ryan hung back to tie the boat. She pointed and said, her voice cracking slightly, "The flat area by the seawall is where my mother fell in the water on the day she drowned. I suspect she was murdered."

Murdered? That was a bombshell. Ryan didn't know what to say. He remembered the drowning and the fact that Martha had found the body, but the other details were a blur. Beth's death had consumed all his thoughts at that time. He started to tell Diane he was sorry for what she'd been through, but the words seemed trite. Instead, he said nothing.

***

Diane

*D*iane watched Ryan's expression and wondered if she had just spoiled any chance she had to talk with him about the circumstances surrounding the two deaths. She'd been too focused on her plan and had lunged when she should have glided.

"Sorry," Diane said, looking away from his eyes. She paused a moment longer, hoping he might say something; anything. He didn't. She tried honesty. "All evening I've wanted to bring up the subject of my mother's death. I knew if I waited much longer, we'd be with Martha and Maya again and wouldn't be free to talk." She sucked in a breath. "My mother was working in her garden that day. Apparently, she'd been drinking wine."

"Is that why she fell in the lake?"

"That's the million dollar question. My mom drank to relax, but never so much she would lose control. Yet that's what the police say she did. They say she drank so much she lost her balance, fell in, and was too drunk to stand up in shallow water. I don't believe it, but they don't seem to care what I believe. They dismissed my concerns as if I were a child. It was frustrating, to say the least."

"Still, she was drinking," Ryan said. His eyebrows were raised, and his head tilted slightly. His skepticism couldn't have been clearer if he'd called Diane a liar. But he was listening. She was glad about that.

"I wanted to speak with you because I know how you lost your wife," Diane said. "I thought you might have similar concerns."

Ryan nodded, but looked uncertain.

Diane said, "The two drownings were close together in time and place and I believe they were both violent."

"I'm not sure our situations are the same and even if I thought they were, people who live by a lake sometimes drown. It's sad, but generally there's no one to blame."

Diane wanted to argue, but instead she asked, "What did the police say to *you*?"

"That it was an accident." Ryan paused for a moment then added, "I'd doubled the ropes on my boat bumpers. They said she had her foot between them and when she slipped, the ropes tightened on her ankle like a snare, leaving her dangling in the water. I had my doubts, of course, but I accepted their theory. My focus has to be on taking care of Maya."

Diane knew Maya had been hiding under the boat cover and knew the young girl hadn't been able to recall anything. Judging by what Ryan was saying, those lost memories hadn't come back in the months that followed.

She reached out and took his hand. "Maya deserves the truth as much as you and I."

She dropped his hand as they turned to walk up to the house for coffee and ice cream, but he stepped beside her and took it back.

Chapter Four
Ryan

€arly the next morning, Ryan sat in front of his computer, searching for the story Diane had mentioned, about the hypnotist who solves crimes by looking into past lives. Ryan discovered the man's name, Glen Wiley, and found a number of articles he'd written for various publications. The hypnotist had traveled all over the world recalling people's past lives. He'd worked with people in France and Japan, as well as closer to home, in Vermont and North Carolina. He claimed past life events tend to repeat. Success in one life can lead to success in another and, of course, tragedy can lead to more tragedy as well.

Maya was still asleep. They had returned home from Diane's at ten o'clock, an hour and a half past his daughter's normal bedtime. But he had rationalized the break in their rules, because the next day was Sunday and neither of them had to get up early. He woke early anyway, giving him extra time to read about Wiley and to think about Diane's ideas. The theory that her mother's drowning was a murder rather than an accident seemed outlandish, even though Ryan had the same thoughts about Beth's death.

If someone *had* been involved with the death of Diane's mother, then Beth's death was suspicious as well. And if that person worried about Maya's memory coming back, she might be in danger. The police had closed the case, but a hypnotist-detective presented a different way to look into the tragedy.

The articles by Wiley focused on his ability to help his subjects recall their past lives. Ryan had never had a strong opinion one way or another about the subject, but it was clear he could also bring out repressed memories from his subject's present lives.

Ryan's email to Glen Wiley read as follows:

My daughter and I live in a lake community in Northern New Jersey. Violent crime is rare in our area, yet ten months ago, two deaths occurred within days of each other. One of the people lost was the mother of a friend of mine, who officially died by accidental drowning. My friend does not accept that conclusion.

Two days after that first tragedy, my wife also drowned. The police declared her death to be an accident as well, but two such similar deaths so close together seem suspicious.

Our daughter, Maya, was with my wife when she died, but has lost all memory of the event. Recently she has experienced episodes during which a woman, a stranger, has come to her in her dreams and has drawn her into dangerous situations, including an episode of sleep-swimming. If I had not discovered her missing from her bed, Maya might also have died. My daughter has been in therapy, but she continues to have the dreams.

My friend and I want justice for our loved ones, but what is most important to us is that Maya be healed. I plead with you to consider our case. You are our best hope.

Ryan reread the note twice to ensure it wasn't overly dramatic, then appended his street address along with his phone number, and pressed SEND.

***

A few days after Ryan sent the email, his landline rang. He was on the patio, husking a couple of ears of corn for the night's dinner while watching Maya play ring toss on the front lawn. Ryan warned his daughter to stay away from the water as he went inside to answer the phone.

"Mr. Jensen?" a man's voice asked.

"That's me."

"This is Glen Wiley, the regression hypnotist and I'm interested in your case. I'd like to spend time with you and your daughter."

***

Diane

After her mother died, Diane closed out her parents' bank account and transferred the car and the house to her name. She took over the banking and went through the paperwork they kept downstairs. But there were years of old bills and credit card statements up in the attic. Because she had doubts about the events leading up to her mother's death, Diane decided to go through everything. There could be a piece of paper upstairs that would reveal a motive.

Diane climbed into her modest attic through a pull-down door with a folding ladder located in her bedroom. The great room had a cathedral ceiling, so only the space above the bedrooms had room for storage. She used a flashlight because only a limited amount of light came through the roof vents. Since the light took one of her hands, she had to carry the twelve portable files down the ladder one at a time. She had the most trouble with two of the older plastic boxes which were cracked. Still, when she reached the floor all the files were intact.

Diane spread an old tablecloth on the dining room table to protect the surface, then began to separate the papers into piles. She picked the boxes in no particular order and finished each one before going on to the next.

A receipt for the Sunfish her father had bought her when she was twelve triggered the first memory. Diane had been too young to sail on her own, so her father always went with her. They would lean back to balance the boat as the wind tipped it to a steep angle. At first, Diane held the rope controlling the sail while her father held the rudder, but she wanted to steer so she argued until he let her control both. She would make the boat skim across the water like a huge surfboard. Then, when the wind was calm, they would talk and share jokes, laughing aloud while the water splashed across their bare legs and the sun warmed their shoulders.

Diane found a stack of orthodontist bills for the braces she'd had to wear when she was thirteen. Even though she needed to wear them for less than a year, she winced at the memory. She also found a bill for art classes with a teacher who kept talking about colors and perspective, and never gave his students a chance to pick up their brushes. Her mom had pulled her out of those classes quickly.

Then a wonderful memory came rushing back.

Her mom had held on to a pair of tickets from twenty years ago, to a performance of *The Fantasticks* at a small theater in Chester. Diane shook her head as she turned them over in her hands. When Diane was a child, she had fallen in love with the original cast recording. Her mother's CD was long gone, but here were the tickets to the show that was supposed to let Diane see real singers and dancers performing the music.

They'd allowed extra time to get there even though they lived only thirty minutes from the theater. Pouring rain made it hard to see, so Diane's mom decided to get out to the highway rather than sticking to the winding roads around the lake, but when she reached Route 80, the traffic stopped. Later they learned a multi-vehicle accident had blocked all the westbound lanes, leaving cars parked in the middle of the interstate, unable to move at all.

Diane had been on the verge of tears when her mother, reaching for a Kleenex, said, "You want to hear someone sing your favorite song? I'll sing it." She could still hear her mother's voice over the rain on the windshield, soothing Diane's disappointment. Although she didn't know it then, her mom's performance had been a thousand times more memorable than anything she would ever see in a theater.

After the tickets, Diane found countless papers reminding her of how her parents had kept her life problem-free for years. Then she chose a folder containing old newspaper clippings, and felt the blood drain from her head. The first article was an announcement of the birth of Elizabeth Chapin. Diane knew the woman's maiden name, because she'd read her obituary. She was the woman who would become Beth Jensen, Ryan's wife. This certainly showed a connection between the two victims. Diane flipped to the next article, cut from the *Star Ledger,* a story about athletics at James Caldwell High School, which included a picture of the woman's track team. Beth stood third from the left in the second row.

Other articles included a note about Elizabeth Chapin's graduation, *cum laude* from Drew University, the engagement notice for her and Ryan, and the birth announcement for Maya. The folder was a brief synopsis of the high points of her life. There were also candid photos of her as a little girl, then as a teenager, then as a young woman.

Why had her parents been tracking Beth?

Diane felt dizzy, as if the air in the room was not breathable. She sat back for a while, holding on to the old pieces of paper, swaying back and forth, trying to wrap her mind around what all of this meant. Her mother had cut out articles about Beth years before their deaths. The articles she'd found suggested a connection between Diane's family and Ryan's. There had to be more to this than what the police thought.

***

Ryan

Ryan brought Glen Wiley home from Newark Airport and called Diane a couple of hours later. It had been three days since the dinner.

"You know the hypnotist you mentioned when I was at your house?" he asked, pacing while talking. He was more nervous than he'd realized. "I contacted him," he continued after a brief pause.

"Really?"

"He's got a website. There are articles about him all over the Internet."

"The man specializes in past lives, right?"

"Well—past memories might be more accurate. The articles are mainly about past lives, but he can bring out repressed memories as well." Ryan didn't want to mention his own dreams, although they were a factor in his decision to make the call. Instead, he said, "I know Maya's reaction to her mother's death led to her middle of the night swim, but I hope Glen Wiley might put *me* under rather than her. He might discover specifics that could help me understand what I need to do to help her. At the same time, we can test the process. While speaking with him, I mentioned your case. He's sitting on my patio right now and wants to meet you."

"Oh?" Her voice sounded uncertain.

Ryan moved away from the cabinet and stepped toward one of the windows where he could look out over the lake. There were only two boats on the water.

"I thought you'd be excited about this," Ryan said, thinking how different she was from Beth.

"There's something I have to tell you. Can I come over now? I don't want to say it over the phone"

"Of course, I'll let Glen know you're coming."

***

Diane

*D*iane pulled her hair back, wrapped it with an elastic ponytail holder, then grabbed the folder. She headed to her car to drive to Ryan's home and, in less than five minutes, was walking to his door.

"I need to show you what's in here," Diane said, holding up the folder as she stepped inside. She walked past him to his dining room and placed it on the table.

"I assume this is about your mother's death," he said, shutting the door.

"About her life, I suppose. And about Beth's."

"Beth?"

"You need to look at the papers." She turned to Glen, who was quietly watching, and added, "You must be Glen Wiley. I'm glad you're here. Maybe you can help sort this out."

Diane opened the folder.

"I found these while going through my parents' papers. I don't understand how or why they were there, but I can promise you this—if Mom knew something bad was going to happen to your wife, she would have tried to help. That was her way."

"Nice to meet you," Glen said, stepping toward her with his hand held out.

Diane took his hand and shook it. "Same here," she said, smiling. "I'm hoping you can help us, because the papers I found make things more confusing than ever."

Glen was a bookish man in his mid-forties with dark rimmed glasses. He was Diane's height, a few inches shorter than Ryan. Next to Ryan, Glen appeared unkempt. Where Ryan had neat, short, dark hair, Glen's brown mop looked well overdue for a cut. He wore baggy, blue slacks and a light blue long sleeved shirt.

"I'll do what I can." Glen turned toward the dining room table. Ryan was reading with his back toward them.

Diane spoke to Glen. "I'm starting to think everything is connected: what happened to my mother, to Ryan's wife, and to Maya."

Glen raised his eyebrows and said, "Ryan said his daughter was sleep walking and ended up in the lake. An argument might be made for a connection between the drownings, but Maya told him a woman had spoken to her that night, in her dreams, luring her into the water. There's no evidence of your mother or Beth experiencing anything similar to that, is there?"

"I can't say anything about Maya's dreams, but the clippings seem to confirm my theory about my mom and Beth's deaths."

Diane looked toward Ryan. He had turned so she could see his face. He was crying—not bawling like a child, but she could see his hands shaking and could tell his eyes were moist. She and Glen moved toward him.

Diane put her hand on Ryan's shoulder. "I should have warned you."

"Why would they be spying on Beth?"

The strength of the word *spying* surprised Diane.

"May I see the articles?" Glen asked.

Ryan gathered the papers into a pile and handed them to the hypnotist, who sat beside him and began skimming.

Ryan stood and moved close to Diane. "I know you try to tell me everything, but maybe there's something else, something important, something you don't think has anything to do with Beth..."

Diane felt her eyes twitch and moisten. "I brought the papers to you, didn't I? Ask me anything. I'll tell you whatever I know."

"There's another approach," Glen suggested, pointing to his place on the paper with his index finger as he turned to speak to Diane. "I might be able to bring out your memories. Perhaps you saw one of your parents reading something. Or maybe you picked up a clue from a conversation."

Glen Wiley had solved crimes, including murders, by bringing out past life memories. His method was to regress the friends and family of the victims looking for witnesses to crimes in other lives. This is where things got fuzzy, at least to Diane.

"I could use a drink," Ryan said. "Would either of you care to join me?"

Diane thought drinks would probably do them all good.

"I'll have wine if you have an open bottle."

"Water for me," Glen said.

When Glen finished the last article, he stood and moved toward the den. Diane followed. She took a seat on the sofa facing the television. Glen sat in one of two recliners. "Tell me what you think about past lives," he said, tilting his head while looking in her eyes.

"I thought you said we're after a memory of my parents from when I was a child."

"I did, but that's just a beginning."

She stared over his shoulder, through the patio doors. She tried to keep any quaver out of her voice. "As you know, my mother is dead. I feel certain she was murdered, but the police don't agree. I found your name while searching on the internet, but I wasn't looking for anything spiritual. I was looking for someone who might use nontraditional methods to help me find the truth. I neither believe nor disbelieve in past lives, but I do feel there's something after death. I can sense my mother's presence, so I know a part of her still exists. Maybe the part I feel is her soul and perhaps, somehow, she'll come back in another life. To be honest, I haven't thought much about past or future lives."

Glen shook his head. "Maybe not multiple lives, but it sounds as if you've thought a great deal about souls."

"I live alone and spend most of my time with the woman who used to be my mother's best friend. There's plenty of time to think about Mom's soul."

"For many people, past lives are less about their own souls than about the souls they love. You sound as if you're in that camp."

Ryan walked in with a glass of white wine in one hand and a glass of water in the other.

"Here you go." He set the two glasses on the coffee table.

"Doubt is the greatest roadblock to successful regressions," Glen said, as Ryan went back to the kitchen for his own drink. "But a belief that's too strong can be a problem as well. I think you're a perfect candidate. Open-minded people don't try to steer or resist. They just let the process take them where they need to go."

"How about me?" Ryan asked, as he returned with what appeared to be a scotch on the rocks.

"Only time will tell." Glen turned to Diane. "When would you like to start?"

"I'm ready right now, if you are."

"Tomorrow would be better. I'd like to settle in here first."

"Sounds good. How about after lunch?"

He nodded, then sipped his water as Diane tasted her wine.

"Remember, a regression is not a scene from a movie," he told her. "Films have a tendency to exaggerate and skim through the highlights. Regressions are more like day-to-day life. You won't be able to change anything that happens, but you'll see your parents, hear them, and when they touch you you'll feel them."

Diane had sifted through plenty of old pictures and videos of her parents' lives, but what Glen offered was more. If what he said was true, this was a chance to relive rather than remember. The idea amazed her.

She had just dropped a bomb on Ryan with the documents she'd discovered, so she couldn't let her focus drift from the reason Glen had offered to regress her. "I wasn't around when Beth was born, but I was alive when someone cut out that engagement announcement. If you think it would help, I'd like to try." Like to, she thought. *There's* an understatement.

Ryan invited Diane to share lunch with them before the next day's regression. "I was just planning soup and sandwiches. One more person won't make a difference and I'd like your company."

"How about two more?" Diane asked. "And we bring bagels."

"We?"

"Martha would kill me if I left her out of this."

***

The next morning, Diane ate breakfast, then tried to read a few more chapters of a novel she'd started a week earlier, but she couldn't concentrate. The regression excited her too much. So she switched to a few chores she'd been putting off. She stripped her bed and threw in a load of laundry, then dusted and vacuumed to fill the rest of the time. At eleven o'clock, Diane changed to a pink, long-sleeve T-shirt and a pair of red exercise shorts (Glen had suggested comfortable clothes). She slipped on a light jacket and went down to wait for Martha by the water. The only people she could see on the lake were a couple of fisherman in a bass boat by the two small islets near Raccoon Island. Then Martha appeared on her dock.

A quarter of a mile of water separated Diane's dock from Martha's, so her friend appeared no more than a spot in Diane's vision. But since she had seen Martha prepare for a canoe ride many times, she knew exactly what the woman was doing.

As a soft wind blew small waves against the dock and seawall, creating a heartbeat-like sound, Diane watched Martha make her way across the lake and thought how wonderful to do things with the woman who had been her mother's best friend, as if something of her mother persevered. The thought made her wonder about Glen's description of the permanence of the human soul.

***

After lunch, Ryan offered coffee refills to his three guests. Maya was in school.

"I think I've had enough caffeine," Martha told him. "Your coffee's good, but strong."

"Diane probably shouldn't have another cup, either," Glen said, then to her he added, "If you're too jumpy you won't have a successful regression."

Diane smiled and nodded.

Glen stood and walked to the striped couch in the living room portion of the great room. "This would be a fine place to lie down."

The other three moved toward the couch. Diane sat to remove her sandals. Ryan and Martha stepped back to the den area to bring in a couple of straight back chairs, while Glen positioned a pillow for Diane's head.

"Lie on your back and look up at the ceiling," Glen told her. "Pick a spot for your focal point. Have you ever been hypnotized before?"

She shook her head, then wiggled into a comfortable position. Her feet were touching the arm of the couch, so she shifted and crossed her right foot above her left ankle. Glen reached over and uncrossed her feet.

"Try this," he said, bending her right knee. She shifted her left leg to match her right and leaned sideways against the back of the couch. "It's important to fit your body to the surface, so you can relax. You want to look up, but that doesn't mean you need to be stiff."

Glen's touch was like a yoga instructor's, personal but not sexual. He seemed so different from Ryan. Glen wore his blue shirt buttoned all the way up while Ryan wore jeans and a tight black T-shirt. If Ryan had positioned her legs, it would have been more intimate.

Glen paused for a moment, then said, "Tell me about the woman your mother was when you were young. Did she stay at home? What was her relationship like with your father? Was she different when she didn't know you could see her?"

Diane told him everything she could think of. His request was like a release valve for all the thoughts about her mother she'd had since the drowning, emotional, but not difficult. She talked so long he had to interrupt her.

"I'm going to help you reach back into your memories. Hypnotism can't make you do anything you don't want to do. You have to be willing to let me bring out these episodes from years ago."

She nodded to let him know she understood.

He added, "If you relax, we can find out more about what happened."

"I'll try."

"That's all I ask." Glen said. "Is there a place where you go when you want to be alone, a place where you feel most at peace?"

"Yes."

"Tell me and we'll picture it together."

"My dock."

Diane surprised herself. Her mother had died near the place she had chosen, yet she still believed water was peace.

"Perfect," Glen said, his voice turning soft and smooth. "I'm going to step you through scenes you should know then step you back into your subconscious by guiding you to places in the recesses of your mind. Start by picturing yourself alone on your dock in the cool, early hours of a summer morning. In this picture you are wearing your favorite bathing suit, breathing in the fresh smell of the mist on the lake and listening to the water gently lapping against the shore."

Diane heard soft, synthesized music combined with water sounds, waves on a shore. Glen must have had an audio player in his pocket. She allowed her thoughts to drift away as she entered the world of his words.

"Imagine you are lying on your belly, reaching over the edge of the dock to touch the water. It's wet and warm. You enjoy how it feels so much, you stand up and dive in. The power of the water has pulled you. You recognize the feeling, the floating sensation as if life has you in its control and all you have to do is go with the flow."

She arrived where Glen's words had pulled her, feeling the familiar weightlessness of swimming underwater, letting him guide her in a way that made the flow of water against her skin more intense than any other time she'd been in the lake. She wasn't just in the water, she became one *with* the water.

Glen continued. "The water swirls around your body as you move through it without effort. You've been here before. It's all familiar, except now you don't have to go up to the surface to breathe." He paused, then added, "Now *you* describe what it's like."

Diane began to speak without turning her eyes from the ceiling. "I am swimming the way I swam as a young girl, floating through the water rather than pushing toward a goal."

"Excellent."

"My world is underwater like an unborn child's. I can breathe, so I can smell the sweet odor of fresh water, like rain in spring. I open my eyes. The water is clear, but everything more than a few yards from me is blurry. I swim to the bottom, to a place near the dock where there are no weeds, old leaves, or rotting sticks. I push my hands into the clean sand and pull out a smooth stone the size of my thumb. I hold it up in the light from the surface and see yellow and gray patterns. Its appearance reminds me of a tropical fish my father kept when I was a child. I drop the stone, then look around for real fish."

"Good, but before you can find any fish, you see a light. You can feel its power, pulling at your soul. You swim into it. Scenes from your life drift past until a current seems to catch you and pull you in a single direction. You're moving through time. You are a young girl."

Diane feels the water swirling, just as Glen said. It is neither cold nor hot. The motion becomes slower, but keeps pushing her. She doesn't resist, and as she moves, she becomes a child, hiding behind a chair, eavesdropping on a conversation between her mother and her father.

***

𝒟iane was hiding behind her daddy's big chair watching *Three's Company* when her mommy came in and turned off the TV. Her daddy stood. At first, Diane was too surprised and upset to understand what her parents were saying, but soon the words became clear.

"We had no relationship," Gary said, his voice shaking. "It was just something that happened. It would be over if there wasn't a child to consider."

"Two children," Lori told him. Her voice sounded loud and mean. "Do *not* forget about Diane."

Diane tensed when she heard her name.

"I never meant to hurt either of you."

Hurt? young Diane thought. Daddy wouldn't hurt me.

"Does that woman still work in your office?"

"I can't fire her, if that's what you mean, not with her daughter on the way."

"A daughter?"

"That's what her doctor told her. They wouldn't survive."

"You should be worrying about *our* family surviving."

"Of course I worry about us. You and Diane are everything to me."

"There's another lie. You'll think about the child every day of your life. I know because that's how often I think about my first daughter. If anyone knows how bad choices can affect your life, I do. But I never betrayed you."

"It will never happen again."

Diane didn't like hearing her mommy and daddy arguing. She wanted to get back to her room.

She tried to crawl away, but her mommy saw and called out. "Diane? What are you doing here?"

"I couldn't sleep. You were shouting."

"You see?" Lori said to her husband.

Although the regression was as clear as living in the moment, the adult Diane still had the sense of who she was. She watched her parents, absorbing the way they moved, her father pacing with his constant, long strides; her mother moving away from him, fast and smooth as a cat. Her mother smelled of *Charlie*, the perfume she had worn when Diane was a child. The scent reminded Diane of how safe she had felt back then, but while the smell awoke old memories, she could feel, with immediacy, what the four-year-old version of herself felt. Young Diane was anything but secure.

Lori leaned over and picked her daughter up. "Don't you worry, hon. Everything will be all right. Sometimes grown-ups argue like kids do, but Mommy and Daddy still love each other."

Her mommy was holding her tighter than usual. She carried her toward her room, while Diane watched her father walk to a window and stare into the darkness.

***

Glen's voice sounded to Diane like leaves rustling in the wind. "Come back," he said. "Return through the years." The session ended with his soft, lullaby tone. What had happened was exciting, yet the secret she'd learned had left a dark feeling in her heart. Glen's pleasant voice continued, "On the count of three you will awake and remember everything you've experienced. One. Two. Three."

Diane stretched her arms and wiggled her legs. She slowly twisted so she could shift into a sitting position. She noticed Ryan looking at her, then at Glen, then back at her again.

She felt dizzy. Her mixed up, crazy emotions combined with the amazement of the experience causing her heart to race. She pulled in a deep breath and tried to calm down. Both her mother and father had been there—as physical, as emotional, and, despite their fighting, as beautiful as they'd ever been, as if they had never died! And it had all seemed so real! But there were also two children she didn't know about, two half-sisters. She'd heard the argument once before, when she was a child. So she knew all this, but she must have forgotten. And neither of her parents had brought it up again.

Glen had told her to describe what she was experiencing as she was regressed, so the three who'd been listening knew what she'd been through and every emotion she'd felt along the way. She trusted Martha. She didn't know the two men nearly as well, but she had decided to trust them also, so she could find out more about her mother's death.

"I wasn't comfortable with the regression," Glen said, standing as he spoke. "It was your first session and the memories you were recalling seemed..." He paused then said, "painful."

Painful was a good word, although *torturous* would be better. A miracle, but she had experienced this miracle in a memory so horrible, she'd suppressed it for more than twenty years.

Her mom had told her dad he'd betrayed them both. She was right, of course. The session had restored her life's most agonizing memory and revealed the man she had idolized to be nothing more than a bad cliché. Yet for all the revealed truth, she still didn't know the name of her father's lover or either of her half siblings.

Martha stood as if she'd read Diane's thoughts and put her hand on Diane's shoulder. "Your mother told me what happened at the time. Bella Cox was the woman's name."

"You knew about this? Why didn't you say anything?"

"It was a long time ago. Your mother didn't think you had understood what you'd heard and believed bringing it up would cause more harm than good. But your parents loved each other. I knew them well enough to know that."

Diane looked toward the bay windows at the front of the house. It seemed as if it had been only a couple of minutes earlier when her father stared out the same window. She turned back toward Martha. "What people do is more important than what they feel."

"I don't agree. Besides, he stuck with you and your mom."

Diane was about to argue when Ryan said, "I know Bella Cox's daughter. She's Heather, the woman who was in my house when you dropped by the other night." Ryan turned to Glen and added, "Heather is an employee of mine."

Ryan's revelation put a face to what her father had done, a pale face with dull blue eyes. "The young blond woman is Bella's daughter?" Diane asked, her jaw shaking as she spoke.

Ryan nodded.

"There has to be a reason this memory was the first to come out," Glen said. "I want to hypnotize Bella, to explore the events from a different angle. Would you object if we took that approach?"

As Diane shook her head to say she didn't object, Ryan said, "Heather's mom died a few years back."

Diane gasped. Life had gone on after the first time she'd learned of her father's relationship with Bella. She'd been young and unaware. Her parents had never brought it up again, but Bella knew and had probably told the entire tale to her daughter. If so, Heather had known they were sisters, even if Diane hadn't. To the best of her knowledge, she'd never met Bella, but the woman's death meant Heather was alone—a lonely person with a powerful reason to hate Diane's mother.

"It was totally unexpected," Ryan added, answering one of the questions Diane was about to ask. "Heather took it well. She was back at work the next day."

"The next day?" Diane remained on the couch. Martha sat beside her.

Ryan nodded. "She's tough."

"Or incapable of caring," Diane added in a quiet voice.

"Apparently Heather is your half-sister," Glen told Diane, ignoring her comment, "a fact coincidental enough to give me pause. It could be a piece in the puzzle. Our souls don't move from life to life alone, we move as a group. We stay close to the same souls in our various incarnations, but the relationships generally change. A sister might have been a friend in another life."

"Or an enemy," Diane added.

Glen said, "Heather might have been important to Maya in another life. Or maybe Bella was. That could be the connection you're looking for."

"Or maybe your other half-sister was the important one in her past life," Ryan said, looking straight at Diane, "because, given the articles your mother was keeping, I have a feeling that my Beth was your other sister. And no one was more important to Maya than her mother."

***

Ryan

"I'm home," someone shouted from the kitchen, interrupting the conversation. The voice belonged to Maya.

"Why are you here so early?" Ryan asked his daughter.

"Dr. Kari picked me up," Maya told her father as she set her backpack on the floor.

"Dr. Kari?" Ryan asked. "You're not supposed to have a session today. And why would she bring you home instead of going to her office?"

"I don't know. We talked in the car. I guess that was enough."

Ryan looked confused. "I'll have to call her."

"Hope you had a good day at school," Glen said to Maya as she moved toward the adults.

"Anyway, I'm glad you're home early," Ryan told his daughter. "Dr. Wiley has agreed to stay with us for a while. He's going to help us understand your dreams."

Glen said, "I'm looking forward to working with you, Maya."

Ryan needed to be clear about what working with Maya would entail. She wasn't to be hypnotized until he was certain the procedure was safe.

Maya nodded to Glen, but kept addressing her father. "Will I still see Dr. Kari?"

"Of course," Ryan told her. "I've said all along we're going to do whatever it takes to help you."

"It's raining," Maya said, changing the subject.

"Is it?" Ryan looked out the window. The glass was wet, but falling rain wasn't visible and the house was too far from the lake to see ripples on its surface.

"Not hard," she told him.

Diane stood and spoke to Martha. "We should head home." She turned to Ryan and added, "You'll need to make lunch for Maya."

"Would you cover the boat, Maya?" Ryan suggested, "Perhaps Glen could help you before the drizzle turns to a downpour." It would be good for Glen Wiley to talk to Maya, but Ryan would not let his daughter be hypnotized, not yet.

Ryan had been overcome by grief on the first day back in the lake house and had even considered selling, but he'd quickly determined the best way to help his daughter adjust to life without a mother would be to move forward with as little change as possible. He treated their house as he had always treated it and pushed Maya to do the same. He didn't want his daughter to be afraid of her home or boats or water. And although he often felt a wave of grief when he went out on the dock, he hoped Maya did not.

"I'm cooking steaks for dinner," Ryan said, after Maya and Glen headed to the lake. "You're both welcome to stay."

"What do you know about Bella Cox?" Diane asked.

"First, let's talk about this connection we have through Beth," Ryan said. "It's weird."

"I'll grant you that."

"But it's nice, too."

"I hope you're not thinking the way that sounds, because I'm not Beth, just like I'm not Heather."

"I know, but you were her family, even if neither of you knew it."

"Please, let's talk about Bella Cox."

"OK." Ryan looked at the ceiling for a moment then started. "On snowy days or when Heather had car problems, I would swing by their house in Mt. Arlington to give her a ride to work. Bella would always invite me in for coffee. She seemed nice enough, although she'd get irritated with Heather from time to time. I just figured that was a mother-daughter thing."

"Do you think Glen could help you remember more details?"

Judging by the intensity in Diane's voice, what she said was more of a suggestion than a question. Ryan worried this Bella thing might be taking focus away from Maya's problems. However, it appeared she was right about Lori and Beth's deaths being related. At times, it seemed as if everything was related.

"I don't want any regressions while Maya's home, not until we're ready to involve her. And I won't be ready until I'm certain the sessions are safe."

"Would it help if we came back tomorrow while she's in school?"

Although Heather and Diane had blond hair, they looked less like sisters than Beth and Diane. He could see Beth in Diane, in the way they walked, or rather, the way Diane walked and Beth used to walk before...

There were pictures of Diane's family on a sideboard in her house, so Ryan knew the appearance of the father Heather and Diane shared and the mother Beth and

Diane shared. Beth had been the only dark haired woman in the group.

"Tomorrow is a good idea," Ryan said.

The door opened then shut as Glen and Maya came back into the house.

"We beat the hard rain," Glen said. "Maya handled the cover like a pro."

"She's strong for her age," Ryan told him.

Maya shrugged her shoulders. "Covering a boat isn't hard."

Diane told Glen, "We're leaving, but we'll be back tomorrow. I'm looking forward to working with you again."

"Breakfast?" Ryan asked. "Around eight?"

"See you then."

Chapter Five
Diane

The next morning, when Diane and Martha arrived at Ryan's house, Maya was already on the bus headed to school. When they finished breakfast, Diane asked Glen to regress her first. She said she wanted a longer experience this time.

Ryan told the others to leave their dishes on the table; then they all moved back to the living room. Diane sat on the striped couch, swung around, and lay down while Martha took her place in the matching armchair. Glen returned to the straight-back, kitchen chair where he'd been sitting the first time he hypnotized her.

Diane saw Glen pull the audio player out of his pocket, a small thin device but with its own speaker. He started playing the same track of water noises and new age music. The sound had a tinny quality, but served its purpose by helping her relax.

"I'm going to handle this session in the same way I handled your last one," Glen said. "This time, however, I will guide you further, way back into another existence. Are you ready?"

She nodded slightly without moving her gaze from her focal point on the ceiling.

He smiled and spoke softly. "Take a deep breath and imagine you are lying on your dock, again. It's a warm, summer afternoon. You are enjoying the heat of the sun on your back. There are constant waves from passing boats, all splashing under the dock."

The soft sound of the gentle music helped her thoughts float away as she envisioned waves of water. She imagined herself looking through the spaces between the boards on the dock's surface, watching the waves break on the pilings underneath. She felt drawn to the water, so she stood, walked to the dock's edge, and jumped in. The water swirled around her. This time she let it pull her deeper. A spot drew her attention, a reflection, something shiny, half-hidden in the muck at the bottom of the lake. As she got closer, the water started to spin.

Diane tried to relax so she would be free to slip into whatever memories came. She let the image of flowing water wipe all thoughts from her mind. The weightlessness of floating under the surface of the lake was ingrained in her from her childhood. That feeling led her to a blurry image of her life as someone else. She still knew she was Diane, but she was this other woman as well. As the strength of that presence grew, Diane understood the other world. She stood beside a woman, a friend. They were in a clearing surrounded by a forest.

***

Oota Dabun

Oota Dabun was picking blueberries when she glimpsed a spot of light, like a reflection off the surface of the pond but in the woods, away from the water.

All the Lenape women participated in the important work of berry picking, along with their children, the boys as well as the girls. Even the babies who were too young to do anything other than sleep and eat were brought along. Oota Dabun's best friend, Pules, had brought her infant daughter, Nuttah, into the forest, carrying the child in a flat cradleboard she wore on her back.

Pules and Oota Dabun had been friends since their own mothers had carried them on berry picking days. Pules was older, but only by a few moons. They were similar in height, but Pules was heavier. While Oota Dabun wore her dark hair loose, Pules parted hers in the middle and gathered it to both sides using ties decorated with seashells as round as her face. She had softer features than Oota Dabun, whose nose was long and straight and whose chin was flat. They both had dark eyes, although Oota Dabun's were different because they were often circled with darkness. Pules said the darkness might be a sign of sickness, but Oota Dabun felt healthy and Abooksigun, the local man of medicine, told her not to worry. He said the darkness was a sign of an ancient soul.

Oota Dabun and Pules had wandered off where they could talk as they gathered. Pules took the cradleboard off and hung it on a tree while she started to collect the berries. Most of the berries would later be dried to be used in corn cake or eaten on their own.

Although Pules led a traditional life, she was the only person Oota Dabun could talk to about her hopes. A few men had asked Oota Dabun to marry, including her friend, Chogan, who would have made a wonderful husband, but Oota Dabun had refused them all. She wanted a vision quest first, despite the fact that the quest was a ritual rarely undertaken by women. Pules' baby reminded Oota Dabun of what she was missing. If she waited too long, she might never have a child of her own. Yet Pules' life wasn't perfect. Her husband had died during a hunt, before their child was born.

"Something is in the woods," Oota Dabun said.

"Something wrong?" Pules asked.

"I'm not certain, but it's bright and out of place."

Oota Dabun shifted from one foot to the other to look from different angles. She tilted her head and stepped to the right. The reflection reappeared, but only for an instant. They had been picking at the edge of thicker woods, where the berry bushes grew well. Oota Dabun stepped toward the place where the forest was dense.

"Careful. It could be a bear." Pules voice was tense and sharp.

"A shiny bear?" Oota Dabun smiled wide. When she laughed all her teeth showed.

"You know what I mean. It's dangerous to follow what you don't know."

Nuttah made a soft cry. Pules set down her basket and went to the tree where her baby was tied in the cradle. Both Oota Dabun and Pules were dressed for the heat of the summer, in wrap around skirts with no tops, making it easy for Pules to feed her daughter. She carried Nuttah in her left arm, stepped back to the bush and continued to pick, filling her basket where it sat on the ground.

Oota Dabun turned away from Pules and Nuttah to look back.

Pules said, "There isn't much light in the woods. The sun would have to be peeking through a break in the leaves to reflect off a surface. What is the chance of that?"

"Are you saying I imagined it?"

"I'm saying it's unusual."

Oota Dabun leaned to her right to try to see clearer. "Perhaps it's a sign," she said.

"I'll show you a sign. See how I'm picking more berries than you despite working with one hand? That's a sign of someone not doing her job."

Oota Dabun looked at Pules. She noticed Nuttah's face was turned from her mother's breast. "Is your daughter done feeding?"

Pules dropped a handful of berries in the basket then re-positioned her baby on her other breast. Oota Dabun smiled and stepped toward the woods again. She saw something move. At first, she thought it was a deer, but she noticed a head of thick hair which she could tell belonged to a person dressed in buckskin clothing.

"Someone's lying on the ground."

"A shiny person?"

Oota Dabun didn't have time to respond to Pules' sarcasm. "There really is a person there, someone who may be hurt." She started to take another step, but Pules had hold of her skirt.

"What if it's a white man or an Iroquois?"

"We have to help."

"You watch from a distance. I'll get one of the boys to run for Abooksigun." Pules turned and headed toward the others, still holding her child.

Oota Dabun knew Pules was right. If someone was faking, the situation could be dangerous. If not, the injured person needed a shaman. She stepped back and breathed deeply. What if this is the sign I've waited for? she thought.

Oota Dabun glanced in the direction her friend had run. Pules would come back after she sent a boy to run for Abooksigun and others would come with her. She had only a few minutes to be alone. She breathed deeply and walked into the woods.

A white man with light brown hair and a thick beard lay there, breathing unevenly. His right arm was under his body, but she noticed a portion of a large gash in it. Oota Dabun knew she had to stop the bleeding.

She pulled on his unconscious body, rolling him so she could see the wound clearer. A long blade had been partially caught underneath him and now wasn't. She picked up the enormous knife. She saw blood on the blade and a glittery, red stone in the decorative handle. The blood caused her to wonder if the man had defended himself. Could he have survived a bear attack? Also under his body was a long object which looked like a case for the blade. She shoved the blade beneath a bush, then undid a belt that held the case to the man's waist. She put the case and its belt beside the blade.

Oota Dabun needed something to stop the bleeding. She looked at the man's clothes. They were dirty and it would be hard to get them off. She thought of the light beaver blanket in Nuttah's cradle. It would be a good size. She stood up and stepped back into the clearing. Pules had left the blanket there and at the foot of the tree was a gourd water bottle. Oota Dabun grabbed both items and returned to the man.

She used water from the gourd to clean the wound as thoroughly as she could, then wrapped the blanket around his arm. If the blood had been flowing quickly, she would have placed the blanket closer to his shoulder and twisted it with a stick, but the man had been lying on his arm. His position had caused the wound to fill with dirt, which helped to slow the bleeding.

She heard steps behind her. Pules had brought their friend Chogan along with the medicine man.

When Pules sent for Abooksigun, Oota Dabun had been certain Chogan would come, too. The men were together more often than they were apart. If she had not known them her entire life, she might have thought Abooksigun was Chogan's older brother. Although Chogan was taller by the length of one of his hands, their square jaws and long, dark hair made them look similar. But the hunter, Chogan, with his simple attire, was smooth and clean like a river rock, while the shaman, Abooksigun, with his tasseled wrist bands and powerful necklaces, was like a garden stone, moss covered and draped with vines.

"He's been bit," Oota Dabun said, as Abooksigun unwrapped the blanket to treat the wound. Chogan took her by the arm and helped her stand.

"You shouldn't have approached him alone," Chogan scolded.

"That's what I told her," Pules said.

"The man is a gift from the life-spirits," Oota Dabun argued.

"You don't know that," Pules told her.

"I saw him. The sun shone through the thick trees and reflected off a jewel in the handle of his giant blade. The spot of light came to my eyes and my eyes alone. It was a gift."

"What blade?" Chogan asked.

Oota Dabun took him by the hand and led him to the bush near the man. Abooksigun had finished treating the wound and had started to chant. Oota Dabun held the blade up so Chogan could see it. His eyes grew like two moons.

"It's an animal bite, a bad one," Pules said, looking at the man. "He might not survive."

Oota Dabun turned toward Pules. "He will," she said, "The bite was not to kill him. It was to send him to me. The spirits will be good for our village and especially good for me."

Abooksigun and Chogan made a stretcher from two tree branches and mats they'd brought with them and used it to carry him toward the village. One of the women would be asked to take care of him. Oota Dabun had not mentioned anything, but intended to volunteer. Pules would say she was crazy, but someone had to do the work and Oota Dabun had the most to gain.

Pules put Nuttah back in the cradleboard then Oota Dabun helped her strap the baby to her back. They picked up their berry baskets then followed the men.

They walked in silence for a short distance until Pules spoke. "Do you wish you were born a man?"

Tradition specified distinct gender roles, but Oota Dabun's desires weren't based on a simple tendency to break routine. There was a spiritual side to her interest in men's work.

"I'm happy to be the person I am," Oota Dabun answered. "I don't care if I hunt and build houses or plant and make clothes. It's the answer to a bigger question that concerns me. The Great Spirit speaks to all and I want a chance to listen."

"We women have our time in the sweat lodge."

"True, but we don't spend time alone in the wild, seeking guidance."

"We search in other ways, in our own ways." Pules turned her back toward Oota Dabun, so her child was facing her friend. "Look at Nuttah's eyes. I never felt closer to the Great Spirit than on the day she came to the world. Men can't have that."

"Any animal can bear young." Oota Dabun regretted her words as soon as she spoke. She hadn't meant to disparage Pules's choice to marry and have children, but Oota Dabun had a path of her own. Pules turned away without speaking and Oota Dabun knew she had hurt her friend.

***

Ryan

Ryan watched Diane sit up and stretch. She seemed as awestruck as he felt, but not stressed. The woman in his dreams and the woman in Diane's memories shared the name Oota Dabun, which meant her regression had established a connection. If that woman was Diane, no wonder he felt drawn to her.

"Are you all right?" Glen asked, leaning toward Diane from the kitchen chair he'd pulled over.

"That was astonishing," Diane told him. "and not as if I was in some virtual reality program or 3D movie. Everything I experienced was as clear and sharp and physical as any event I've ever lived through. And if I can be Oota Dabun years before I was born, then doesn't that mean I can be someone else after I die?"

"I believe that's true, but we can't know for certain," Glen answered. "These are memories I've helped you recall. You can't have memories of something that hasn't happened. When it comes to the future, we can guess based on patterns from the past, but that's all we can do."

"And have faith," Martha added.

"Let's talk about what you saw," Ryan said, still thinking of how Diane's regression related to the woman in his dreams. "Does any of this relate to the deaths of your mom and Beth?"

"I'm not sure," Diane told him. "When I was Oota Dabun, an object caught my attention. It was a medieval sword with a red stone in the handle. I was drawn to it. I'm not sure if that feeling means it was important to me while I was looking back into my memories or if it was important to Oota Dabun during her life. But I do know it impressed me."

"The Lenape Native Americans were using stone tools when the Europeans first encountered them," Glen said, "so Oota Dabun had reason to be impressed with a sword. But you're right. Feelings from a current incarnation can sometimes get mixed up with feelings from a past one, even if the subject isn't in the middle of a regression. That's what we call déjà vu."

She grimaced. "We need to find out more. And I want to know what happened to the injured man."

"I can help you recall those memories. I can guide you to a time that's a week or so later, when the woman you were would know more about the person you saved."

Ryan interrupted. "I dreamed about a Native American woman whose name was Oota Dabun. The woman kept coming back in recurring dreams." Diane was staring at him, tilting her head slightly as if trying to understand. "If you were Oota Dabun, then you were that woman."

Ryan couldn't read anything more than curiosity in Diane's expression. Was she hiding her feelings or was he looking for something that wasn't there?

Martha leaned forward to speak to Glen. "You said something about our souls, how they move through time together. Are we all related somehow?" Ryan wondered if her question came from the confusing connection between Martha's Native American heritage and Diane's memory of life in a Lenape tribe. One was genetic while the other was—spiritual?

"We move in groups," Glen answered.

"So could Ryan have been the injured man Oota Dabun found?" Martha asked.

"That's possible. Memories from our other lives are generally buried in our subconscious minds, but events from those experiences can show up in our dreams. There's only one way to know. I can regress Ryan to see if he goes back to the time and place Diane experienced."

"Let's do it." Ryan went to the couch and wriggled into a comfortable position, then nodded to Glen, who took his position in the straight back seat. Diane sat in the upholstered chair where Ryan sat when she was regressed.

"You seem to love this lake as much as Diane does. Do you have a favorite place?"

"I like to fish, to be out in my boat, in the morning when it's peaceful."

"Perfect. Pick a spot on the ceiling and use it for a focal point, then imagine you're in your boat."

Ryan shifted, but kept his focus on the ceiling. He thought of a lake scene, a summer morning when the only boat on the open water was his. Everything was quiet and peaceful.

Glen spoke to Ryan in the same soft voice he'd used for Diane's regression. "Let your problems float away. You're alone on the lake, just you casting your line across the still water. Imagine how the rod feels in your hands.

You cast. As you reel the lure back, you tug at the line every so often so your lure looks like a meal to the hungry fish out there. You'd like to catch something of course, but if you don't that's OK, too. It's peaceful. You feel as if God has made this place just for you."

Ryan breathed deeply and let it out slowly, allowing his thoughts to get lost in Glen's words. He pictured a light near the shore. Then he moved the boat, because he was drawn toward that light. When he got close, he slowed the engine. The light pulled him out of the boat, through the water, and into its glow.

Ryan felt as if he were sailing through the water, floating in a swirling tunnel until he was a different person, walking along a wooded path, holding the back end of a crude stretcher.

***

Chogan

"Will he live?" Chogan asked, as he and Abooksigun carried the man toward the village.

"I asked the spirits to heal him, but in my heart I hope he dies."

It wasn't the answer Chogan had expected. He'd heard the rumors of the unfair ways some Lenape had been treated by the white-faces and the giant blade worried him as well. But this man was only one among many and Oota Dabun had taken his weapon.

"Oota Dabun stopped his bleeding and I treated his wound. We've done what we should do."

"But why wouldn't you want him to live?"

"Two white men came to one of the villages of the turtle clan where my brother lives. One of them was sick with blisters on his skin. Soon after they arrived, many of our people developed sores like the ones the white-face had. But his health improved, while most of the Lenape who lived there died. The white men were planning to move on, but one of the men in the village killed them before they could go. It was for the best."

"Yet here you are carrying this one back to our village so he can be nursed."

"He's wounded badly, but he's not sick like that other one. Leaving him untended would be the same as killing him and although I hope he dies, I won't kill him unless I know he's a threat."

They walked in silence for a short distance except for the sound of sticks and old leaves crunching beneath their feet. Chogan wondered about Abooksigun's dilemma and if it was right for this man to be held responsible for harm caused by other white men.

"Did your brother die?" he asked.

"The last I heard he wasn't one of the sick, but I have no way of knowing what has happened recently."

Abooksigun stepped over the trunk of a thin, fallen tree without losing his hold on the stretcher. Chogan followed, still carrying the back end.

"What should we do if our people get sick?" Chogan asked.

"We?"

"I am not a healer," Chogan replied, "but healing may not be the answer."

As they walked into the village, Oota Dabun and Pules caught up to them. Oota Dabun said, "Take him to my house. He's my responsibility."

Oota Dabun lived in a typical village home, a bark-covered frame structure built from thin tree trunks and branches. The man was too hurt to cause harm, but Abooksigun's talk worried Chogan.

"The white-faces may be dangerous," Chogan said. "There are signs. Abooksigun was telling me..."

Oota Dabun interrupted. "I was guided to this one, a sign greater than any other." There was no arguing with her when she had her mind set.

Abooksigun and Chogan carried the man to Oota Dabun's wigwam and put him on a pallet of grass covered with deerskin, the place where she had slept. She would have to make another before the night came.

"This won't be easy," Chogan told Oota Dabun. The man was barely alive. If his wounds turned worse, they would have only to bury his body, but if he grew healthier, Oota Dabun would have to feed him, clean him, and treat the bites he had suffered. It would be a long time before a man in such a state could do anything for himself. "He's a man, not an animal. His spirit is not so simple."

"Which is why caring for him is important. For this man to live through such an attack is a miracle and I am part of that miracle." Oota Dabun looked at the injured man. "I believe he'll bring us a gift from the animal that attacked him."

Years ago, when Chogan was on his vision quest, he spent days paddling along the shore of the great pond, watching animals, including the crows he'd been named after, looking for clues about the meaning of life. When he went down river, he encountered a family of otters and stayed there for two nights. He took the otter spirit into his heart, which helped him understand the importance of living and working with friends. This animal spirit influenced how he lived his life and even helped him listen to Oota Dabun's words. But *her* experience was different.

"Gifts aren't always good," he told her.

"Perhaps." Yet Oota Dabun's smile told Chogan she felt no doubt in what she was about to do.

Abooksigun touched Chogan's shoulder and nodded toward the wigwam's exit. Chogan followed his friend, but glanced back at Oota Dabun, who had taken water to the injured man and was trying to get him to drink.

"This is the first of the white men to find his way here," Abooksigun said, when they were outside. "He won't be the last."

***

Diane

𝒟iane had been right about knowing Ryan in her past life, but had expected his soul to be in the injured man. Oota Dabun had felt only relief when Chogan and Abooksigun had arrived to help. The injured man, not Chogan, held her interest. Yet something had changed from the past life to this one, because when Diane was near Ryan there was no confusing the attraction.

"It seemed so real," Ryan said, as he twisted into a sitting position.

"It *seemed* real because it *was* real," Glen told him. "Every memory is permanent, part of a universal consciousness."

"Or part of God?" Martha asked.

"I don't think it's possible to believe in God without believing in the permanence of what happens," Glen told her. "Think of the quote from Jeremiah—*Before I formed you in the womb I knew you...* It's the Judeo-Christian tradition, everything goes on forever, both ways. The same is true in the Buddhist and Hindu faiths. Eternal life is at the core of almost all religious belief. So yes, part of God is a way of saying the same thing, or part of Yahweh or Allah or Vishnu.

"How do we find the others in our spiritual family?" Diane asked.

"We hypnotize people," Glen said.

"People like Maya?" she asked, turning toward Ryan.

Maya had been with her mother when she died. She had also experienced a vision that could have been the same woman Ryan saw in his dreams. She seemed a logical choice.

"Not yet," Ryan told her.

"It could help," Glen argued.

Ryan shook his head. "Or it could hurt. Regress me a few more times, so I'm certain the process is safe. After that, we'll talk. We have to be careful. She's fragile."

Diane understood why Ryan might be cautious or possibly want to check with Maya's psychiatrist. Retrieving a bad memory could upset her. Yet none of this was simple. Ryan's daughter deserved to know what had happened to her mother as much as Diane deserved to know what had happened to hers.

"There was a pond by the village in the memories," Ryan said. "Do you think it was one of the ones that formed the current lake?"

Glen paused then said, "People can love places as much as they love anything else, so I suppose it's possible a location could draw souls. Perhaps I should see more of the lake."

Chapter Six
Glen

Martha offered to take Glen for a short, lake tour in her canoe. They rode to Diane's house in her car, where Martha's canoe had been pulled up on the dock. "I paddled here," she told Glen as they slid it back into the water. "It's easier than taking the ferry."

"There's a ferry on the lake?"

"A small, two car barge people use to get to the island where my house is. I'll show you."

"I'm looking forward to it."

Martha told Glen to take the front seat, so she could steer from the back. Once out on the lake, Glen realized he would have to turn around and raise his voice to be heard, an effort that ran counter to the feeling of peace instilled by the flow of the water around them. Neither of them spoke much, providing a chance for Glen to be alone with his thoughts.

He was looking for something dark.

Glen had researched this lake before coming to New Jersey and had learned that the water could be busy on summer weekends when multiple ski boats circle the wide areas and gas-guzzling powerboats try to outperform each other. Autumn now, the water could still be rough, but most of the waves were made by the wind.

When the canoe entered the narrow area Martha described as the channel between Raccoon Island and the mainland, Glen saw the ferry she'd mentioned. It looked like a pier as it sat motionless on the island side. The ferry had a bright yellow cabin on one side, which apparently contained the engine. There were warning signs on it, telling other boats to keep their distance for safety concerns. It wasn't pretty, but was clearly functional.

Two drownings had occurred as well as what had happened to Maya. Glen understood how evil can hide within beauty. He looked across the water's surface and wondered what lurked below.

There was a dark undercurrent in the regressions as well, beneath the surface like the essence of whatever Glen was searching for in the lake. Chogan and Abooksigun had spoken of death in one of the other Lenape clans. The danger was too distant to be a threat to anyone in their village, but it meant there was something worth investigating. Glen might find a connection between the dark of that life and the force that had tried to drown Maya.

Aspects of this case were progressing quickly. Diane and Ryan were the only two people he'd regressed so far and they had shared a previous life. Finding two people who shared another existence is fairly common, but it doesn't follow that everyone in the social group was part of the same incarnation. Maya's soul was key to solving the puzzle, which is why Glen was frustrated by Ryan's reluctance to allow him to regress her.

Each time the blade of Glen's paddle broke the lake's surface, he would hear a splash accompanied with the sweet aroma of fresh water and the musky smell of seaweed. The wind was gentler in the sheltered waterway.

Oota Dabun's touch must have been soft and healing on the wounds of the white man she discovered, something Chogan might not have liked. Glen wondered if jealousy might have led to acts of violence within this group of souls, acts significant enough to repeat in later incarnations. He needed to perform more regressions. Working with Diane or Ryan again would be easy, but discovering someone else in their circle would be more productive.

Glen thought about the woman seated behind him. She was of Lenape descent and had studied the culture, which wouldn't affect where her soul had been in past incarnations. But if she had a presence in that village, she might understand aspects of their life in ways others wouldn't. Martha had also been Diane's mother's closest friend and was now as close to Diane as she had been to Lori. He knew from experience that three souls so intimately connected probably shared multiple lifetimes. If he wasn't allowed to work with Maya, Martha seemed to be his next best choice.

Glen twisted in his seat to face her. "I think I have a better feel for the lake now. Can we head back to Diane's?"

"There's something else important for you to know—the lake's sense of time. Look over there." She pointed as she spoke. "The boathouse set back in that cove and the other two along the shore have existed for as long as I can remember. Change happens at a slower pace here than the rest of the world, but things do change. The lake was formed from two ponds when the dam was built. My ancestors lived on the shore of one of those ponds when the Europeans first arrived. They wouldn't recognize it now."

"Your knowledge of this area is important," Glen told her. "I'd like to regress you next."

"I'd like that, too."

They paddled in a circle and headed out of the channel in the direction from where they'd come. The open water was rougher because there was more wind, but there were no waves from other boats. They were alone on the lake except for a tiny blue spot off to their right. Glen could tell the spot was a powerboat, but the distance made all other characteristics indistinguishable. As they headed for Diane's home, Glen tried to picture what the lake had been like during the Lenape years.

***
Maya

$\mathcal{D}$r. Kari picked Maya up at the end of the school day. They didn't speak the entire way to her office and since the doctor never turned on the radio, all Maya could hear were road noises: the brakes of trucks, the creaking of a school bus, the whir of tires against the pavement. When she closed her eyes, it seemed as if she'd entered a magical place, like the world of her most vivid dreams. Dr. Kari smelled of lake water, which helped Maya feel her presence, like the lady who had called her to the lake on the night of her swim.

"I picked you up for a reason," Dr. Kari told Maya as she pulled the car into her driveway. "There's something I need to show you. I think you'll like it."

After Dr. Kari unlocked the front door, she led Maya through the green waiting room, then opened the door to her office. The shades were pulled, so it was dark in there, except for the glow from something against the right wall. Maya turned to see a large, colorful, aquarium with small, bright fish darting among clusters of weeds. She ran to the tank and touched the glass.

"They're pretty," Maya shouted as she stared at a fish half the size of her palm.

"Yes, they are, but there's more to the aquarium than fish, plants, and colorful stones. There are lessons in the water."

"You mean about the night I went swimming?" That was, after all, the reason Maya was here.

"Of course, and about water in general."

"Tell me!"

Dr. Kari reached for Maya's hand. She led the young girl to the couch. There was a piece of green construction paper on the table between the couch and Dr.

Kari's chair. The doctor leaned over and began to fold it without explaining what she was doing.

"What is it?" Maya asked as the doctor began to crease the paper.

"You'll see."

She held up what appeared to be an upside down hat.

"I don't understand," Maya said.

"I'll show you," Dr. Kari stood up and stepped back to the aquarium. Maya followed. The doctor opened the top of the tank and placed the paper on the water revealing it to be a boat, a tiny, canoe-like boat.

Maya's eyes grew wide as she stared and said, "It floats."

"Throughout our lives we're drawn to water. The more we learn, the more we are amazed. Perhaps it's because our bodies are more than half water. No one knows for sure, but people use it for worship and meditation. Everyone is drawn to water, not just you."

Maya looked down at the floor and shuffled her feet. The office had a wooden floor with a throw rug under the couch and the seats, but there was no carpet by the fish tank. She used the toe of her sneaker to trace a grain in one of the boards.

Dr. Kari leaned over and touched Maya's face, turning her until their eyes met. "The border between water and air is confusing. There is a world above and a world below, just like the concept of heaven. You can see both worlds in my tank, but you can't in the lake, even though it's just as true. So when the lady called you, she called you from one world to the next."

"Is my mother there?"

"I would have to ask *you* that."

Maya didn't understand Dr. Kari's answer. But if her mother was in the other world, why didn't she come out? Maybe she couldn't.

Maya reached into the fish tank and touched the surface. *Another world*, she thought. If there was a chance she could see her mother, she needed to know more about the other world and about the lady who called her to it.

"Borders are meant to be crossed," Dr. Kari told Maya, "and worlds are meant to be explored. I'll help you find your mother if she's there, but don't tell your daddy we're doing this. It will be our secret."

***

Martha

Martha woke the following day eager to be regressed as Glen had promised. She loved her heritage. The strength of that love made her certain that her soul had been among her genetic ancestors. If Diane and Ryan were there, then she must have been there as well.

But hypnotism worried Martha, because she didn't want Diane to discover the secret of what Martha's ancestors had passed to her through generations—at least not yet. Martha had researched enough to know that people can keep secrets even when hypnotized, so she would just keep it in her mind that all comments concerning the jewel were off limits.

It was a Saturday, which meant Maya would be home, so they moved Martha's session to Diane's house. Ryan arranged for Heather to babysit.

Diane had a circle in the center of her great room formed from gray couches facing each other, with two armchairs on one end and a freestanding fireplace on the other. Either one of the couches would make a good place for Martha's session. She picked the closest one.

The smooth ceiling in Diane's house made it difficult for Martha to find a focal point. She tilted her head toward her feet and noticed two directional ceiling lamps.

She picked one and focused on it, inhaled a deep cleansing breath and tried to relax as Glen began to speak.

"That's right, relax. Take another breath and release it slowly. You're in a perfect place. Your mind is free of worries. Picture yourself in your canoe on a crisp, autumn day with the sun shining.

"Concentrate on the image of water in your mind. You see a strange whirlpool in the water. You paddle toward it and when you are close, it pulls you to its center. You aren't scared because there's a feeling surrounding the whirlpool that's warm and familiar. Your boat starts to spin slowly."

Martha followed Glen's words and started to sense scenes from her life appearing briefly in front of her, before slipping away. Many of the scenes were major, but others were everyday events. When the jewel entered her mind for a brief moment, she let the thought of it drift away. The whirlpool started to pull the canoe down. The events kept passing by, but now they were from a different era. She stepped back in time, yet the scenes she saw were familiar.

Martha was drawn into another existence. When the details came into focus, she realized she was a man in this other life, an injured man.

The hurt from the man's wound overwhelmed any surprise Martha felt from the discovery that she had once been male. She couldn't think of anything but the intense pain she felt through the person who shared her soul. Yet there was also relief, because someone wonderful was helping him, cleansing his wound.

Martha started to describe what was happening.

***

Phillip

A woman knelt to wash Phillip. She had cleaned the gash in his arm and was now treating it with a soothing poultice.

The paste appeared to be working, because the pain was easing.

He had awoken days earlier, but hadn't left the pallet where he slept. His clothes had been removed, and he'd been given a blanket.

His legs were uninjured, so he thought he could walk if he could get to his feet. The problem was that each time he attempted to stand, he felt great pain and the woman yelled at him. She also motioned for him to remain still. She didn't speak a word of English and Phillip didn't speak her language. But she made herself clear and he felt too weak to do anything other than obey.

She brought him food and helped him when he needed to relieve himself.

Phillip had been around members of the Lenape tribe before, in a village along the Hudson. They seemed to be a peace loving people and offered him food in exchange for English tools such as knives and axes. He dealt exclusively with the men in that village who could speak limited English. The women remained at a distance and never tried to communicate with him.

The woman, his nurse, grew more attractive to him as his wound healed. She had the dark hair and tan skin common among her people. When he had first opened his eyes, that's all he had noticed, that and the dress she was wearing: buckskin with tassels and blue trim. But after he had been awake for a full day, he began to see how her large eyes were close set. Her cheeks were high with more red in their tone than the rest of her skin. Her nose was narrow and straight, giving her a strong appearance justified by the way she set about her tasks. Her lips were delicate and always formed a slight smile, as if she felt happy to be tending to him no matter how difficult the labor.

Phillip understood how serious his wound had been and how he owed his life to this Lenape woman. He didn't understand how to express his gratitude. He realized she didn't know his language, but he had to try. So he smiled and said "Thank you" each time she did him a favor. It didn't take long for the woman to imitate his phrase. By the third day after he awoke, she was saying "Thank you," over and over. She said it as a greeting. She said it when she began to replace the poultice. And she said it when she brought him food. To her "Thank you" seemed to mean "hello," "goodbye," "how are you," and "would you like something" all rolled into one. Her use of the words seemed nonsensical, but she tried to communicate with him and her effort filled Phillip with enough joy to forget the pain for a moment.

When she finished treating Phillip's arm, the young woman pulled the blanket away, helped him move off the pallet, reached for her bowl of water, and continued to wash the rest of his body. He tensed slightly in response to her touch and cried out when he felt pain from his wound.

The woman said, "Thank you," then put her hand on his chest. He could tell she wanted him to lie still. After he stopped moving, she continued to wash him.

The woman's touch was softer than beaver pelt. Phillip wanted to reach out to her and hold her. His body began to respond to his attraction. He knew any sign of what he felt would be wrong. He tried to think of walking through a forest on a spring day and tried to focus on something from his daily routine—on the process of setting a snare, how to position the loop so when the animal poked its head through, the twine would tighten.

But as much as he tried to fight his arousal, Phillip couldn't keep his focus on anything other than the woman's touch. He grew hard. There was nothing he could do to stop it. He was embarrassed, but more than that, he was worried about what she would think. He didn't want to make her uncomfortable or worse—anger her.

The woman stopped washing him. She remained on her knees, but leaned back. She stared at his lower body, then her eyes darted to his face, as if she was trying to compare what Phillip felt in his mind to what he felt elsewhere. Then she laughed and said, "Thank you."

Phillip replied with his own laugh. He knew the reason behind her laughter was different from the reason behind his own, but that didn't matter. She would stay with him, to continue to treat his wounded arm as well as his wounded soul.

The woman finished washing him, then helped him slide back onto the pallet. She covered him with the blanket and said, "Thank you" one more time.

If Phillip was going to get to know this nurse and avoid further weirdness, he needed to teach her more English. He pointed to himself and said, "Phillip."

The woman tried to imitate the sound, but what she said came out more like "filly" than his name. He repeated "Phillip" and she tried again. After a few attempts, she said it in a way that was close enough. He smiled and pointed at her.

The woman said, "Oota Dabun."

He repeated her name, but she laughed. He tried again and this time she smiled. She pointed to herself and repeated, "Oota Dabun." He tried a third time. After this attempt, she smiled without saying anything. He must have gotten it right.

Then Phillip picked up his blanket and said, "blanket." The woman shook her head and replied, "Elemokunak." She turned and walked out of the small wigwam.

He turned from the door and stared at the ceiling. There was little else to do when the woman left. He lay on his pallet and studied the wigwam, a structure made from flexible branches two to three inches thick. The branches were bowed into a rectangular frame with a round top, then covered with what appeared to be a combination of birch bark and mats woven from reeds. He wondered what held the bark in place.

The house didn't seem as if it had been difficult to build, yet it did a good job of keeping the rain out. He was lucky this friendly tribe had been the ones to discover him and especially lucky the woman was among them.

**

Martha

"Having a past life as someone of the opposite gender is common," were the first words Glen said after bringing Martha out of her regression.

"You think that upset me?" she asked.

"Not exactly, but I hope you weren't too surprised. I was a woman in one of my past lives. I know what it's like to learn your assumptions are wrong. One of the best aspects of a regression is the opportunity to experience life from a different perspective."

Martha raised her left hand to stop him from talking, while taking hold of her bear claw necklace with her right. "What surprised me was the white European part, not the man part."

Glen looked away for a second, then turned back to her.

"You haven't lost your heritage, if that's what concerns you. Except in rare cases, the body your soul was in is not genetically connected to your current body. But what I said still applies. Try to see the value of experiencing life from a different perspective."

Martha closed her eyes and swallowed. She knew she should be happy. She'd had a successful regression and hadn't mentioned the jewel.

"The woman with you—she was me, right? Diane asked Martha, who opened her eyes but didn't answer. Diane seemed confused and agitated. "She had to be unless there was someone else named Oota Dabun taking care of a white man who'd been bitten by an animal."

Oota Dabun and Phillip had existed in another time, but their souls were a part of *now* as much as they had been a part of *then*. And there had been sexual tension between them. Souls are not physical, but still, she could understand if Diane was confused by the idea that in another life they might have had a different kind of relationship.

Martha had visited Lori in the hospital on the day Diane was born and had kept up with Diane throughout her childhood. She had been Lori's best friend and was now almost as close to her daughter. Martha and Diane both needed to know everything that happened between the injured man and the Lenape woman.

"Can you send me back?" Martha asked Glen.

"Not a good idea. Your first regression can be a strain, emotionally," he told her. "I'd rather wait at least a day."

"Then how about me?" Diane asked.

"Since you were Phillip's nurse, I should be able to pull those memories. Would you like to try?"

Ryan said, "We need to keep our focus on what will help Maya." Martha noticed that his voice cracked slightly.

Glen responded, "Right now we're fishing for clues and this is as good a spot as any other."

Martha took her cue from Ryan, who nodded in agreement. She got up from the couch and signaled for Diane to take her place.

Glen spoke his instructions softly once more and, in a short time, Diane was again recounting a day in her life as Oota Dabun.

＊＊

Oota Dabun

When Oota Dabun found Phillip in the woods, she thought he was a gift, an animal spirit in human form. She was convinced of this possibility, because the white-faces seemed as different from the Lenape as many animals were.

Abooksigun was the only person among the wolf clan who had first-hand knowledge of men like Phillip. Because her friends were ignorant concerning the ways of the white people, Oota Dabun had thought she could learn more from the wounded man than she could learn from traditional spirit guides.

What Oota Dabun hadn't considered was human attraction and once she understood that Phillip could respond to her touch like any other man, she became aware of her own feelings. She wasn't certain how to act under these circumstances, but since she had brought him back from the edge of death, she wasn't about to turn his care over to someone else.

After Phillip was healthy enough to clean himself, the situation became less confusing in some ways, but more in others. Oota Dabun's own feelings were growing stronger, although she could only see his attraction to her in subtle ways. He would turn away quickly when she caught his gaze, look at her lips when she spoke, and hold his breath when he watched her change her clothing.

Communication was less of an issue, because Oota Dabun had learned enough of his words to speak to him. Phillip, however, made only a few attempts to learn hers, causing her to wonder what his indifference meant.

Phillip helped with her work—women's work. Oota Dabun was not sure if he did this to express his gratitude to her or because he was unable to hunt. She wasn't certain what his actions said about his character. Pursuing women's work was generally a sign of weakness for a man, but Phillip had survived on his own at least long enough to reach places where white men had not been before. He must have hunted or he would have starved. Only the strongest of men could survive a bear attack.

Oota Dabun had to step out of her house to think, to get away from the puzzle of Phillip. She walked alone so she could contemplate her thoughts. She tried to understand what she had learned from this man as well as what she had begun to feel about him.

She went down to the pond, to a spot where tall grasses met the water's edge. The wind was soft and the water quiet, except for small waves lapping along the narrow shoreline in front of the trees. She often sat there looking at the birds, mostly little ones such as cardinals and jays but also, hawks, ducks, heron, and once in a while, a turkey, although hunting had driven most of them away from the village.

She turned away from the pond and noticed Chogan near Abooksigun's home. She approached him.

"How are you, my friend?" Oota Dabun asked.

"Very glad to see you—alone."

Chogan's response took her aback slightly. He was her best friend, yet there was anger to the tone of his words. She decided not to ask what bothered him, but instead to continue with the reason she'd approached him.

"I think it is time to return Phillip's knife. He still can't use it with his right arm, but he may get use out of it with his left."

"Abooksigun and I don't intend to return it."

"But it belongs to him and it was always our intention to give it back."

"It was your intention. I never agreed."

It was not like Chogan to keep what wasn't his. Something was bothering him.

"Are you troubled?" she asked.

He stood as tall as he could and stared in her eyes. "That knife is as big as an axe."

Oota Dabun had known Chogan for as long as she could remember. They had played together when they were young: games such as the bowl game in their early days and Pahsaheman when they were a few years older. They had always been able to talk to each other. Oota Dabun had told him things about herself she wouldn't bring up to anyone else, even Pules.

She stared back at him and said, "I trust him."

Chogan stepped back as he seemed to collect his thoughts.

"Abooksigun speaks of a village of the turtle clan where some of the people died after white men arrived."

"The men in that village were not attacked. They died of sickness."

"Abooksigun told you his story?"

"Yes."

Chogan shook his head and held his hands up as if he was appealing to the Great Spirit.

"Then why do you trust this man? Abooksigun said the white-faces have powerful magic."

"Maybe the disease had nothing to do with the white-faces."

"Only the Lenape died. One of the white-faces grew weak and spots appeared on his skin, but he recovered. The other never was sick."

"Phillip has been here for moons and I am not sick. He's had many chances to hurt me with or without magic. He chose not to for the same reasons I chose not to hurt him."

"And that reason is?"

"We like each other."

Chogan jumped at her and stomped his feet, as angry as she had ever seen him. "Don't say that out loud. I'm afraid of your feelings for him more than I am of his sword. He could never be your husband. He's not capable of hunting."

She stepped back. "I said nothing about becoming his wife. Listen to me. The magic I am certain of is that the Great Spirit brought Phillip to this village and to me. I realize now that he cannot be a traditional guide, because he is as human as you and me. Yet he is still a gift and we have a lot to learn from him."

"All I am saying, is you need to be careful with the way you learn from this *human*."

Chogan turned and left abruptly. Oota Dabun no longer wanted to be around her Lenape friends, so she headed back to her home. With each pace, her own anger grew. By the time she arrived at her house she felt furious and no longer cared what Chogan or Abooksigun thought. This might not be a traditional vision quest, but it belonged to her and she would see it through to the end.

Phillip was outside, cleaning fish, always a sloppy job, but much worse when done with a single hand. Blood and scales were all over his body.

Oota Dabun touched his shoulder. He jumped slightly, then turned to see her. She signaled toward the door.

"We go in," she told him in English.

"I'm almost done. Can it wait?"

"Go in. Clean you now."

He seemed confused. He put down the knife he'd been using and followed her. She stepped toward him and pulled at his buckskin top. "Clean now," she repeated.

He let her help him off with his top. Then she got down on her knees to pull at his boots.

"Wait a minute. I've got to sit to do that."

She backed off, but as soon as he got down on the ground, she bent over and took off his footwear. While he was sitting, she found a bowl of water and began washing his arm with her hand. He let her do that as well. He still wore a confused look. Then she pulled at the belt holding his leggings in place. By this time, he had apparently decided to let her do whatever she wanted. It only took a short time for her to remove all his clothing.

She stood, looked at Phillip's body from his head to his toes, then began to take off her own clothes.

***

Glen

"Come out slowly," Glen instructed, "and peacefully. Release your memories and return to us."

He was concentrating on Diane, but he noticed Martha in the corner of his eye and turned. She looked confused, nervous. She frowned, bit her lower lip as Diane moved her right arm slightly, and started to rock her head.

Glen understood how important this discovery was to both women. He'd brought Diane out because their past life relationship had taken a turn that might affect their present day relationship in ways he could not predict. But Martha shook her head and stared at him. Maybe he'd moved too quickly. Maybe they needed to know where this was going.

He made a split second decision.

"Don't return all the way," Glen instructed, still speaking in a gentle voice, but with a slight increase in intensity. "Move forward in time. Focus on an experience further along. Where were you and Phillip a half year after what you just went through? Think of that time. Slide into that memory and tell us what you see.

***

Oota Dabun

The baby growing inside Oota Dabun kept her warm and comfortable. Phillip didn't complain, but she knew he had to feel the chill. The ground had snow on it and the pond was frozen. In winter, it was always cold inside their home even with a fire going. Oota Dabun would have been surprised by how little the temperature bothered her if Pules hadn't told her it was normal to feel warm when carrying a baby.

The longhouse might have been more comfortable for Phillip with its multiple fires, but he said he preferred to be alone with her. Except for a few words, Phillip still did not speak Unami and couldn't communicate with the others unless she was near to translate. She didn't think he liked being so dependent. He used gestures, but that method was only enough for the most basic ideas.

When Chogan and Phillip came back from the last hunt, it had been clear something had gone wrong. Phillip acted confused and needed Oota Dabun's help to learn what he'd done. They had gone after deer and Chogan claimed Phillip had not hidden himself well enough to fool the animals. Now that Oota Dabun and Phillip were back at their home, he told her Chogan was wrong.

"I'm a hunter," Phillip said. "I've stayed alive for moons by outwitting animals. It was Chogan who could not stay still. He was angry again and let his anger affect his hunting."

"Chogan wanted me for his wife," Oota Dabun said. She had told Phillip this many times before.

"And he still does. You're a beautiful woman. I don't blame him, but he takes his frustrations out on me."

"I do not understand your word."

"Beautiful?"

"You know what word I speak of."

"I suppose I do. Frustration. It can mean lots of things, but in this case it means you chose me and that makes Chogan angry."

Oota Dabun nodded. "He is a man."

Phillip smiled and poked at the fire with a stick. Oota Dabun smiled, too. Their conversation made her happy, but she wasn't sure why. Maybe she was happy being with Phillip. She felt that way most of the time. Maybe she liked the way he called her beautiful. Of all the words, he'd taught her, that was her favorite. Maybe she liked the way Chogan still wanted her. Oota Dabun was having Phillip's child, but he was not her husband, not yet.

Oota Dabun was looking at the fire when she heard the sound of ice breaking. She turned toward Phillip and saw that he'd heard it, too. He had stopped poking at the fire, sat straight up, stared out the door, and clenched the stick as if it was a snake he was trying to kill.

Winter was always a hard time for the village. Animals such as deer and turkey could still be hunted, but others disappeared for the season. Fishing was impacted even more. The fish swam in deeper water, so spears were useless and to drop their nets the men had to break through ice as thick as the length of a beaver tail. The task wasn't easy with their stone axes, but this year, thanks to Phillip's large knife, they had a new tool that could break through ice with much less effort and wasted time. This meant they could open more places to catch the fish where they were hiding.

Phillip said he wanted to help the Lenape people, but wasn't happy with the way his knife was being used. Chogan was the one who had thought of using the knife as an icebreaker and Oota Dabun wondered if Chogan had been trying to make Phillip angry.

She moved behind him and rubbed his shoulders. "You are upset."

"The sword is valuable in ways I've never told you, spiritual ways. I brought it from my home in England and it kept me safe. It's much more than a weapon. I wouldn't have been alive for you to find me if I hadn't had it."

"The people need food in cold weather. The knife helps. You should be happy."

"This village has survived many winters without the sword."

"Most of our people move to the ocean every winter, where we can fish in the cold season. This year, because of your sword, more of us have stayed here. Chogan thinks it will help us survive."

"Chogan's trying to get to me by destroying what I own. Next he'll be attacking you."

"He would never attack me." Chogan was a friend, Oota Dabun's best friend and protector. Phillip had no right to make such an accusation against him. "He helped you when you could not use your arm, when all you could do was women's work. He hunted for us, fixed our house, and took our side at the council when Abooksigun spoke against allowing you to stay with me while your injuries healed. Is this how you repay his kindness?"

"He helped you, not me."

"He helped us both."

"If Chogan could make me go away and keep you, that's what he would do."

"No one keeps me, not him, and not you. Maybe it is different in the white villages, but here, we women keep ourselves."

"I understand how proud you are and love you for it."

Oota Dabun said nothing. She fought her impulse to smile. But when Phillip used the English word *love*, she understood it to mean *ahoaltowagan*, a word that could bring joy to her heart.

Phillip seemed to recognize the change in her mood and took advantage. He said, "I want us to leave the village."

His words made her mood change back. "You leave if you wish, but I stay with the people here."

"Don't you love me?"

There was the word again. This time it didn't warm her. Oota Dabun turned toward the fire as she spoke. It felt too difficult to look in Phillip's eyes. "I have always lived with my people. I feel the quality of their spirits. I have not known you for long and you were weak for much of that time. My heart needs more."

"You are carrying my child." Phillip's voice cracked.

Oota Dabun worried at his sign of emotion. She wondered if the baby meant enough to Phillip to keep him in the village. If that was his only reason, he could grow bitter.

She also wondered if his attachment was a weakness. Fathers were important, but children belonged with their mothers. It was a truth that could not be different among the white-faces. At least she hoped it could not.

"I could stay." As Phillip made this pronouncement, Oota Dabun noticed the sound of the breaking ice had stopped.

She heard voices and although they were too muffled to distinguish specific words, it was clear there were English-speaking visitors in the village. She looked at Phillip as he cocked his head, then stepped out of the wigwam. Oota Dabun followed and looked toward the longhouse.

Chogan, Abooksigun, and six other men were talking to two white men dressed in clothes similar to the ones Phillip had been wearing when Oota Dabun had found him. Phillip ran toward them. He patted them on their shoulders and shook their hands. He appeared excited to see the outsiders, but Chogan looked worried and Abooksigun was clearly furious.

Oota Dabun walked toward the men. Unless one of the strangers understood their tribe's dialect, she would need to translate.

"What is going on?" Oota Dabun asked Chogan, speaking Unami.

"These men know Phillip. Abooksigun says we will soon see waves of white men, so many they will overwhelm our village. Death followed their arrival in his brother's homeland and he's convinced it will follow them here as well."

"What does he want to do?" she asked, trying to hide the fear in her voice.

Chogan turned back to look at the three white men.

Phillip was beside the two strangers. Abooksigun was facing them, close enough to hit anyone of them with the turtle rattle he was holding. It wasn't a weapon, but could be used as one.

Oota Dabun knew she had to act quickly or someone would be hurt. She glanced at Chogan, then stepped forward and began to speak in English.

"Friends of Phillip?"

"You speak English?" the short one asked.

"I learned your words from Phillip. He was hurt. He stayed with me as he grew strong." Oota Dabun hoped to assure the men that he had been in the village a long time and had been treated well by the Lenape. She could tell these strangers had their doubts.

Abooksigun had been shouting at them in words they could not understand and the others, including Chogan, wore scowls and furrowed brows.

The white men had rifles. Both men were clutching them as if their weapons were their only chance to survive, but the opposite was true. She needed to convince the men to hand them over.

"A bear attacked me," Phillip said. "I was badly bitten and unconscious when Oota Dabun found me. She nursed me back to health. All the people in this village treated me well."

"Oota what?" The short one asked. He had long brown hair, a crooked nose, and a jaw that stuck out like a ledge on a cliff. He had a beaver skin hat that looked like an upside down pot and a blue coat. His friend, the quiet one, was wearing a red shirt and a similar hat. He had no coat and it was cold, but he appeared to be wearing another shirt under the red one.

Phillip told them, "You can call her Day Star if you prefer. That's what her name means. She's an intelligent woman. I'm the first white man she's met, so she's learned our language quickly."

"What are you called?" Oota Dabun asked.

"I'm Elias Broome," the man in the blue coat said. "This man is Noah Hooks. We're trappers. We met Phillip when we were all in New Amsterdam." The one called Noah was still quiet, Oota Dabun wondered if there was something wrong with him.

"Are you looking to trade?" she asked Elias.

"We might be, if you have beaver. Noah has an axe we might give up and I have a hammer, but we prefer another type of trade. We've set our traps, but haven't circled back to see what we caught. With luck we'll have all the pelts we can carry in a few weeks. We'll share them with you in exchange for food and shelter. We'd like to stay here for the rest of the winter and possibly into spring."

"You believe you'll have more than you can carry?" Phillip said. "Luck is the right word for that belief."

"True."

"Trading tools might be the safest way to go and it would prove you're friendly. A couple of the men here could use proof. They accepted me, but I was in no condition to hurt them. You two are strangers with guns."

Oota Dabun knew Abooksigun's worries had nothing to do with the guns these men carried. The men of the village could defend themselves against weapons like those. He feared the sickness, but if their God was strong enough to bring death to an entire village, then fighting these trappers wasn't the right choice.

"Are you hungry?" she asked the trappers. "Tired? Phillip can bring you to our home for food and rest."

She noticed how Elias looked at Noah with an odd expression.

***

Diane

When Glen brought Diane back, she felt tense. The emotions Oota Dabun had experienced were still in her. She had watched Oota Dabun's interactions with Phillip, but had never lost the knowledge that Phillip and Martha had the same soul, causing her to feel confused in ways the Lenape woman hadn't.

For most of Diane's life, Martha had been her mother's friend, not hers. They had known and liked each other, but hadn't shared problems or dreams. Diane's mother never intended to keep the two women apart, but she had been a filter, removing any opportunity for them to share intimacies by being the one they would both turn to when they needed to talk. Everything changed when Diane's mother died. Diane was certain Martha never intended to replace her mother, but in many ways, she had. Now this already complicated relationship had become confused even further with a sexual relationship from another life.

"Do you think there was a child?" Diane asked. "They didn't have modern medicine, so I imagine there were plenty of pregnancies back then that didn't come to term." She looked at her friend, but Martha was focused on Glen.

"If there was a child there must have been another soul, right?" Martha asked Glen.

He nodded.

"And today that soul would be someone we know?"

"This is all so confusing," Diane said.

"Even if the pregnancy wasn't carried to term there's a chance the fetus had a soul," Glen told the two women. "No one knows for certain when a soul enters a body."

"We still should find out if there was a child," Diane said. After she spoke, she looked at Ryan. He was shaking his head.

"We're going to look back many times," Glen said. "When we're finally through, we'll know about the child, we'll understand Maya's situation, and, hopefully, we'll know the truth behind what happened to Beth and Lori. We're on the right track. We just need to keep going."

Chapter Seven
Kari

A YMCA pool was Kari Montero's swimming hole when she was young: memories of chlorine and old people swimming laps. But there was always room to play.

Her friend Dot would go with her on Saturday mornings. The girls would ride their bikes to the old, three story brick building, climb the stairs from the street to the front door, then step through the lobby, down the winding stairway to the women's lockers, and, after changing into their suits, head into the pool room. It was their weekly ritual during the warm months—until one day Dot tripped on Kari's foot, fell off the side of the pool, and choked on a mouthful of chlorinated water. She recovered physically, but didn't get over the embarrassment or return to the YMCA.

Dot took up with another girl who was a dancer, played the piano, and owned a Yorkshire Terrier named Clark; all things she said were more interesting than swimming. Kari kept going to the pool alone for a month or so, but lost interest when the weather turned cold.

She saw Dot the following April, on a rainy day, in the parking lot of a drug store. Kari was getting drenched as she waited for her mom to pick her up. Dot and her new friend Susan sat in a blue Dodge, apparently also waiting for someone. Dot opened the window to say hello, but didn't open the door to let Kari get out of the rain. When her mom arrived, Kari was as soaked as Dot had been the day she fell into the pool. Dot had been wearing a swimsuit, while Kari was in her street clothes.

Kari caught a cold and stayed out of school for five days. Her mom told her she should have waited in the store, which made sense, but hadn't been the plan. Kari blamed the rain and the pool. Water was always causing harm, but, as with Maya and Diane, the harm didn't temper its draw.

Peg Brodsky, who was a year behind Kari in school, became her new best friend. Unlike Dot, Peg would do anything Kari suggested, including sneaking out late at night to place a pie tin of antifreeze beside the rhododendron where Susan's dog relieved himself each morning. Clark died and Peg won Kari's friendship until they both grew bored with each other and went their separate ways.

Kari learned two lessons that year. She discovered the delight to be found in carefully executed revenge. She also learned how insecure people, like Peg, will do anything you ask them to do—if you're careful how you ask.

***

Kari's next important lesson came a couple of years later. Her parents had been busy, career oriented people. Her dad was a salesman who was on the road more than he was home. Her mom was an event planner, with an office in their den. She wasn't away as much as Kari's father, but she was so busy, she had little time for her daughter.

When Kari was thirteen, her mother had been working on a wedding anniversary that was to take place in Charlottesville, Virginia. Her father also had clients down that way, so her parents decided to pull Kari out of school for the first family trip they'd taken in years. While they were waiting for their flight, her mom and dad began fighting. Kari wasn't sure what the argument was about, but it grew loud enough for the people around them to start changing their seats.

Kari turned away from her battling parents, trying to concentrate on something other than their shouting. She heard a song playing in another part of the airport. She wasn't sure if it was playing on the airport PA or if one of the passengers had a CD player. She got up and walked off to find the source.

After a few minutes of searching, the music stopped, but by that time, Kari had walked far enough to be lost. She felt afraid and reacted to her fear by picking a direction and running as fast as she could, weaving in and out among the people. Fortunately, she soon found her parents. When she reached them, she sat in the chair she had left a short time earlier. They were still fighting.

What her parents did in response to Kari wandering off impacted the rest of her life. They did nothing. As far as Kari could tell, they hadn't even realized she'd left. Kari was a teenager, too young to leave without anyone caring enough to notice. She kept thinking about that incident for years. If her parents didn't care, who did?

Kari could point back to that day at the airport as the time when she decided she had to work hard and succeed enough to be noticed. She threw herself into her schoolwork and, in response, her grades skyrocketed. She was easily accepted at the colleges she applied to and eventually established a good career, but at thirty-six, with medical degrees and her own psychiatric practice, she continued to believe she needed to make a mark in the world at any cost; she needed to publish. Kari decided to produce a case study in her field and to achieve her goal she needed to set up circumstances worth writing about.

She had always been drawn to lakes, especially the lakes in northern New Jersey, as if something from her past was calling her there. Kari set up her home-office in

Randolph, a fifteen-minute drive from the Hopatcong State Park. She would go there sometimes to think about a rough case or just to de-stress. She would pack a picnic lunch and sit in the shade, watching the boats go by or the swimmers wade. Every once in a while, there would be a child who was afraid of the lake, which made Kari wonder what would cause that particular fear.

Had there been episodes in the lives of the people who suffered with aqua-phobia? Perhaps they'd been witnesses to people drowning or they'd experienced near drownings themselves? It was an interesting question and one that would be popular among the general public as well as her peers. There was no definitive study on the prevalence of this phobia, but the best statistic she could come up with was that one in fifty Americans suffered from the affliction. Plenty of people would be interested in her work.

The trick would be finding the best cases to study. She could search for people who had suffered through the traumas, then hope she could get to those people before anyone else did. Or, if she was smart and careful, she could create her own cases. She'd messed with her data in a similar way in smaller studies. But this was different. This had the potential to be huge.

***

Dr. Montero had met Heather when the young woman showed up at her office without an appointment. The doctor had a free slot on the following day, but Heather insisted she needed to see her sooner, so Kari offered to stay late. She had nothing else to do that evening and generally didn't eat her dinner until after eight.

Heather sat in the waiting room from two o'clock until five fifteen when Kari allowed her back into the room where she held her sessions. The problem Heather related was typical. She was raised by a single mother and didn't learn her father's name until she was a young woman. What was unusual was the amount of rage and jealousy she expressed.

She had a half-sister and, in Heather's opinion, this other young woman had a better life as the *legitimate* child.

"Don't get me wrong," Heather told Kari. "I respected my mother for what she did. She spent as much time as she could with me, but she was always working late and always depending on me to do the stuff around the house, like the cooking and most of the cleaning. There was never time for me to do things that were important, you know what I mean: school plays, soccer, shopping trips for pretty clothes, all the things *normal* girls get to share with their *two* parents. I put up with this and I never complained. I mean it—*never*. But when I found out the son-of-a-bitch who had knocked my mom up was her boss, I flipped out. Think about it. That bastard was the one who kept her working overtime. Excuse me. That's the wrong word. I'm the bastard, aren't I? He had two parents. My *sister* had two parents. I'm the one who was left with a single mom who never came home on time. And what were they doing during all those late nights at the office? Like I said, I respected my mom. But she had to keep earning money, right? She needed the job or we'd have been homeless. When you think about it, she had no choice. The son-of-a-bitch turned her into his whore."

"Take a deep breath," Kari said, thinking how Heather had transmuted the love for her mother into hate for her father and was responding to out-of-control emotions. "It won't do any good to work yourself into a frenzy."

Kari touched the young woman's shoulder in what she thought was a motherly way. Heather jumped a little, then stared. The intensity of Heather's stare was enough to cause Kari to draw her hand back. Heather breathed heavily, but Kari's touch seemed to have made her nervous rather than angry. She was leaning forward slightly. Her right hand was gripping her right knee and her left was pushing down on the seat beside her.

"You said your mom spent as much time with you as she could. Tell me about one of the good times you remember."

Heather's body language eased somewhat. She looked up at the ceiling for nearly a half a minute, then back at Kari. She breathed easier. "OK. I know a day that was fun. It was a Saturday. My mom took me out to lunch and a movie, just the two of us. That doesn't sound like much, but it didn't happen very often around my house. Like I said, it wasn't Mom's fault. It was his."

"Where did you eat?" Kari asked, trying to keep Heather focused.

"We had pizza. I don't remember the name of the place. It closed years ago."

"How about the movie? Do you remember what you saw?"

"*Almost Famous.*"

The choice surprised Kari. "How old were you?" she asked, thinking Heather had to be twelve or thirteen when that film was out, young for a story about drugs and rock n' roll. She noticed Heather tensed at the question, so she added. "It sounds as if you had a good day. You're right. She was special."

Heather relaxed again. She told a couple of other stories that were pleasant memories, about her tenth birthday when her mother called in sick to work, then kept Heather out of school, so they could spend the day eating popcorn and playing *Clue*. And another time, when she was allowed to have a friend stay overnight. Both those stories seemed normal enough, but not enough to ease Kari's fears about Heather's emotional state. This wasn't the first time the doctor had seen a patient with this type of issue. Kari asked her to return the following week.

"I can't afford to come regularly," Heather told her.

"We'll work something out," Kari wanted to keep seeing this young woman because she seemed to have a capacity for rage Kari hadn't seen in years. And if Heather's emotions were as far out of control as they appeared, she could probably be manipulated in a way that might be helpful.

During the twelfth session, Heather confessed something that confirmed Dr. Montero's feelings about her. She'd been "involved" (Heather's own word) with two drownings at Lake Hopatcong and Kari was connected to one of those deaths, since she'd been treating Maya, the daughter of the victim.

Heather didn't regret what she'd done. She claimed the two women got what they deserved, but she felt a need to talk her actions over with someone who might understand. Kari knew why she'd been the one Heather confessed to. Doctor-patient privilege kept her from giving the information to the police. Kari smiled. While she had been thinking of useful ways to manipulate this young woman, Heather had manipulated her. Kari would have to be careful as their relationship continued.

She recognized the deaths as events that were similar enough to be interesting and loved the fact that they weren't on anyone else's radar. She started thinking of Maya and Diane as potential case studies. She also knew she could use Heather's rage the way she'd used Peg's insecurity, if she ever needed help collecting additional data about Maya and Diane. Kari kept that option in the back of her mind.

***

$\mathcal{D}$uring one of her recent meetings with Heather, Kari told her, "I met with Maya a number of times after her mother was gone. I found that she is receptive to hypnotism, so it was possible to put her in an interesting situation without detection. But Diane is a different case. Since the purpose of my project is to gain an understanding of an adolescent's reaction to the drowning of her mother and compare it to the reaction of an adult in a similar situation, I need to orchestrate something for Diane, something similar to Maya's midnight swim."

"Are you asking me to help with that?"

Kari smiled and nodded. "There has to be water involved and the circumstances must be life threatening. But I want her in counseling when this is done, so be sure to leave her an escape route."

"I understand," Heather said, as she returned Kari's smile. Then in a sudden, unexpected movement, like a snake darting after prey, Heather reached out to Kari, wrapped her arms around her neck, and hugged her.

Kari stiffened, but quickly forced herself to relax. She returned Heather's hug and patted her back. She started to speak, but was torn between words of encouragement or a lecture on discipline. She chose silence instead and waited until Heather broke away.

"Diane's weak," Heather said. "Remember that if things don't work out the way you want."

Kari's smile returned as she said, "Of course."

***

Ryan

The note Ryan left for Glen read: "I took the boat out to have a chance to think. There's fresh coffee in the pot, eggs and milk in the refrigerator, and cereal in the cabinet beside the stove. Help yourself. Maya's on the bus to school. I'll be back in an hour or two."

He headed around Halsey Island toward Byram Bay, but before he entered the cove, he realized being alone with his own thoughts wasn't enough. He needed to hear Diane's opinion.

He understood enough about past lives to know that unless a major, unresolved event was destined to repeat, the relationships between two souls could be entirely different in different incarnations. But still, in the here and now, Martha and Diane knew they'd once had a child. How would they react after that fact had time to settle in? And how would this affect Diane's feelings toward him? If she had any feelings toward him.

Ryan turned his boat and headed toward Diane's dock. He knew calling her first would be the polite thing to do, but didn't want to give her a chance to tell him she wasn't in the mood to talk. When he was close enough to see that Martha's canoe wasn't at Diane's house, he knew this would be his best chance to catch her alone.

He tied his boat beside her dock, bow facing out. This time of year, the direction didn't make much difference, but if he tied it the other way in the summer, the water could be rough enough to send waves over the transom. Ryan felt as nervous as he had years ago when he first called on Beth. He hadn't backed away then and he wouldn't now.

Diane took five minutes to answer her door, causing Ryan to worry she might not be at home. When she arrived, she was dressed in a short, white robe with satin trim over a two-piece swimsuit, blue with a camouflage pattern. The robe was open. She wore no makeup and her feet were bare. Her shoulder length hair was loose, but neatly brushed and dry.

"I hope I'm not catching you at a bad time."

"Not at all. I was going to have coffee. Would you care to join me?"

Since they were by a lake, a bathing suit was common attire, even for morning coffee. Still, it was early and chilly both outside and in her house. Ryan was wearing jeans and a T-shirt.

"A cup of black coffee sounds nice," he told her.

She smiled then turned toward her kitchen. As she stepped away from him he said, "Yesterday's regressions confused me. I wanted to talk to you, to find out what you were thinking." It was easier to speak to her back, although in that robe she looked beautiful from any angle. Her ass was so much like Beth's, he felt a wave of grief. He tried to shake off the emotion. Fortunately, Diane didn't turn around to respond until she was by her coffee maker.

"You're confused? I feel as if the world I was living in was fake. And my life as Oota Dabun is the least of it."

***

Diane

Ryan wanted her input about his mixed up feelings. It would have been nicer if he'd said he was concerned rather than confused, if his first thought was about her reaction to her strange new relationship with Martha rather than his own.

Her feelings about Martha now had elements of intimacy akin to what lovers feel. But she wasn't gay and wasn't interested in a romantic relationship with *anyone* from her parents' generation. So this intimacy felt forced. But how could she say that to Ryan? And, when the time came, how could she say it to Martha or the person who now had the soul of their child?

"I wanted to talk to you alone," Ryan said. He seemed nervous, which was unusual. "These past life experiences have been a revelation with implications for our future as well as our past. I'm going to see Beth again someday, but I don't know what our relationship will be. She could be someone who can't be my wife, like your relationship with Martha. So do I spend the rest of this life looking forward to her return?"

There was a moment of silence as Diane thought how Ryan sounded as if he'd rehearsed that speech. Finally she said, "No."

"That's it? That's all you have to say?"

"Our lives should start out fresh. Maybe unresolved events and relationships from other existences can influence our behavior, but there is so much more to who we are. We should make each life the best we can have."

"That makes sense."

"I wasn't sure how to treat Martha. But after thinking about your situation, I can see I need to deal with my own."

"Glad I could help."

Diane smiled as Ryan stepped toward her, touched her left forearm and held on. She took his hand in her own and pulled him close. When he kissed her, she wasn't surprised.

"I've wanted to do that for a while," Ryan said.

"So have I."

He kissed her again, this time he wrapped his arm around her waist and pulled her body close.

"I saw you tying up at the dock this morning," Diane said softly. She had her head on his shoulder and spoke into his ear as if they were dancing. But they were barely moving. She could feel his body swell with each breath he took. "I was running around in a tizzy, brushing my hair, putting on this suit and robe. I wanted to look good for you."

"You couldn't look bad."

She laughed as she backed away from him. "You didn't see the old sweats I slept in."

He stepped toward her again and reached for her robe, pushing it off her shoulders.

She wondered how she should respond. She could pull the robe back up or let it fall to the floor. The suit wasn't as skimpy as some of the ones she'd seen on the young girls around the lake, but the bottoms hugged her hips and the top pushed her breasts up. It was the sexiest one she owned, which is why she'd worn it.

She held her arms against her sides, keeping the robe in place as she watched Ryan. He was staring at her body with the look of a man who had been without his wife for too long. Diane had expected that look, but there was something missing. If he'd glanced up at her eyes long enough to show an emotion other than hunger, she'd have led him straight to her bedroom. Since he hadn't, she pulled the robe up and tied the sash. She said, "I think I'd like to go swimming. Do you want to continue talking on the dock?"

He looked surprised rather than disappointed. All he said was, "The water has to be cold!"

***

Kari

If Heather was going to work her magic, Diane had to be away from her house at a defined time. Kari invited her along with Ryan and Maya to a dinner at Kari's home, in the same house as her office. She told Ryan that Maya had mentioned Diane a number of times and explained that if she was becoming an important part of the young girl's life, it would be helpful for Kari to get to know her. She wanted to meet with them together in an informal situation. She told him she didn't plan to discuss Maya's case, she just wanted to watch how Diane and Maya interacted.

Kari called Heather to make the arrangements. "She'll be at my place next Friday evening, from seven until nine or later if I can keep them talking."

Heather laughed then said, "That should give me plenty of time. I'll need to get into her house while she's with you. But can you get a drug?"

"I have roofies." One of Kari's patients had handed the pills over to her as part of a recovery process that hadn't worked. He was in juvenile detention now.

"That ought to work."

"If you can get Diane to take it."

"Yeah. If I can get her to take it."

Heather said "if" but her voice was confident, as if she knew a way that couldn't fail. Kari would have to be careful to stay on the good side of this young woman.

***

Ryan

Ryan watched Diane swim, mainly to be certain someone would be there to pull her out and administer CPR, if the frigid water stopped her heart. It didn't. She jumped in and immediately climbed out, moving so quickly the only effects the cold had on her were goose bumps and nipples hard enough to see through her top. She shook her hair, bounced up and down a couple of times, then wrapped herself in a towel. She ran toward the house, shouting as she went that she had to put on clothes before she caught her death.

Ryan yelled back, telling her he would call. When she disappeared into her house, he untied his boat. He planned to ask Glen to regress him again. He wanted to find out more about Chogan and Oota Dabun's relationship. Maybe that would help him understand the feelings he had for Diane.

***

"You don't want the others here?"

Ryan had known this would be Glen's first question. Up to this point, they'd participated in the regressions as a group. At each session, only one person would be regressed, but the person would relate the experience as it happened. This method meant they all had the same knowledge and everyone could participate in the discussions of how the past might affect the present.

"This is personal," he told Glen. "I haven't dreamed about Oota Dabun since my regression, but I feel a connection to Diane. I'm confused by the relationship between Oota Dabun and Phillip. I want to understand more about Chogan and *his* relationship with Oota Dabun. I spoke to Diane this morning on her dock, but that didn't go the way I expected. I'll be more comfortable if we do this alone."

Glen appeared to be thinking about Ryan's request. It surprised Ryan that the hypnotist might have qualms about it. He started to argue his case, but Glen spoke first. "What you're requesting will require us to pull one of your memories from a time later than the ones we've looked at previously. When I'm investigating a case, I generally like to keep the regressions in the order they occurred. My thinking is the facts make more sense if we discover what went on as if we were living it rather than remembering it. But it isn't a hard-and-fast rule. I don't see how it will hurt and if you think it will help you work with Diane, I'll make an exception."

"It will."

The men got into the positions they'd used previously with Ryan on the couch and Glen in a straight back chair beside him. It didn't take long before Ryan was looking through the eyes of Chogan.

***

Chogan

At first Chogan was annoyed, but his irritation quickly turned to worry. It wasn't like Oota Dabun to let her baby cry for so long, especially when the rest of the village was sleeping. He rolled off his sleeping pallet, left his wigwam, and headed toward hers.

Inside Oota Dabun's home, Chogan found two people: Phillip, who was lying unconscious on the dirt floor, and her crying baby, Kimi. He checked on Phillip. When he saw the man was breathing, he picked up Kimi and carried her to Abooksigun's wigwam.

"She's nowhere to be found?" the medicine man asked.

"I ran to you. Phillip appears ill. I am worried this may be the sickness you spoke of. Oota Dabun could be in trouble if it is."

"We need to find her."

Abooksigun stood up from the pallet where he'd been sleeping. He grabbed his spirit mask and the medicine bag containing his bear and wolf bones, his hawk and eagle feathers, and his turtle rattle. He quickly looked at Kimi, then followed Chogan to check on Phillip.

In Oota Dabun's wigwam, Abooksigun got down on one knee beside Phillip, then turned to look up at Chogan. "He is in a place between this world and the next, much like the place our young men go to during their vision quests. The white-faces have a drink that puts them in this state. The two men who arrived this past winter have brought it with them."

"Will he be all right?"

"I believe so. But we need to find Oota Dabun."

Chogan knew how many times Oota Dabun had expressed her desire to have a vision quest. If Phillip offered her the chance to have her wish, she would have taken it.

"We need to find the ones who call themselves Elias and Noah."

The two white visitors were staying with Etchemin, the canoe builder. They were all asleep, but only Etchemin woke when Abooksigun and Chogan entered his small wigwam. Abooksigun bent down to examine the men.

"These two have also had the drink we spoke of earlier. They cannot help us find Oota Dabun."

"She was here earlier, visiting them," Etchemin said. "She was with the man, Phillip."

"They left together?" Chogan asked.

Etchemin nodded.

When the men reached the pond, Etchemin noticed that one of his canoes was missing.

"We must search the pond," Abooksigun said. "I will head toward the large cove. You two go the opposite way."

Before they could leave, they heard a noise behind them. Six people from the village were approaching, one man, and five women. Pules was among them, alone and standing apart as she always seemed to be, now that her child was gone.

"Sakanon heard Oota Dabun with Phillip last night," the man said. "They were laughing, making too much noise for night. She meant to speak to them, but when she leaned out of her wigwam, she saw Oota Dabun was leaving the village. Sakanon said she seemed to dance as she walked."

Chogan turned away from the villagers to look over the pond once more. He saw something in the moonlight. He pointed over the water. "What is that?"

"It could be a boat," Abooksigun said. "We need to look."

"We can use my other canoe," Etchemin told them. "Who will go with me?"

"Abooksigun must be the one," Chogan said. "He will know what to do if Oota Dabun is hurt."

As the canoe with Abooksigun and Etchemin left the shore, Chogan kept his eyes trained on the blurry, shadow like object on the pond's surface. He prayed Oota Dabun was there. If she wasn't floating in that boat, she might be dead. She could have drowned or been attacked. What did he know about these friends of Phillip? Nothing—except they were with her just before she disappeared. His heart beat rapidly as he thought of the horrific possibilities.

Before Oota Dabun decided she wanted a vision quest, their world had made sense. It had seemed to Chogan that everyone in the village knew they belonged together. He had thought he understood Oota Dabun's desires the way a bird knows how to build a nest or a wolf knows how to hunt. He had been wrong. The only thing more confusing than her desires were his own.

Now she had a child with Phillip and in exchange for her intimacy, the hunter stayed in the safety of her wigwam. The white did not deserve her and Chogan swore by the otter, his animal spirit, that he would win her back.

But first, she had to be found.

Chogan felt his last thought throughout his body. His jaw quivered and his stomach turned. He felt fear and although he wanted to hide his weakness, he needed to know if Oota Dabun was safe, the way a drowning man needs air.

More people gathered at the water's edge. A few of the women tried to ask Chogan what he knew, but he kept his focus on Etchemin and Abooksigun as they approached what he hoped was Oota Dabun in the other canoe. He did not even acknowledge the questions.

The canoe with the men became difficult to distinguish as it drew closer, but Chogan could still see their silhouettes in it. There were no such shadows in the other boat, causing Chogan to be scared that it might be empty. When they reached their goal, one of the men appeared to grab the boat as the other began to paddle back toward shore. It didn't take long for the men to reach a point where Chogan could see both canoes clearly, but with only one man paddling, the rest of the wait would still take a while.

Chogan was at the front of the crowd when Etchemin and Abooksigun neared the shore. Oota Dabun was in the bottom of the canoe that had been floating loose. Chogan could feel his heart race as he stared at her. He could see her body, but did not know if she was alive or dead. He looked from Etchemin to Abooksigun, but neither man's face revealed her state. He would have to wait until he could touch her before he would know for certain. He prayed again as he waited for a time that seemed as long as the Great Spirit Kitanitowit had existed.

Chogan ran into the water to reach for the woman who had shaken his soul. He grabbed her, lifted her, and felt joy as her body twitched in his arms. She was alive, but sick. She vomited as he held her, on his chest and side. Still, he held her tight and cried out his gratitude to Kitanitowit.

He set her on the ground. Her wrists were bound together and so were her ankles, so first he untied the ropes, then touched her forehead with his own and wailed another prayer that this sickness Oota Dabun suffered with was not the same disease the white-faces had brought to the village of Abooksigun's brother.

***

Ryan

He squinted his eyes, as Glen brought him out of his hypnotic state. Ryan tried to wrap his mind around the experience. "Did she live?" he asked, his voice shaking.

"She was fine a few hours before the canoe incident, which means the vomiting was an isolated symptom. It came on too quickly to be smallpox or measles. I think it's safe to say that Oota Dabun was drunk. She would be hung-over in the morning, but that's about it. The fact that her wrists and ankles were bound worries me. Someone put her there."

"Then why did you bring me back? I might have learned who did it."

"Chogan's feelings about Oota Dabun were clear once you felt his reaction. The regression had served its purpose and I pulled you back."

Ryan smiled and nodded knowingly, but his emotions weren't any clearer than they'd been before. Prior to the regression, he'd been wondering why he felt so much. What he was feeling now seemed like nothing against the scale of Chogan's feelings, causing him to wonder if he felt enough.

"Is it normal for two souls to change their relationship?" he asked.

Glen smiled slightly, as if he found the question to be cute. The look annoyed Ryan, but he was still glad he'd asked.

"Relationships change over time, even within a single lifetime, but there are many more factors if you're talking about more than one incarnation. Chogan was a young man and Oota Dabun a young woman, so I would guess that your soul and Diane's are more likely to maintain a similar relationship than Martha and Diane's."

He paused and smiled again. "But both relationships will be influenced by emotions from the past. We just don't know how or to what extent."

Glen's answer pleased Ryan until he remembered how he still didn't know the feelings of either Diane or Oota Dabun.

Chapter Eight
Heather

The night would be cold, so Heather asked Martin Malek for advice. When he wasn't working, Martin loved being outdoors: hunting, camping, and fishing. He loaned her a cheap pair of binoculars, a down jacket, and a pair of camouflage pants. The clothes were too big, but they were warm. She held the pants up with an old belt.

They worked together at Ryan's cabinet shop where she was the CAD drafter-receptionist and he was the carpenter-installer. She was the one who had convinced Ryan to hire him, but their relationship went back further than work. Martin dated Heather's mother before Heather was born, and spent a few nights with Heather, mostly after she was old enough to be legal. He was close to fifty with a full head of white hair and a matching soul patch beard. He still looked good and was an excellent resource. Thanks to his clothing, the crisp November night wasn't going to bother Heather.

She watched Diane from the lakeside yard. The house had an open design, which allowed Heather to see the living room, dining room, and kitchen without having to move. She hid behind a poplar tree, but didn't need to. The lights were on in Diane's home and it was dark outside. She could see in without any problems and was certain Diane could not see out. The moon was hidden by clouds, which worked to Heather's advantage.

Heather hid in this yard, in the same position for five nights, studying Diane's routine the way a pro athlete studies his opponents. So this night Heather knew exactly what to do. True to form, Diane entered her home from the back. Heather heard Ryan drive off after the back door closed.

She watched Diane drop her coat on one of the couches, then head to the bathroom. Heather waited patiently, knowing that Diane's first time would take less than a minute. The second trip, after drinking her nightly cup of cocoa, generally took longer. It was probably when she brushed her teeth and removed her makeup.

Dr. Montero told Heather to leave an "escape route" for Diane. Heather planned to follow through on that request, but not only because she respected the doctor's wishes. Diane was her half-sister, another daughter of Heather's father. When her mother told her the truth about their complicated family tree, she made Heather promise to respect her blood relatives. Neither Diane's mother nor Diane's other half-sister had shared any blood with Heather, so it had been all right to hate them. And she had.

Heather waited for years after her mother told her about her family. She kept waiting after her own mother died. Then, when the time was right, she acted and achieved the justice she deserved without regret. But this plan of Dr. Montero's affected Diane and Heather intended to keep her promise. Diane would live to see another day whether she deserved to or not.

She worried when Diane came out of the bathroom while brushing her hair, because it was a change in routine from the other nights. But Heather was relieved when Diane set the brush down on the kitchen counter and reached for the cupboard with the cocoa mix. She watched as Diane opened the container and put three heaping teaspoons in a mug she grabbed from the draining rack. Diane stirred it a few times then put the cup in her microwave. Apparently, she hadn't noticed the extra white particles in the mix. The next part of Heather's plan would be both risky and physically demanding.

Diane turned on a lamp, then sat on the couch across from the one where she had dropped her coat. She placed her cocoa on the end table and picked up a book, still in keeping with her daily routine.

She read for a while, pausing to drink every few minutes. After at least ten sips, her head nodded forward. The book slipped from her hands to her lap. Diane rubbed her eyes, sipped more of her cocoa, and tried to read again. She appeared to have problems keeping her eyes open, put the book and cocoa down, and tried to stand. After a single step, Diane turned back to the couch. She half lunged, half fell into the place where she'd been sitting.

Heather moved to a different position in the yard to see the couch more clearly. Diane lay on it, on her side, crumpled in an awkward position like a child who had fallen asleep in front of television. This was perfect. If the drug had left her in a drunken state rather than knocking her out, Heather might have had to cancel the plan, but Diane looked dead to the world.

Heather waited a few more minutes, to be certain it was safe to act, then went to the front door. It was open because she had left it open earlier. Diane had entered through the back door and hadn't checked the front.

The first time Heather went into Diane's house that night, when she laced the cocoa, she sliced a line in a screen beside the front door then slipped a bent coat hanger through the slit and used it to hook the inside lever handle. It had been a tricky process because the wire loop had to be positioned far enough from the center to get leverage, but not so far it would slip off. It had taken her more than a dozen tries before the door opened. As her mother used to say, "Persistence leads to success."

This time, she went straight for Diane and tried to wake her. If she didn't have enough roofies in her system to keep her knocked out, Heather planned to say she saw Diane through the window and came in to save her life, a weak claim at best.

Diane didn't wake, so Heather retrieved the coat from the couch where Diane had left it and started to put it back on the unconscious woman. It wasn't an easy task, especially pushing Diane's limp arms through the sleeves, but the coat didn't have to be arranged perfectly, it just had to keep her warm enough to survive. Next Heather had to get her out of the house and down to the dock.

She went outside and located Diane's wheelbarrow. It was too wide to get through the door, so she left it outside, which meant she had to get Diane's body out the door. Heather lifted her into a sitting position, then got behind her and wrapped her arms around Diane's upper body. From that angle, she could drag her. Her skirt caught on the storm door, but that was the only time Heather had to set her down.

Once outside, Heather lifted Diane's body into the wheelbarrow to bring her to the waterfront. She took her down the four stairs leading to the dock, placed her in Martha's canoe, arranged her on her back, bound her ankles and wrists to the canoe seats, and got the boat into the lake. Diane made a few sounds as she was jostled about and even spoke a few incoherent words, but never came out of her semi-conscious state. Heather went back to retrieve the binoculars. Leaving them would have been a serious mistake.

Heather towed the canoe using the rented jon boat, the same small boat she had used to tow it across from Martha's dock. She set it free on the other side of the point where it could be seen from Ryan's home. After that last step, Heather used the boat to get back to where her car was parked. She needed to get a few hours sleep before work. If she appeared exhausted and Ryan noticed, he might suspect her involvement.

***

Ryan

Ryan's cell rang as he was starting to rinse the breakfast dishes, while Glen sat at the table finishing his coffee. Maya went back to her room to get her book bag.

"I'm worried about Diane." The call was from Martha. "I was going to paddle around the island this morning, but my canoe was gone. I called Diane to find out if she might know something. She didn't answer and she *never* shuts off her phone. I know you went out with her last night, so I thought there was a chance she might be there."

"Diane and the canoe are both missing?" Ryan choked the question out.

Glen's eyes went wide. He stood up and approached Ryan.

"If you know something, tell me," Martha demanded.

"I had another regression yesterday. Something just like this happened to Oota Dabun. I've got to look for Diane right now. I'll call if we find her. No. I'll call either way."

"What are you planning?" Glen asked.

"Maya," Ryan shouted. "Get out to the bus stop before it comes. I'll see you after school."

Ryan darted out the door and ran down to the dock with Glen behind him. He tore at the cover on his boat and tossed it in a clump on the dock.

"I see something across the lake by the bridge," Glen yelled.

They pulled beside the canoe in less than a minute. She lay in the bottom of the boat. Ryan was scared she might be dead, until he saw her move. She was in a semiconscious state, her jaw shaking and her lips tinted blue. The temperature was cold, upper thirties, maybe forty at the most.

"She's tied," Glen said.

Ryan shut off the engine and reached under the deck. He had placed a blanket there after Maya's midnight swim.

"Cover her," he told Glen. "I'll tow the canoe to my dock. We can untie her there. The important thing is to warm her." The canoe had no tie rope, so Glen switched boats, sat in the front seat, and held on to the rope from Ryan's.

"Did it drop below freezing last night?" Glen asked when they reached the dock where they found Martha waiting.

"I don't know how cold it got," she answered.

One of the knots had pulled too tight. Ryan had to cut it with a fishing knife.

"This must be a repeating event," Glen told them as they lifted her to the dock. "It's too coincidental."

"Does that mean the same soul who set Oota Dabun adrift, did this to Diane?" Ryan asked

"Most likely."

They carried Diane into Ryan's home and put her on the couch. She was awake now, but shivering. She couldn't walk on her own and was saying things that made no sense.

Martha assured her she'd be fine as they tried to get her to drink a cup of warm tea. After she finished half the drink, they got her up again and helped her out to Ryan's van.

"Can you drive faster?" Martha asked, "She's shaking—a lot." They were on the way to Dover General. Martha was in the back with Diane while Ryan drove. Glen stayed at Ryan's house in case Maya had a problem with the bus.

Ryan glanced back at the two women. Diane still wore her coat, and was covered with the blanket. Martha held it in place as she stroked Diane's hair.

"What are we going to tell them at the hospital?" Martha asked.

"The truth."

"She appears drugged. They might suspect you, since she was with you last night."

"All I care about is getting her to a doctor."

***

Diane

The doctors kept Diane overnight. They ran tests to see if she had suffered a stroke during the ordeal. The next day, the attending physician said she appeared fine, but Dr. Montero came by her room and offered to help her deal with any psychological issues the attack might have caused.

"Don't you generally work with children?" Diane asked.

"Not exclusively and I'd like to help. I'll cover any costs above what your insurance pays."

Diane agreed to call her office to set up an appointment. Other than a few bruises, she didn't feel any different physically. She remembered falling asleep at home and waking up in the boat for a short time after they found her. But that was all hazy. She didn't fully wake up until she was in the hospital. She had been violated. She hadn't been raped, but she'd been drugged and left where the cold could have killed her.

The tests showed Rohypnol in her system, and at first, the police had suspected Ryan. But they searched her home while she was in the hospital and found the drug in her cup and in the cocoa mix in her cupboard. They said it could have been anyone.

Martha drove her home and offered to stay. Diane sent her away, saying she needed time alone. But as she walked around the house, she knew that her life had changed in ways she was just beginning to realize. She called Ryan and, when he didn't answer, she left a message asking him to come.

Diane looked out a front window at the waterfront. First, her mother had drowned, then she'd been tied to a boat and set adrift in the same place. Her stomach felt queasy. She wished she could eat something, but she didn't trust the food in her house. She would have to make a grocery run before dinner.

Who could possibly hate her enough to do this? Was it a man or a woman? One person or a group? And why?

As she turned away from the window, she noticed the slit in the screen.

***

Ryan

"I brought dinner," Ryan told her when he arrived at her back door.

She was still wearing the clothing she'd had on when she returned from the hospital, a black and white striped top with a blue skirt. Martha had picked the outfit out of Diane's closet because the only clothes Diane had with her were the ones she'd been wearing when she was set adrift.

"Hope you're in the mood for fast food."

"May I show you something?" she asked. There was urgency in her voice, causing Ryan to forget about his Big Mac.

He followed her to the front of her house where she pointed at a window beside the door. He wasn't sure what she was looking at until she got down on one knee and slipped a finger through a slit in the screen. He knelt beside her, still uncertain what point she was making.

She said, "There's no damage on either side of this cut, which means it wasn't torn. It must have been done with a knife."

They were so close he could feel her breath on his ear and smell the soap on her skin. When he turned, their lips almost touched. He backed away slightly to focus on her words.

"If this was here before, I would have noticed it when I was cleaning." She opened the slit slightly. "Someone could have worked a wire through here and got in by hooking the knob. I was certain I hadn't left the door unlocked and this proves I was right."

"The police didn't see it?"

"So far they haven't been very helpful."

She stood up so quickly, it seemed to Ryan she was jumping away from him. As he watched, she began pacing about the room.

Ryan moved beside her and took her hand while they walked. "Easy, Diane." He spoke in a gentle soothing voice as if he was trying to soothe a wild animal. He stopped, pulled her to him, and wrapped his other arm around her waist. She responded by holding him tight and placing her head on his shoulder. Their bodies were together, but hers was still shaking. He was afraid to move or to let her go.

"Someone broke into my house and did God knows what to me before dumping me in that canoe."

He touched her cheek softly with his own.

"I was always secure in this house, even sitting on the dock after sunset. The stars seemed brighter back then and I felt close to God. Now it feels as if He has abandoned me. First my mother, now this."

"We'll find whoever did it. I promise. And we'll also find whoever murdered your mother and Beth." This was the first time he'd acknowledged that both of the deaths had been murders. He wondered if she noticed.

"Thank you."

"And you can stay at my place until we do."

"You and Maya don't have room for me. I'll ask Martha if I can stay with her."

"But I want to protect you, Diane. I can't do that if you're on the island."

"You are sweet, Ryan. But this isn't about what you want. It's about what I need."

"Then call Martha now." He released his grip on her, so she could make the call, but instead of leaving his arms, she moved her lips to his and kissed him.

Ryan's body responded immediately to the soft, wet feel of Diane's mouth, to the feel of her body, and to the smell of her hair. Each sensation seemed to ignite the next. She pushed her fingers into his hair, grabbing hold with both hands. While she kissed him, he reached under her top and under her bra until he cupped one of her breasts. She stopped kissing to bury her face in his neck as they both shivered and she cried out a soft, breathy sound.

They drifted to the floor as if their motions were choreographed, then pulled at each other's clothing until every barrier between them was gone and everywhere they touched, their skin was one flesh. Ryan's heart was racing. His need for her seemed almost spiritual, as if their souls were connecting. He had never experienced anything close to this with anyone else, not even with Beth.

He was Chogan and Diane was Oota Dabun. But Ryan wasn't frightened, not for himself nor for the soulmate he held, because everything felt natural and good. Who they were didn't matter, neither did the color of their hair, their eyes, their skin. The way their voices sounded and what their bodies felt were nothing compared to the draw of their spirits. They knew they belonged together and were surrounded by the power of that knowledge.

Ryan understood the eternal side of their spiritual love, but at the same time that love was in the moment and physical. He felt his release into her body and her acceptance of him. They lay there intertwined, breathing together until he broke the silence to say, "You're beautiful."

She tightened her hold on him before smiling and replying, "So are you. And you saved my life. But I'm still staying with Martha."

Her words didn't make Ryan happy for a few reasons, mostly because he wanted her to stay where he could watch over her. But he also felt a pang of jealousy tied to Martha's life as Phillip. He hid all his thoughts quickly and didn't think Diane could read his mind.

He kept his weight on his arms and legs as he pulled his body off Diane's. She squeezed him one last time then let him go. They sat up, both cross-legged, a few feet apart, staring at each other. He watched her brush her disheveled hair out of her eyes. It was blond and long, long enough to reach below her shoulders, but not to cover her breasts. He was intrigued by her hair after spending so many years with Beth's short, dark cut. Diane had small breasts, like Beth's, but was heavier than Maya's mother had been. She was taller, but nearly identical in the hips. Like Beth, Diane had an athletic body.

Diane seemed more interested in his naked body than in the way she was revealing her own. Ryan liked how she was comfortable in front of him, especially since this had been their first intimacy—at least it was their first one in this life.

Then a sudden look of worry crossed Diane's face. She reached for her skirt and used it to cover her body. Ryan wasn't sure what had caused this change until he saw her looking at the front of her house and the windows without curtains.

Chapter Nine
Kari

*D*iane scheduled an appointment with Dr. Kari Montero for the following Tuesday. Kari thought she was almost ready for the study. Like Maya, Diane had lost her mother in water. And like Maya, she'd survived a dangerous situation related to water.

Maya understood water as a metaphor for life and death. Kari needed to use the same analogy with Diane. She could emphasize the word *border* and show her how two worlds can exist above and below the water's surface, just as she had with Maya. But an adult would not be impressed with a folded paper boat in a fish aquarium.

The phone rang. Kari glanced at the screen. It was Heather's number, which wasn't good. They had agreed to wait at least a month before contacting each other—unless there was an emergency.

"I need to talk."

This was not what Kari wanted to hear. "We agreed you'd wait before you schedule another session."

"I need someone who will listen to me."

"It can't be me. Not now."

"It can't be Ryan either. Or Martin."

"Of course not."

"Well—there isn't anyone else, not since my mom died."

"Just wait a couple more weeks, then we can restart your regular sessions without raising suspicions."

This is what I worried about, Kari thought after Heather hung up. She's a loner, which gives her the freedom to do whatever she wants, but only because she's got nothing to lose.

Heather's life was the antithesis of what Kari desired for her own. The young lady was as close to invisible as anyone could be in this age of mass communication, relatively unknown to everyone except her boss, Ryan, her co-worker, Martin, and a few customers of the cabinet shop. This hard truth was sad, but also a good reminder of the importance of becoming well known.

Kari could only reach the recognition she longed for if her study was recognized by her peers, while also popular with the general public. Water was the key to both those goals. It was the element that would make her study unique, as well as the draw for the huge portion of the general population who found serenity in oceans, rivers, and lakes.

***

Maya

Lucas lived closer to Maya than any of her other friends and often asked her to come by his house after school. It was no surprise when he suggested they meet at the corner of Waterside Drive and Brady Road. Although they generally got together at one of their houses, they usually ended up doing something outside. Most of her friends at school were girls, but they spent too much time watching TV and playing Truth or Dare. An afternoon with Lucas was an adventure. This time they couldn't get together until four thirty because he had homework.

It wasn't close to sunset, so she was surprised that Lucas had a flashlight with him. He led her up Waterside and through a small wooded area to the bank of a narrow inlet. He showed her a hole in the bank surrounded by tall grasses.

"It's a nest for a mother muskrat and her babies. Me and my dad saw the mother from our dock, so we came over here and found the nest. You can look in with the light, but don't get too close. Dad says they bite if you corner them."

Maya grabbed the flashlight from Lucas, pointed it down the hole, and knelt to peak at the rodents. She saw brown fur and the shine from the reflection off a couple of eyes. She wanted to get closer, but knew Lucas well enough to take his warning seriously. They both remained a few feet from the entrance.

"The little ones are called kits," Lucas told her, as he looked over her shoulder. "There are five in the litter. They come out mostly at night, but sometimes you can see them after supper." Lucas had his hand on her arm. He'd never touched her before.

She looked at the nest as she spoke. "Cool."

"You can stay for dinner at my house, if it's OK with your dad. We might see the muskrats come out."

"I've got to get home. My dad doesn't know I'm here." Maya said that last part before she had a chance to think. It wasn't true, just a good excuse. But she didn't want an excuse. Sometimes she said things she didn't mean around Lucas. He made her nervous like that.

Maya thought about Lucas as she started her walk home, but her thoughts turned to the muskrats. They were at home in the water and on land, which meant they crossed the border Dr. Kari talked about. Maybe they could teach her something that would help her find her mother.

***

Kari

There was no indication of aqua-phobia during any of the sessions Kari held with Maya. Also, neither she nor Heather had observed any indications of a fear of water in

Maya's behavior when she was apart from the security of her therapy.

Kari could see the drowning of Diane's mother hadn't changed Diane's relationship with the lake any more than Beth's drowning affected Maya. Both their reactions were probably due to the lake's presence in their lives long before the deaths of their mothers. It was too soon to know if the canoe incident had affected Diane, but it seemed odd that Kari saw such limited reactions from both of them.

Odd wasn't bad. In fact, for a study to have any hope of bringing out something new, odd seemed necessary. It was also important for a study to become popular. The general public loved odd things. A quick sampling of videos that have gone viral proved the point. The trouble was this particular scenario included no phobia symptoms—no anxiety, no poor hygiene, no hyperventilating, and no fainting. The members of the public who didn't share those issues loved to hear about them. The lack of these indicators in their own lives proved to uneducated people that they were sane.

***

Martha

$\mathcal{D}$iane had begun cleaning the table when Martha reached forward and touched her arm. They were in Martha's house and had just finished a meal of Pickerel, brown rice, and green beans. Martha caught the fish a few months earlier and thawed them for her overnight guest. They also started a bottle of Pinot Noir, which loosened Martha's tongue for the conversation with her young friend.

"Leave the dishes. I need to tell you something about my ancestors."

Diane sat quickly. "Anything you can tell me about tribal life is important."

Something about the way Diane used the words *tribal life* irritated Martha, but it was her jealousy over

Diane's past life that had her on edge. She wouldn't let her own petty feelings interfere with their relationship.

"Our tribe has a long standing oral tradition." She was careful to say *our* rather than *my*. "Most of the stories are history, but a few are concerned with the future rather than the past."

"The future? That's a surprise. The feeling I had when I was in the memories of Oota Dabun was that one of the most wonderful characteristics of the Lenape culture was the ability to live in the moment."

That's what people say about dogs, Martha thought. She was irritated and realized it was more than her jealousy. It was her guilt. She breathed, controlled her emotions, and tried to explain rather than criticize. "You think they didn't worry about what the onslaught of Europeans would do to their lives? What about Abooksigun? He was as scared for his village as any leader in the time of a plague."

"I see."

"Good. But we're getting off track. A prophecy was passed down in my family about a golden haired woman who would lose her mother to water."

"Lose her mother?" Diane's voice cracked and Martha knew she had her attention.

Martha sucked in a breath. "I can tell you're drawing the same conclusion I drew..."

"What's the rest of the story?" Diane interrupted.

"There's no specific predictions, just that this woman becomes important."

Martha was comfortable with people, which is why she was good at her job. But this was different. She'd been closer to Diane's mother than any other person, including all the Lenape women she knew. And since Lori's death, Martha had grown to love Diane like a daughter.

"The story came with something, an object handed down from generation to generation. It was to stay in our family until this golden haired woman appeared, then it was to be turned over to her."

"You're saying I'm that woman and you have something to give me?"

"Exactly. I wasn't sure until the regressions began, but the way you described the jewel in the sword handle seemed right to me. Then Glen sent me back to my memories of Phillip. The sword had been taken away by then, but I felt the importance of the jewel in its handle, even through the pain I was experiencing. It was enough for me. I am sure you are the one, the golden haired woman discussed in the stories my family passed down from generation to generation." Martha handed Diane the jeweled band she held, saying, "It's a forehead band."

"It looks medieval," Diane said, "like something from ancient England or Scandinavia. I would think your ancestors would have passed down something Native American, like the bear claw necklace you wear."

Diane stepped into the bathroom to try it on in front of a mirror. She rarely wore jewelry, but this piece would have intrigued her even without Martha's story. It was an ornate chain appearing to be silver, with a red jewel in the center of a pendant hanging down over the arch of her nose. Diane turned right then left and tilted her head to the side as she studied her image. The band seemed to emphasize her best features, her smooth forehead, her high cheekbones, her white smile. But it wasn't the ornamental effect on her appearance that drew her to the pendant. With the forehead band in place, Diane felt like royalty, like a strong medieval queen who could solve any problem.

"I'm honored to give this to you," Martha said. "I never imagined I would be the one to find you."

"You're saying I'm special?"

"Of course. My family has been searching for you for hundreds of years."

"But why?"

"I don't know," Martha said, "but we'll find out soon enough. Like I said, the jewel in the band is the same one that was in the handle of Phillip's sword."

Diane got up from the table and walked to the door that opened to the screened-in porch. She was looking across the lake, presumably at her home.

Martha went on to tell Diane the jeweled band had been handed down through generations of her family and the prophecy of the golden haired woman had been passed with it. But this type of mysticism was unusual among her people. The prophecies of the shamans were generally about problems of the forest and its inhabitants, more akin to warnings from an environmentalist than religious predictions from a priest.

"Maybe that's why it's European rather than Native American," Diane said.

"Perhaps," Martha replied.

***

Diane

"Can we sit on the dock for a while?" Diane understood Martha needed to respect what had been passed down through generations, but she had questions about the prophecy itself, things that didn't make sense.

Martha raised her eyebrows. "It's cold."

"I want to sit with you under the stars. We can bundle up."

Now that Diane was aware of her life as Oota Dabun, she was more attuned to nature. Still, it was an odd feeling to be convincing Martha to step outside when her friend had always been the one with the need to be in touch with life.

Martha kept a few heavy chairs on her dock during the summer, but had stored them at the end of the season. She grabbed a couple of folding ones from a closet. She followed Diane to the waterfront after they had both put on sweaters.

"How do you know I'm the right woman?" Diane asked.

"The sword was in our past life. Also, you're mother died and everything else fit: your hair for one and the fact that her death was a drowning."

"Maya fits the same description."

"Maya's a child."

"Does age matter? And what about Heather? Her hair is blond and she lost her mother. Bella died of a heart attack, but we don't know the circumstances. Maybe she was swimming."

"Maybe, but none of that matters. The stone was in the handle of the sword that drew Oota Dabun to Phillip. And I love you like you're my own child. I think that's important, don't you?"

Diane looked up at the sky. The light pollution was such that the stars weren't close to the canopy that had once covered Oota Dabun's village, but they were still beautiful. She looked for the big and little dippers, the only constellations she knew. She couldn't find them. The mainland trees might have been blocking her view, if the dippers were too low on the horizon.

"Love me?" Diane asked as she felt the pace of her breathing increase slightly.

Martha spoke without taking her eyes off the sky. "The literal translation is 'a woman with hair like the feathers of a golden eagle,' but I still knew it was you. You fit the prophecy. I have no children, so you are my daughter more than any other. No one else could take the jewel and the prophecy from me. And yes, I loved you when you were a child and I love you now that you are a woman.

Those feelings will never change. I never doubted them—even before Glen showed us a new way to view eternity."

Diane thought about Martha and about what had happened with Ryan earlier that day. She continued to look at the sky. The Earth was a miniscule spot among the stars in the universe, yet there were more kinds of love in this tiny world than anyone could count.

She turned her head to Martha and asked, "Hair like feathers?"

They both laughed and Martha suggested heading back up to the house to finish the bottle of wine.

Chapter Ten
Kari

$\mathcal{D}$iane was scheduled for the following Tuesday, which meant Kari had to prepare. The first appointment was always the most critical.

Both Maya and Diane had experienced significant traumatic events and would work well as the adolescent and adult subjects of her case study. Kari already knew Maya did not show any indications of a fear of water. On Tuesday, she would find out if Diane also had little to no reaction to her trauma. Aqua-phobia is partially a reaction to events and partially genetic. Kari would need to find more information about their families. She might also recruit Heather again, if she needed more data.

***

Glen

$\mathcal{M}$uch had happened since the last time Diane and Martha had been involved with a regression. Glen hoped the events of the last few days wouldn't be a distraction for either woman. He looked at Diane. "I hesitated to hold the last session, because Ryan was alone and we work so well as a group. But I'm glad we did. Learning about the canoe incident with Oota Dabun might have saved your life."

"And I'm grateful to you both," Diane said. Glen noticed Ryan was watching her as she fidgeted with her hands, drawing circles on the back of her left with the index finger of her right.

"Thank you," Glen said. "There are other repeating events from that life which may be critical as well. We need to pay careful attention. Two aspects of Ryan's regression jumped out at me, both having to do with children. The first was that Oota Dabun and Phillip had a healthy daughter. The second was that when Chogan saw Pules, his first thought was that she was always alone now that her baby was gone. We need to find out what happened. I want to send you back to a time prior to whatever happened to Nuttah."

"I'm ready when you are," Diane said. She looked around the room at her friends, then walked toward the couch.

***

Oota Dabun

She woke to the sound of voices: a distressed woman and a man trying to console her. She recognized the voices of Pules and Abooksigun. Oota Dabun got up as quickly as she could. Her body was huge, which made rising from her sleeping pallet difficult, but she wasn't the first woman to carry a child.

The day before, Pules told Abooksigun that Nuttah's body was hot and the word spread through the village. When Phillip heard, he ran to Pules' wigwam to see if he could help. Abooksigun blocked him from entering her home and made threatening gestures. Although Phillip's inability to speak Unami kept Phillip from understanding fully, he told Oota Dabun he believed Abooksigun was accusing him of bringing the diseases of the whites to the village.

"I have been with you for moons," Phillip said when he returned to their home. "I could not have brought a sickness even if I wanted to."

But Elias and Noah had arrived recently. They could be the carriers. Still, she did not argue, because at this time all that mattered was Nuttah's survival.

"Can you help her?" she asked, hoping he could appeal for mercy from their God.

Phillip told her he knew a way that might work, but it was risky. Both Abooksigun and Pules would think he was out of his mind and hate him even more if his idea failed.

"Do what has to be done," she told him and in the morning, when she awoke, he was not beside her.

Oota Dabun pushed off the bearskin she slept under and reached for her skirt and buckskin top. The skirt had to be tied higher than she liked because her belly was so big, but that was to be expected. She rushed out of her wigwam. Pules paced in front of her home, turning wildly to look from one direction to the next. She sobbed and tore her hair. Oota Dabun feared Nuttah had died overnight and ran to console her friend.

"She's gone! Someone stole my baby!"

Oota Dabun wrapped her arms around Pules. She thought of what Phillip had said. Could he have taken Nuttah? He said he knew something that *might* help her. She prayed he would appear at any moment with the child in his arms.

Pules pulled away from her. "I have to find her!"

"Tell me the places you have already looked and I will help."

"Abooksigun went into the forest. He told me to wait, but waiting hurts."

"I can stay here while you check the pond."

"You think she went to the water?"

"I don't know, but the only way we'll find her is to check every possible place."

Pules nodded, then ran toward the pond. As Oota Dabun watched, she saw Phillip coming from where Pules was heading. She could tell it was Phillip by his bulk and the color of his hair. He carried something in his arms as

Oota Dabun had hoped, but Pules screamed and she knew this wasn't good.

Oota Dabun started toward them, but couldn't go fast because the baby inside her made running difficult. When she reached them, they were both yelling in their own languages.

Pules had taken Nuttah from Phillip and was cradling her in her arms. The baby was soaking wet as if she had just been pulled from the pond. Pules was yelling that Phillip killed her daughter and Phillip was yelling that he had tried to save her life. Neither one could understand what the other was saying.

Nuttah appeared limp. Oota Dabun hoped Pules was wrong, that her daughter was unconscious rather than dead, but Phillip was not disagreeing.

"I tried to bring down her fever. I used the cold water, but I was too late."

"He wants you to know..." Oota Dabun started to tell Pules, but the woman stopped her from speaking.

"He wants? You are defending him."

"I am speaking his words, so you can understand."

"He killed my child. His words burn in my ears."

Phillip shouted at Oota Dabun. His words blurred because he was speaking too fast. She could tell he wanted to know what Pules was saying, but telling him would only make things worse.

Pules kept yelling. "You choose the white men over the Lenape every day. And you choose this one over your friends, over Chogan and me, even after he has killed Nuttah. This white man is a murderer, but you have betrayed everyone who has ever cared for you."

"What is she saying?" Phillip screamed.

Oota Dabun couldn't speak.

Pules started to walk away, but Abooksigun was running toward them. When she saw him, Pules stopped and wailed. Oota Dabun turned toward Phillip to warn him. The way he was standing and the look in his eyes told her he did not need language to understand. Abooksigun stopped to examine Nuttah. He spoke to Pules, but they were too far away for Oota Dabun to hear what he said. He placed his hand on Nuttah's lifeless head and paused for a moment before he turned toward Oota Dabun and Phillip.

"Tell me what happened," Abooksigun demanded when he reached Phillip and Oota Dabun.

"Phillip was trying to help."

"Maybe he says so, but Nuttah is dead."

"He tried to save her from the fever, but he couldn't."

"By drowning her?"

"Last night Phillip told me he knew of something that might help Nuttah. I thought he would pray to his God, but this is what he did instead. He told me he would be hated if it didn't work and it appears he was right." Oota Dabun glanced at Pules who was keeping her distance, but staring.

"Hate isn't the issue," Abooksigun said. "Phillip killed Pules' child and needs to pay. It does not matter what he was *trying* to do."

"You have been a great medicine man, but some people you were caring for have died. If this justice you speak of is right then you should also pay."

"Not the same. Not at all. Phillip claims he was trying to cure the fever, but the white-faces brought the disease."

"We don't know that. Many of our children became hot and sick before any whites came to our village. Even if this is a disease that came from the white-faces, it did not come from Phillip. He was in our village too long."

"He must pay. Look at Pules. Her heart is breaking."

Oota Dabun did not look at her friend. She was about to repeat her argument instead, when she saw Chogan coming from the longhouse. She would appeal to him. Abooksigun and Oota Dabun both spoke at once when Chogan was close enough to hear.

"Tell me what you're saying," Phillip demanded. But Oota Dabun held her hand out to quiet him. If she lost her concentration, she might lose the argument and Chogan's support. He could influence Abooksigun more than anyone else in the village.

Oota Dabun didn't know what to expect from Chogan. He had been her friend since they were both children and still loved her to this day. He seemed to hate Phillip at times, but she knew his feelings grew from his jealousy and believed he could control his emotions enough to be fair.

"Phillip has been with our village long enough to deserve the right of our justice," Oota Dabun argued.

Abooksigun countered with, "The white-face is not a citizen. He lives in our village because Oota Dabun wants him here. He has no rights. But Pules needs our concern and care. She and Nuttah are the citizens who deserve our justice."

"He was trying to save her life."

"Even a white-face deserves to be heard," Chogan said, looking at Phillip as he spoke. He turned to Oota Dabun and added, "Tell him he must stay in my wigwam while I call a meeting of the tribal council. They will need you as well to translate for him." He spoke to Pules, saying, "You can make your case at that time."

***

Martha

"We need to move forward to the council meeting," Glen said, as he brought Diane back from her regression. "But this time I want to work with Martha. Phillip's perspective is important since he was the one on trial."

After Diane sat up and acknowledged Glen's words with a nod, Martha moved to the couch and took Diane's place. The other time, Martha hadn't known what to expect, but this time she did. She was about to experience the thoughts and emotions Phillip felt when he was on trial for murder. She didn't know what type of penalties the Lenape councils handed out, but she believed death was likely.

When she was lying in the proper position and staring at the ceiling, Glen started to speak softly. Martha listened to his words and his tone as he guided her through memories of everyday experiences into visions of her past life in the Lenape village.

***

Phillip

Lussin was a word Abooksigun had been repeating to Phillip when he was bound on the dirt floor of Chogan's wigwam. He knew from the shaman's hate filled stare that the word wasn't good, but didn't know exactly what it meant until he was in the council house. He asked Oota Dabun to translate.

"You don't need to know," she told him.

"Not knowing makes me worry."

She had touched his shoulder, but looked away from his eyes. "It means burn."

"I see. And that is what they do to murderers?"

"You did not kill her. The sickness did."

"You and I know that, but convincing the others will be hard. They'll want to listen to Pules, who hates me."

"They will listen to everyone who wants to speak. That is what they do."

"Even Abooksigun? He hates me more than she does."

"He knows it was the disease and he will not lie."

"We will see."

Oota Dabun sat beside Phillip on one of the benches along the perimeter of the council house, the largest of the rectangular longhouses with a ceiling that reached the height of two people at the center. The building smelled of smoke and sweat. Abooksigun and Chogan sat across the room along with Noshi, the chief, and six other men. Women were also in the room. The council was all men, but anyone in the room was allowed to speak.

The only trials Phillip knew anything about were the ones run by the traveling magistrates in England. The verdicts of those had less to do with justice than what the wealthy landowners wanted. If this council had similar priorities, he was in trouble. Pules had the support of Abooksigun, one of the village's most respected citizens.

The process started with a talk by the chief, Noshi. He raised his hands and gaze toward the heavens, then spread his arms wide as if he was indicating everyone in the room. Phillip hoped the chief's gestures included him and were meant as a statement that Europeans deserved the same justice anyone else would receive. Phillip turned to look at Oota Dabun to see if she was ready to translate, but she was concentrating on the meeting.

Pules was the next to speak. Her words were fast and angry. She pointed at Phillip, then at her own chest. Oota Dabun had told him that Nuttah's name meant My Heart. Her gesture brought her loss home to the other mothers in the room as well as the men who loved them. Even Phillip felt like crying for her. The people who understood her words had to be filled with sadness and rage.

Abooksigun spoke next. His tone was less emotional than Pules', but during the middle of his speech, Phillip heard him mention Elias and Noah, so he was certain the medicine man was bringing up Nuttah's fever.

He wasn't pleased to have his friends drawn into this situation. Yet raising the issue of the disease worked in his favor. The child had died either from the illness or from the drowning, not from both, and the council had to know that.

When Abooksigun finished, Oota Dabun stood, turned to Phillip, and took his hand. "It is our turn now. You must stand in front of the council while I speak for you."

Phillip followed Oota Dabun to the center of the building. All the people were watching them, some with the anger of Pules in their expressions, but others with engaged looks he didn't understand. He couldn't watch Oota Dabun while she spoke, because his head was lowered in an attempt to appear sorrowful without a sign of guilt.

Her words flowed like creek water around the stone of his presence, a gentle, persistent current smoothing his rough surface while separating him from his judges. The sound of her voice was lyrical, but strong. Its tone offered him hope, but when she was done, he looked up and saw the expressions of the people in the longhouse had not changed. Phillip followed Oota Dabun back to his seat with the knowledge she had told his story and it was the best she could do.

Noshi stood and started to speak, but Chogan interrupted him and stepped to the center. After he said a few words, Oota Dabun turned to Phillip. "Chogan has asked for the right to speak and wants me to translate so you can understand."

Chogan's desire to speak worried Phillip because he believed the Lenape man hated him, but the situation couldn't get worse. He sat tall and listened as Oota Dabun translated Chogan's words.

"When I was a boy I did what the other sons of this village have always done. I went into the woods alone and waited for a vision from Kitanitowit. A family of otters lived along the bank of the river. Kitanitowit taught me that these creatures were to be my animal spirits, so I stayed and watched. I witnessed how they worked, played, and cared for each other during my days by their home and when I came back to our village, I was less selfish and wiser than I had been when I had left. I was a man.

"Most of the time girls become women without the need for a vision quest, but sometimes a special young lady may feel a need for the experience. Oota Dabun was one of these. She spoke of this desire often. She brought it up to me and I know she brought it up to Pules. But no one in our village supported her because she is a woman and does not have the need to understand animals the way a hunter does.

"Then Kitanitowit brought the white-face to her. Oota Dabun believed this badly injured man was her animal guide. Most of you will say that a man is not an animal, but I disagree. People are a type of animal whether they are Lenape, Iroquois, Susquehannock, or white. And what we can learn from a white-face animal is more important than anything I could learn from the otters.

"I do not believe Nuttah had the sickness Abooksigun has described, because she was the only one in our village to grow ill. But if she did and if there is truth in what Abooksigun tells us about the sickness, Nuttah would have died from it no matter what happened in the pond. And many children have died from the common fever, if that is what she had. Either way, Phillip did not kill Nuttah and killing him will not help our people.

"We need to trust Oota Dabun. This is her vision quest. If she says Phillip was trying to save Nuttah, then it is the truth. If she says he did not bring the disease, she is right about that as well. We have known her all her life. She deserves our respect."

Chogan walked back to his seat, Noshi stood again, and Oota Dabun stopped translating. Phillip went back to observing the expressions of the people in the longhouse to determine what was happening. Their anger had lessened. The rage in the eyes of the women in particular had left. But there was a different look now, one of fear. Fear wasn't good.

Pules was the one person in the room whose face still showed rage. Phillip watched her as the men on the council began to speak briefly. He understood this was their method of voting and thought a clue from Pules' expression might tell him which way the vote was headed. But she was staring straight back at him. He looked down and waited to hear the verdict from Oota Dabun.

Noshi spoke last. When he was done, Oota Dabun leaned over to tell Phillip he was free to return to her home.

"Ahhh," Phillip sighed. "Then our life will return to normal."

Oota Dabun shook her head. "It will never be normal again."

***

Diane

$\mathcal{D}$iane watched Martha sit up after Glen called her back. The older woman's body was shaking as she leaned forward, and breathed deeply. Glen touched her shoulder to reassure her. Diane knew what it felt like to be regressed, how the memories belonged to Martha as much as they had belonged to Phillip. Martha sat through the trial feeling Phillip's fear of being burned alive. And if it hadn't been for Chogan, he might have been.

Diane turned her head to look at Ryan and knew she loved him. Were her feelings tied somehow to what he'd done for Phillip when he was Chogan? Then she looked at Martha and wondered if there would ever be a way to get a handle on what she felt for her. She loved her before she knew anything about her life as Phillip. She loved her before her mother's death. But what she felt when she was Oota Dabun was different. She hadn't understood until

Chogan explained the importance of her vision quest. Phillip wasn't a man to her, he was a gateway to a part of her life that had been missing. Even the intimacy of Oota Dabun carrying his child couldn't change how she felt.

Chapter Eleven
Maya

Dr. Kari spoke of the border between the surface world and the world beneath the water. The place between worlds seemed as difficult to imagine as the heaven a few of her friends talked about—until Lucas showed her the muskrats. Maya got a book from the school library to read more about these animals.

She learned that their name might have come from "muscasus," a Native American word meaning "it is red." It also might have come from the way they smell, which sounded awful, but had truth to it. She also learned muskrats live in and out of the water and have lots of babies. If the lady who had called her to the lake was not trying to harm her and if Dr. Kari was right about the magic of the border, then these interesting animals might be the key to finding her mother.

Maya decided she would sneak out on Saturday to see the muskrats again. The book said they came out just before sunrise and after sunset. If she watched at the right time, she might see something important.

There was frost on the ground when Maya sneaked out of her house. Her jeans, sweatshirt, and thick jacket made her too warm while she was walking, but she would need them when she was sitting by the lake. She could get in trouble if her father discovered she was missing, yet the chance to learn something about her mother made the risk worth taking.

Maya remembered the place on Waterside Drive where she needed to step off the road, so she had no trouble getting back to the muskrat hole. She sat on a stone, half hidden by a poplar tree, and watched. After waiting at least ten minutes, Maya saw activity. A large muskrat popped up in the water and was followed by six more. The six were much smaller, each one-half the size of their parent.

The water was high, but Maya could see marks on rocks at the water's edge indicating it had once been higher. That morning the muskrats were using an underwater entrance to go in and out of their home, but the book had said they needed at least one entrance above the waterline. The entrance Lucas had shown her was high enough, as long as there wasn't a flood.

There was a slight breeze rustling the leaves of the trees as well as the tall, grass like plants growing in the shallow water. The wind also created ripples in the lake's surface, but nothing as large as the ripples created by the swimming muskrats.

One of the young muskrats lumbered around a section of a fallen tree half in the water. Maya had a distinct feeling she'd seen a rodent take that path once before, around a similar dead tree. She thought back to when Lucas had brought her here, the only other time she had been at this place. She hadn't seen any muskrats outside of their burrow that time. So where was this feeling coming from, this sense that she'd been here before?

Maya had looked at a couple of muskrat videos on YouTube, but the feeling didn't come from them. The early morning lake smell was part of it, along with the breeze on her face and the sound of tiny waves splashing through the tall grass near the rocks. None of those were in the videos.

She also felt as if her dad was with her and looked around for signs of him, but he was back at the house and probably furious if he had discovered she was gone.

She needed to get home as quickly as she could.

***

Ryan

"She's coming up the road."

Glen's voice carried down to Ryan, who had been pacing by the lake for twenty minutes or so, since the moment he discovered his daughter's empty bed. His mind flooded with images from her night swim: pictures of her head bobbing among the waves and of her thin, naked body tumbling over the side of his boat as he pulled her out of the water. He'd been cursing himself for letting this happen a second time and, worse, he'd been cursing Beth for not being alive to help him protect their daughter.

He ran in as soon as he heard Glen shout. They were both at the door when Maya reached the porch. Ryan wrapped his arms around his girl, lifted her up, and cried into her hair. "I... I thought you were gone! I was so scared!" The relief turned to anger as he let her down. "Where did you go?" he shouted. "How could you do this after all that's happened?"

"I was looking for Mommy." Maya was crying now, harder than her father. "Dr. Kari told me there's a border between the world above the water and the world below. She said Mommy might be there, but only I could know. Then Lucas showed me the family of muskrats. They can live above and below, so I thought they might be able to help. And then I felt like I'd been there before—with you."

"Oh, Maya. I have no idea what Dr. Kari was talking about. Mommy is not under the water. But we'll see her again someday, I'm sure we will."

"I know. That's what everybody says. But when?"

"Nobody knows. But it has nothing to do with water or muskrats. It's about getting by day to day and trying to care for our friends and our family and living the best lives we can live."

"You mean I shouldn't sneak out, ever."

"Yes. And I mean you should never scare me like that."

Glen suggested they step inside. He said he wanted to hear more about the muskrats.

They moved to the couch and chairs where Glen had conducted the regressions, and sat in a circle. He looked at Maya and said, "So you felt as if you had been in that place before?"

"Not really," she answered.

"I thought that's what you said."

"It wasn't that place, but it was a lot like it. And I was watching muskrats, which is weird, because before Lucas showed me the burrow, I couldn't care less about them. They look like rats."

"I see. So something drew you to the burrow Lucas had shown you."

Ryan was starting to worry about this conversation for multiple reasons. What Dr. Montero had said about borders didn't sound like the words of a psychiatrist, which made him wonder what she was up to. Glen was interrogating Maya with the force of a prosecutor, which worried him to no end. And Maya's déjà vu claim rang true, because he felt as if he had experienced the same event. Could there be déjà vu for two people? He thought so, since souls travel together from life to life.

"I think we've talked about this enough," Ryan said. "Maya, you are never... never to sneak out again. Understand?"

She nodded.

"And Glen, we need to have this conversation later. All right?"

He nodded the way Maya had, but the look on his face told Ryan his mind was wandering.

***

Glen

Ryan told his daughter she would not be leaving her room for the rest of the day and while she was there, she needed to clean it.

"Cleaning her room is her regular responsibility," he told Glen after Maya had left the room. "So it isn't much of a punishment, but I think she gets the idea."

"I'm sure she does. She's an intelligent young lady."

"Thank you. Sometimes I worry she's too smart."

"She's something else as well," Glen told him. "Maya's the key."

"There you go again. That's what I thought you were after when you were questioning her before."

"Déjà vu experiences are past life memories poking through the complexities of living our current lives. If I could regress her, I could find out more."

"I'm sure you could, but I won't let you try."

"You brought me here for Maya."

"That's right, but I can't have you hypnotize her while she's still seeing Dr. Montero, not without checking first."

"Speaking of which, what's going on with this border thing?"

"All I know is what Maya said."

Glen bit his lip. He understood enough about child psychiatry to know it wasn't helpful to tell a ten year old girl her dead mother might be somewhere on the border of life above water and life below.

***

Kari

"Make yourself comfortable, Diane. Would you like a cup of coffee or tea?"

Kari realized it was important to make this session work, but more important to keep Diane coming regularly.

"Coffee would be nice with cream and sugar, please."

She stepped around Kari's office before taking a seat on her couch.

"Is this your first session with a therapist?"

Diane nodded.

"The process is easy. We just talk. You've been through a couple of traumatic events. The idea is to make sure you have everything you need to cope."

Kari handed Diane her coffee in a thick, ceramic mug she'd bought years earlier at The Metropolitan Museum of Art in New York. It was white with a picture that was worn, yet still recognizable as a copy of a Seurat painting.

"Everything I need?"

"Yes. Often it's just someone to talk to. A sense of isolation is common with any trauma. Thoughts of the event push everything else away, including friends and family." Kari was sitting in the wing back chair across from Diane, studying the young woman. Even though this was her first session, Diane was acting as if she'd heard it all before. No harm there, Kari thought. "Guilt is another common emotion that doesn't make sense, but occurs often when someone dies. People ask themselves why they are still around after that person is gone."

"I don't feel guilty and I have more friends now than I've had in years."

The defense mechanisms have kicked in, Kari thought. I'll lose her if I can't give her something to keep her coming back. "First you lost your mother. Then you were drugged, attacked, and left without any knowledge of who did it or why. It's possible you didn't react the way most women would, but something about those events must have affected you. You need to talk about it."

"With you?"

Kari heard resistance in her tone. Most of Kari's patients either came to her of their own volition or were assigned to come by juvenile authorities. Either they wanted to talk or they had to. Diane was different. "Let's try another direction."

"OK."

"Tell me what you think about the lake—what the water means to you."

***

Diane

The question was one Diane thought about every day since her mother died. The lake was responsible for her death. So why didn't Diane hate the lake? If she'd lost her mother to a disease, she would have hated the disease even if it was proven that someone had intentionally infected her. Why was it so different with the lake?

"Did you notice I have an aquarium?" Dr. Montero asked. "Having one in a psychiatrist's office generally reduces stress and anxiety among my patients. Sometimes I'll catch someone staring at it and we'll take a break; spend ten minutes or so watching the fish swim."

"People pay you for that?"

"For whatever works." She wrote something on a legal pad she was holding, then said, "Do you find peace in the aquarium? Or does it have the opposite effect for you?"

Diane didn't like the doctor's tone. "Are you trying to get a rise out of me?" she asked.

"Rise has a negative sound to it. I'm trying to get a response."

Her first inclination was to say, "I know you're trying to help, but I have other concerns." However, since

Glen wanted to learn more about Dr. Montero's methods, she controlled her anger and tried to answer the question.

"I like to sit by the lake. I like the quiet days when the water appears solid, with only ripples raised by the wind. But sometimes people bring conflict, sometimes a powerboat breaks the surface, creating waves larger than the ones the wind made. When that happens, the wind seems to say, 'Just you wait. I can do better.' And before too long, there's a storm with even taller waves. So to me the water says, 'I am you. And like you I can be love or hate, forgiveness or anger, peace or war.' I choose love, forgiveness, and peace, then go on sitting by the water."

***

Glen

When Diane and Martha arrived at Ryan's on Wednesday, Glen pulled Diane to the side to ask how her session with Dr. Montero had gone.

"It was confusing. I was expecting questions about things like grief and fear, but all she wanted to know was what I thought of water."

"Water?"

"That's right, about the lake in particular. I suppose she expected the lake to give me flashbacks to the horrors I've been through. She probably wants to know why it doesn't and so do I. I made another appointment."

"I'm glad. Keep me posted."

"I will."

Diane and Glen joined Martha and Ryan in the center of Ryan's living room, where they'd been positioning the furniture for a regression. Glen sat in the same kitchen chair he'd used for the other regressions.

"Today we are investigating the time when Oota Dabun was set adrift in her canoe. After what happened to Diane, I think it is safe to say this is a repeating event. If we can solve it, we are well on our way to solving the attack on her. Although Pules is a suspect due to her anger over the death of her daughter, we are not certain she is guilty. She is, however, the person on whom we're concentrating. I'll hypnotize each one of you.

"I'd like to go first," Martha said as she stepped toward the couch.

"Good. I'll guide you back to a time prior to the canoe event."

***

Phillip

"We should meet, alone," Elias whispered, when Oota Dabun's back was turned.

Phillip looked at her to see if she heard Elias' comment. If she had, she hadn't reacted. She was stoking the fire with wood he cut, too busy to eavesdrop. He was back to full strength now, or close to it, pulling his weight with the day-to-day chores.

He leaned toward Elias. "When? And where?"

"In the canoe builder's wigwam where we've been sleeping. Tonight after sundown."

Phillip enjoyed Elias and Noah's company more than he thought he would. He chose a life as a trapper because he enjoyed being alone. Then, after the bear attack, he woke to find Oota Dabun nursing him. He gave himself over to her because he was injured. But after a while, he came to trust her more than he trusted himself and that trust became crucial when they first had sex.

She seemed to like him, which was a new sensation. The other women he'd been with had all been whores. Some of those were good at pretending, some didn't try. They all eased the tension in his body, but only Oota Dabun made him want to stay by her side forever. And now she was the mother of his child.

She studied him, asked questions, learned from him, the way he might interrogate a trapper who caught more beaver than he did. At first, he liked the attention. Yet her desire for knowledge of his people scared him. He never knew a white woman to be so curious about fighting. He appreciated what the Lenape had done, but did not want to betray his own people.

Oota Dabun stepped out of the wigwam without a word as to where she was going. Elias' gaze followed her with a look that appeared focused on her backside.

"She's getting firewood," Phillip told Elias.

"Pretty—for a savage."

"Watch yourself, Elias. She's like a wife to me."

"I meant no harm. Are you still planning to meet me tonight?"

Phillip hesitated but agreed. Only three other people in that place spoke his language. Oota Dabun was beautiful and kind, but Elias and Noah had whiskey. No reason he couldn't enjoy both.

***

Martha

"Come back a little," Glen's voice called to Martha, "not completely, just enough to shift to a memory of later that same day. Think of the time when the men were drinking, then gently ease into that memory."

Martha released her focus, so she could drift into the other memory.

***

Phillip

"This stuff is good," Phillip told Elias.

"It's imported Irish whiskey. I wanted you to have a taste, but most of what I have is home brew. I brought the liquor to trade with the savages. They don't know the difference."

Phillip was disappointed, but he would take whatever was offered. He wanted the sweet blindness. It had been way too long since he'd had that feeling. He handed the bottle back and reached for the jug.

"I'll take whatever you got and be in your debt."

"Glad you realize that. We have a limited amount. We wanted to check our traps soon, but the savages have our mules."

"You traders carry a heavy load, don't you?"

"We hoped you could get your woman to speak for us."

They passed the jug around three more times before Phillip noticed Oota Dabun. It appeared she'd been standing at the entrance to the wigwam, staring at him.

"We were just talking about you," Elias said. "Noah and I think you're just about the prettiest thing we've seen in—in forever. Right Noah?"

The large man grunted and nodded.

"You know that, don't you? Pretty thing."

Phillip spun toward Elias and took hold of his jacket. "I told you she's mine."

"Easy, friend. No harm meant." Elias turned back toward Oota Dabun. "Care to join us?"

"You're not giving her liquor. She's not used to it."

"Is that fire-water?" she asked.

"It is. Perfect for you. Would you like to try?"

"No!" Phillip shouted.

"He says you belong to him. Is that right?"

"I healed Phillip. He is mine, but I belong to no one."

Phillip knew he could do nothing to stop her. She sat between him and Elias, who handed her the jug. She drank, coughed twice, and passed the container to Phillip. He chugged as much as he could before handing the jug on to Noah. The whiskey took affect and the room began to rock, like the pond during a storm. But Phillip didn't care about anything other than his next turn at the whiskey jug.

***

Diane

The last regression had left Oota Dabun chugging homemade whiskey with three men, so Diane was confident Glen would pick her over Ryan for the next session. She listened as he gently pulled Martha back and watched when her friend opened her eyes.

"How could Phillip have been so different from the person I am today?" Martha asked when she was sitting up.

"In what way?" Glen asked.

"He was self-centered and thoughtless."

"Really? I didn't get that feeling," Diane told her. "He didn't want her to drink, but couldn't stop her. She's got her own mind and he respected that."

"You weren't Phillip. You don't know what he was thinking."

"Which was?"

Martha stood, then stepped toward Diane. "That he wanted to get drunk," she said, speaking softly as if she was confessing, "so he could forget how he had fallen in love with a squaw."

"Love!"

Martha stood up straight, her eyes wide. "You're missing the point. Phillip was a bigot."

Diane thought *bigot* was too strong a word. "People thought differently back then," she said.

"That doesn't make it right."

Glen held a hand up as if he was a traffic cop. "Let's move on. Diane, you're up next."

After time on the couch, Diane was feeling everything Oota Dabun felt. But she was still aware of the experiences of her 21st century life. Those included many glasses of wine and/or liquor. Once, at a party, she had so much to drink, the next day she couldn't remember what she'd done. So, inside Oota Dabun's memories, Diane was in the odd position of going through the experience of a first drunk, while knowing what to expect. Although she understood what was happening, she felt Oota Dabun's impulsiveness and confusion. Since the 21st century woman could not affect the 17th century woman's thoughts, Oota Dabun was responding to the alcohol without the benefit of Diane's knowledge.

***

Oota Dabun

She choked after her first turn at the whiskey jug, causing Elias and Noah to laugh. She was annoyed by their reaction, but theirs didn't bother her as much as Phillip's. He lifted the jug again, choosing to ignore her.

"Vision quests are the ceremonies that change boys to men," Oota Dabun told Phillip. "Girls don't have ceremonies. We take a different path. We become women when our bodies change."

The jug came back. Oota Dabun understood the burn now, so she was able to take a longer drink without choking. The fire-water caused the wigwam to spin, but she controlled that feeling as well. Her mind loosened, drifted into feelings and impulses she'd always kept below the surface.

"I was soooo jealous." Her words were slurring, but she didn't care. "Chogan goes out in the woods. He… he looks around and picks the animal to teach him. Then he's proven himself a man. All we women do is wait for our breasts to grow and our blood to flow. Becoming an adult should be something we earn rather than something that happens to every girl child."

Phillip held up a hand while he took another drink. Oota Dabun thought he was telling her to keep quiet, but she didn't care. He had no right. He wouldn't be alive if she hadn't healed him.

Elias and Noah were wrestling and exchanging punches. Oota Dabun had no idea why. She turned back to Phillip.

"You taught me the white-faces can be strong. You said you would be dead no matter what medicine I used, if you weren't ss... strong. Also, you taught me talking is important. I learned this by you *not* trying to speak our language. So I learned from you... your weakness and your strength. I think you like me, but only if I go to you, not if you come to me. This is a bad thing for you and for me. Also for our people. If we do not talk, we do not learn. If we do not learn, we fear. If we fear, we fight. Our future does not seem good."

Phillip smiled at Oota Dabun, swallowed, then passed the jug to her. She drank again, then felt very sleepy. She curled up on the floor and drifted off.

***

Ryan

Ryan knew his regression was next. Since Oota Dabun and Phillip had drunk themselves unconscious, there was nothing left to learn from them. It was Chogan's turn.

"I'm going to guide you back to a time shortly after Oota Dabun was rescued," Glen told Ryan. "People must have been talking about what happened to her. I'm certain the village had many situations they had to deal with, but this one had to be unique."

He'd already gone back to the memory of the night when Oota Dabun was set adrift in a canoe. It was clear Chogan didn't know who had committed such a dangerous prank, but he spoke regularly with everyone in the village.

The trick would be to listen carefully to the people. Glen was suggesting Ryan might pick up a clue or two that hadn't registered as important to Chogan. Second hand knowledge wasn't as helpful as first hand, but could still have value.

"You don't want me to focus on Pules or Abooksigun?" Ryan asked.

"Your subconscious will lead you to what's important. I'll be surprised if they aren't involved."

Ryan moved to the couch and took the spot where Diane had just been.

***

Chogan

Phillip and Kimi were not in Oota Dabun's wigwam when Chogan checked on her after the canoe rescue. She was alone, lying on her pallet next to a pile of vomit. He ran to her side and knelt.

Kimi was missing, but the women of the tribe shared responsibilities. Someone was tending to the child, probably Pules. After Chogan was sure Oota Dabun was all right, he would look for her daughter.

"Are you awake?"

Oota Dabun turned to look at Chogan. Her eyes were glazed and her smile was weak. He'd never seen her like this.

"I finally had my vision quest."

"Is that true? You learned something from Phillip?"

"I did. Ow."

"What's wrong?"

"My head hurts and my stomach is as twisted as it was the day Kimi was born."

"Abooksigun told me you will feel bad most of this day, but will be fine after."

"Still, last night was good. I learned from Phillip, of course, but also from Elias and Noah. They shared the… Wait! Where is Kimi?"

"Maybe she's with Pules?"

"Pules! She's been angry with me since Phillip stood before the council."

"Kimi will be fine. You know what happened last night, don't you?"

"Kimi was asleep, so I joined Phillip and his two friends. We were drinking the fire-water, then I woke up here."

"You went missing. The entire village searched for you until Etchemin discovered one of his canoes had been set adrift. We found you lying in the boat with your hands and feet bound and we carried you home. Kimi was here, crying. I held her for a while before placing her back on her pallet and leaving. I will look for her if you are feeling better, but Kimi was fine last night and she'll be fine today."

Oota Dabun tried to stand, but fell back on her pallet.

"Are you all right?"

"I need to find her, Chogan."

"I'll look. You need rest."

The men of the village were preparing for the day's hunt. Chogan would normally have been with them: gathering his arrows, tightening his bow, sharpening his knife, and taking a few practice throws with his spear. But today his mind was focused on something different, on finding Kimi. He headed straight to Pules' wigwam, passing many of his friends on their way into the forest.

Pules muttered to herself, loudly enough that Chogan could hear her from outside. When he stepped in, she looked up at him. She was bending over her fire, cooking corn bread and johnnycakes in two clay pots. She pulled her food to the side and stood.

"Do you know where Kimi is?" he asked. Her expression didn't change, but that was no surprise. It had remained mostly the same since Nuttah's death. Abooksigun still claimed the white-faced men had brought the disease, but Chogan no longer believed him. No one else in the village had fallen sick.

"I haven't seen her."

Pules used to laugh. Now, her mouth always turned down and her eyes seemed dull. She lost weight, causing her facial skin to hang loose, which made her look old.

"Oota Dabun doesn't know where she is."

"Have you checked with her white man?"

"With Phillip?"

"Call him what you want."

"He wasn't in Oota Dabun's home. If you have no other ideas, I'll look for him next."

Pules crouched by the fire again and moved her pots back into the flames.

Phillip normally stayed with Oota Dabun, but Chogan knew he wasn't there and went instead to Etchemin's wigwam where the other two whites slept. He found Phillip there, but not Kimi. Phillip was cooking, as Pules had been. He was frying venison.

"Mimenteta?" Chogan asked. But the whites didn't appear to understand. He cradled his arms as if he were holding a baby. They didn't understand the gesture any more than they understood the word. It had been a bad idea to come to this wigwam.

Chogan went toward the pond, toward the place where Etchemin kept his canoes and where he helped save Oota Dabun the night before. Miracles often have a cost. He prayed Kimi's life had not been the cost of that one.

He looked over the water of the pond, as he had most every day of his life, and saw it as the gift it was. He didn't believe all the spirit stories, but was certain there was truth in the power of the pond. He'd seen enough births to know that babies came out of their mothers in a flood of water. And he had chosen the otter as his spirit guide, an animal equally at home on land or in water. He said another prayer to the water, then noticed something moving on the bank by the pond. It wasn't a muskrat. It was a baby.

Chogan picked Kimi up and lifted her toward the sky. "Praise the Great Spirit! Praise the water! Praise!" he shouted, then turned back toward Oota Dabun's home.

***

Diane

"Pules put Kimi by the water," Ryan said. "If she wanted revenge for what Phillip had done to Nuttah, it makes sense that she would try to drown Oota Dabun's child. She must have had a change of heart at the last minute."

Abooksigun was another possibility, but he did not act guilty and helped with Oota Dabun's rescue. This didn't add up, since it was likely the person who set Oota Dabun adrift was the same person who left Kimi beside the pond.

Glen suggested regressing all of them the next day and, at that time, pulling as many memories of Pules as possible. Diane offered to cancel her appointment with Dr. Montero, but Glen said no. He wanted a better feel for the psychiatrist. The next regressions were scheduled for Wednesday.

Martha headed back to the island after Ryan's session. Diane decided to stay with Ryan for the rest of the day and probably the night as well. She had an alarm system installed, but still felt scared to be in her home alone. Ryan and Diane were sitting on his patio while Glen was in the house answering a few emails and revising the notes about their case.

"Pules was with Oota Dabun on the day she found Phillip in the woods. They seemed to care about each other."

"They did, before Nuttah died. A tragedy like that can change everything."

Diane turned to Ryan. "It can't change a person's soul."

"You think so?" he asked. "An experience like that can make someone angry enough to act with violence. Pules blamed Phillip and Oota Dabun is the friend who brought that man into her village. She hated them both and if memories of past lives are part of who we are, then anger and vengeance are as well."

"That's basically what Glen said."

Diane switched to a chaise lounge so she could put her feet up, lean back and look at the stars over the water. Ryan followed. He took the seat next to her, turning the chair so they were facing in the same direction. He rested his hand on her thigh and she placed her hand on top of his.

Chapter Twelve
Kari

Kari remembered the lesson she had learned from her school friend, Peg; how needy people can be manipulated to do anything, no matter how illegal or upsetting. She had practiced manipulation on a few patients from time to time, but hadn't reused her skills for any serious purpose until Heather showed up in her office. It takes discipline, Kari thought, but if you're careful, ruthless, and capable of pushing a person to think with her emotions rather than her brain, the possibilities are endless.

The subjects were where they needed to be. Kari had to interview Diane and Maya, then write up what they told her, but that was all. The case study could lead to further studies by other psychiatrists. Her work might be discussed in classrooms, her name on the lips of her peers. There could be money to be made as well. Water parks, resort areas, and boat manufacturers would all pay to know how to deal with the fears that kept many people away from their products. And those opportunities didn't even touch on the money people with aquaphobia might pay to find a cure.

Kari would have been a poor psychiatrist if she hadn't recognized that her thoughts were fantasies. She understood there was no certainty as to where her work would lead. Still, she had the firm conviction that her life was going in the best direction possible.

**

Glen

"We set the tone yesterday," Glen told his three subjects. They were again at Ryan's, preparing to go through the regression process. But first Glen wanted to discuss the previous day.

"Tone?" Martha responded. "All Phillip felt was a desire to get drunk. The more I learn of my other self, the more I'm ashamed and confused. It doesn't make sense. I take pride in Native American heritage. Why would he disparage it?"

"He took pride in *European* heritage," Diane told her. "It's what he was, just as Lenape is what you are."

"Pules still seems the most likely suspect," Glen said, turning to the topic of the day's plan. "I suggest we work in the same order we did yesterday and we continue to concentrate on the canoe incident. I'll guide you to a short time after the memories we pulled yesterday. We'll see what happens."

**

Phillip

Oota Dabun stayed with Phillip after he was declared innocent, but her relationship with Chogan grew. He was the one who spoke up for Phillip and for her. They had always been friends, but her gratitude changed their friendship into a deeper relationship. After Kimi was born and soon after the canoe incident, she and her daughter spent most of their daylight hours with Chogan, while Phillip spent more of his time with Noah and Elias.

Oota Dabun was on her pallet when Phillip returned to their wigwam. She was lying on her side, breastfeeding Kimi who was beside her. Chogan was on the ground next to them, with his hand on Kimi's back, apparently helping to keep the child in place.

"How are you feeling?" Phillip asked Oota Dabun. She groaned in response.

Chogan yelled, "Ikali a" and gestured wildly with his free hand, signaling for him to get out of the wigwam. Phillip shouted to Oota Dabun as he left, telling her the sickness wouldn't last long. She didn't acknowledge his words, so he wasn't sure she had heard him.

Pules stood alone between Abooksigun's wigwam and one of the community gardens. It appeared she was looking into Oota Dabun's home, but diverted her gaze when Phillip noticed her.

Phillip turned away from Pules and walked toward the pond. He felt her gaze on his back and sensed her starting to follow. What could be on her mind? She'd been avoiding him since Nuttah's death and there was no reason for her to change now, but she was back there. He heard a young girl greet her by name.

When he reached the pond, he heard her footsteps grow loud. He stopped to look back. She was moving quickly, slapping her feet on the ground, heading straight for him. He instinctively braced for contact, but when she reached him, she brushed her arm against his and kept walking. Phillip didn't know how to react to her strange behavior, but decided she was trying to switch roles, to get him to follow her.

Pules moved along the bank, into the woods. There was a rough path that had probably been followed by more deer than men, but was clear enough for Pules to keep her quick pace. When Phillip was in the woods a distance equivalent to twice the length of the village, Pules disappeared behind a tree and three men appeared from similar hiding places. One of the men was Abooksigun. Phillip recognized the other two, but didn't know their names.

The two men with Abooksigun grabbed him by his arms and held him against a tree while the shaman shook his turtle rattle, looked in Phillip's eyes, and chanted.

Phillip tried to break free, but the men were strong and held him tightly against the oak tree. The rough bark didn't scratch because he was wearing a buckskin top, but the pressure against his back and shoulders hurt and the men were gripping his arms hard. The men did not hit him or hurt him in any way not related to their efforts to hold him in place—until Pules returned.

Abooksigun moved over to allow Pules to take his position after she stepped out of her hiding place. She was now the person directly in front of Phillip. Abooksigun stood to the side, but still close enough to grab and hold Phillip's hair. Pules removed the necklace she was wearing, a bear claw on a rawhide thong. She held the claw like a knife, dug the sharpened tip into Phillip's right cheek. When she was done, she spat in his face.

The men released Phillip, who fell to the ground in a pile of wet leaves.

***

Martha

Martha felt a wave of dizziness as she sat up. She said, "God, that was frightening!"

"You're safe now. Be still for a moment," Glen told her.

She lifted her bear claw necklace and stared at it. "Is that why this thing has been so important to me?" Before the last session, she would never have called it a *thing*.

"Does this mean Pules is the one we're after?" Diane asked.

Glen shook his head. "It means Pules and Abooksigun worked together to attack you. Beyond that I don't know."

"Heather cut Maya's cheek," Ryan said. "She held up a knife while we were sitting at the breakfast table. The blade caught her when she turned her head. It was just a scratch and healed in a week or so. This happened right after Maya's midnight swim, so it's been a while. I still think it was an accident, but I'm mentioning it because it was similar to what Pules did to Phillip."

"I'm not sure the two incidents are connected," Glen told him, "especially since Maya was the one cut on the cheek, not Martha. But there might be a link between Pules and Heather. It's always good to hear anything you can think of that seems related."

Everyone was quiet for a moment and Martha was thinking of the forehead band. She still hadn't told anyone about it except Diane. She looked at her friend, who said, "We need to move on to Oota Dabun." Both women stood after Diane spoke.

Martha shifted over to the wing back chair where Diane had been and waited to hear the next part of the story.

* * *

Oota Dabun

Kimi was crying again. It was too soon for her to be hungry, causing Oota Dabun to believe the baby was uncomfortable. Kimi was generally up by this time, riding around the village on her mother's back. But Oota Dabun hadn't felt well enough to get herself up, much less her daughter. At this point, there was no choice. Kimi had probably soiled her blankets and since Oota Dabun felt dirty inside and out, they both needed a good cleaning.

Oota Dabun pushed off her blanket, struggled to her feet, and straightened her skirt. She was wobbly, but felt better now that she was standing. She needed to relieve herself, so she left Kimi alone in their wigwam while she went into the woods. When she returned, she wrapped Kimi in a clean blanket and placed her in her cradleboard. Getting her baby and herself up was the first step toward feeling human again. The next step would be the sweat lodge.

No one was in the sweat lodge, which was lucky because women and men did not use it at the same time. Oota Dabun leaned Kimi's cradleboard against a tree, wiggling it to make sure it was stable. Her baby could be comfortable there, and also see what she was doing.

The lodge was a small hut, half buried in the bank of a hill. The exposed side was covered with wood to hold the heat better than the wigwams did. Oota Dabun bent over so she could step inside. There were a number of stones on the ground, a pile in the center and others scattered about. She gathered the stones and started to bring them out of the hut. They needed to be heated, then brought back in.

When she had all the stones in the fire pit, it was time to start the fire. If the weather had been cooler, there might have been a fire somewhere in the village and she could have gone for an ember. But that wasn't the case, so she would have to use the fire starter bow.

There were plenty of logs and kindling in the lean-to near the lodge. She took what she needed, then placed the dried leaves and grass under some small sticks. She picked up the bow, wrapping its rawhide thong around the shaft, then placed the tip of the shaft in a hole in the base and added more dry grass.

She began to use the bow to spin the shaft. The object was to create enough friction in the spot where the shaft met the base to make heat and eventually fire. It was hard work, keeping the spinning shaft at a fast speed. And since she wasn't used to working this tool, it took a long time.

Both of Oota Dabun's hands began to ache, the right from moving the bow and the left from gripping the wood block she was using to hold the shaft upright. A few drops of sweat went into her eyes, forcing her to blink. Another rolled down her forehead and threatened to fall on the grass she was trying to light, but she shook it off. Finally, she saw a thin plume of smoke and a tiny red-yellow glow. She stopped spinning the shaft and started to blow. It caught and, after adding leaves and sticks, she had a fire.

After the flames caught on a few small logs, she had to shift the stones from the edge of the fire to the center. Oota Dabun accomplished this by pushing them with a log that was among those waiting to go in the flames. When the stones were hot, Oota Dabun used the same log to move them out of the fire and into the lodge.

She checked on Kimi before dropping her skirt and entering the sweat lodge. Oota Dabun was alone, so after she closed the entry with the two buckskin flaps, she took a seat in the center of the tiny hut. She couldn't see Kimi, but she could hear her.

The air in the lodge quickly turned hot. She could feel it in her lungs. At first, her breathing was difficult, but the heat seemed to open her chest. She breathed deeply, through her nose, and released the air slowly. The sweat lodge had always been the place where her mind freed itself, where problems faded and new ideas came. But this time she was here to cleanse herself and Kimi.

Her body felt broken from the events of the night before, but she wasn't certain which events. The last thing she remembered was drinking the fire-water. That alone might have caused her to feel sick. However, Chogan and Abooksigun had found her floating in a canoe and the near tragedy could also have been the cause of her issues. Oota

Dabun hoped the sweat lodge might clear her mind enough to restore her memory.

She sat cross-legged on the floor of the lodge, feeling her body sweat as the toxins left. She felt her blood flowing evenly and could tell the process was affecting her mind. A sense of space was returning, providing room for the memories she needed.

She remembered someone's hands on her ankles and someone else lifting her by her shoulders. The memory was fuzzy, but the feel of the hands under her arms came to her. They were larger, rougher, and stronger than the hands on her ankles.

Kimi made a noise. It wasn't the cry she used when she was hungry or the call that told Oota Dabun her daughter needed to be cleaned. This was the sound Kimi made when she was lonely or bored. She wanted her mother to pick her up.

The timing was perfect. Oota Dabun crawled out of the hut, took Kimi's blanket off her, and brought her into the sweat lodge. Young children and infants could experience a sweat lodge, but only for a short time. Oota Dabun watched her child carefully, until sweat began to form on her belly, then she left the lodge, grabbed her skirt along with Kimi's blanket and cradleboard, and headed to the waterfront where the women of the village bathed.

The pond was shallow enough at this shore for Oota Dabun to wade rather than swim. Once in the water, she held Kimi's face against her shoulder so she could dip down as she stepped backwards and dunk her child without a risk of Kimi breathing the water. This was the way they always bathed. In addition to getting the job done, it was Oota Dabun's favorite thing to do with her child: intimate and fun.

She turned her face toward the shore after she had swirled Kimi around in the water and noticed Pules walking toward the woods. Oota Dabun wondered if Pules had been watching her bathe her daughter. Pules had lost her own daughter to the pond and the memory of that tragedy made Oota Dabun feel guilty for enjoying her time with Kimi.

She wondered what Pules was up to. Since Nuttah's death, she had spent most of her time in her wigwam, only leaving when absolutely necessary. Pules taking a walk alone was as likely as the pond freezing in summertime. She had to be meeting someone.

Oota Dabun was curious and thought she might follow her former friend when she noticed Chogan on the path from the village. She hadn't told him of her plan to use the sweat lodge, so she had no idea how he knew where she would be.

She stood up in the shallow water and walked to shore. If it had been any man other than Chogan, she would have shouted for him to turn away, but if there was one thing she learned from Phillip, it was that Chogan was the man for her. For a while, she thought she'd lost her chance with him. Now there appeared to be hope. She placed Kimi on her blanket and reached for her skirt. Chogan watched from a distance, then stepped forward when she was dressed.

"Was Pules coming here to swim with you?"

"No. She went into the woods over there. I don't believe she knew I was here or she would have chosen a different path."

"Why?"

"She still believes Phillip killed Nuttah and, to her, Phillip and I are the same. Why were you following her?"

"I saw her go into Abooksigun's wigwam. After a short time, she came out and headed this way. I thought she might need help with something."

"Pules knows how to help herself when she wants to."

Oota Dabun turned toward Kimi as her daughter uttered a soft cry. She folded the beaver blanket, placed it in the cradleboard, and swung it all onto her back. Then she picked up her daughter. She had to carry Kimi with two hands as they started back to her wigwam. Pules had been a master at the art of breastfeeding while walking, but Oota Dabun wasn't as good. Maybe Kimi was more restless than Nuttah had been, but it was just as likely that Pules had stronger hands and quicker responses.

Oota Dabun looked down at her child, then over at Chogan, who was walking beside her. Lately, she found herself wishing that he was Kimi's father rather than Phillip. But maybe it wasn't too late. Maybe Chogan would be the man to hold Kimi when she was sad and play games with her when she was lonely. Maybe he would be the one to teach her and care for her. After all, Chogan was a good man while Phillip was just Phillip.

***

Ryan

Martha looked at Diane, and said, "This keeps getting worse."

"Oota Dabun never thought of Phillip as a bad person," Diane told her. "She just liked Chogan more. And it didn't hurt that Chogan was the one who had found her in the canoe." She looked at Ryan. "I can identify with that."

An image came rushing back to Ryan, of the time he'd seen Diane's naked body on the floor of her house. He wondered if Oota Dabun expressed her gratitude with the same passion as her twenty-first century counterpart had. He imagined he would find out.

"Phillip was a drunk," Martha declared, "and I'm not. So how can we share a soul?"

"You have different genetics and a different upbringing," Glen told her. "Having the same soul doesn't make the two of you exactly the same."

"Besides," Diane said, smiling broadly. "I remember a couple of nights you spent on our couch after parties my parents threw. One night doesn't make a person a drunk."

"But one night can change a lifetime and that's what happened to Phillip."

Diane shook her head. "Phillip was a loner whose attachment to Oota Dabun had to do with gratitude more than love. It wasn't meant to be long term."

"This is interesting," Glen said, "but we need to move forward. Are we ready to get into Chogan's memories?"

Ryan nodded, then went to the couch.

***

Chogan

Kimi fell asleep after her feeding, so when they reached her wigwam, Oota Dabun put her down on her pallet. She left the blanket inside the cradleboard after taking it off her back. It was warm enough for Kimi to be comfortable without a cover. Phillip was not there, so Chogan went inside and sat where he could watch the woman and her child. He cared more and more for them every day.

Chogan loved the beauty of a mother's love evident in the tiny details of the life Oota Dabun shared with Kimi: from the protective way she held her daughter while they were swimming to the gentle way she put her down for her nap.

Oota Dabun stepped away from Kimi and almost backed into Chogan. He didn't think she knew where he was standing until she reached down and took his hand. It was an act of intimacy he wasn't expecting. He had to glance at their interlacing fingers to convince himself this was real. She had refused his offer of marriage once and, after that, Phillip and then Kimi had become her life. Was this a sign her heart was changing?

She pulled him closer and hugged him. He felt her smooth skin against his chest and as she held him tight, he felt the warmth of her breast milk. He thought of the beauty of the cycle of life, and how much he wanted to share everything with her.

Chogan understood Oota Dabun's feelings as she pulled him toward her pallet. She took off her skirt while he removed his breechcloth and leggings. They drifted down to the soft blanket and, with the motion of a single soul, wrapped their bodies in the love they shared.

Chogan lay on Oota Dabun for a moment after their love making while they both struggled to regain control of their breathing. He felt her grow tense and when he opened his eyes he saw hers, wide and still as the pond frozen in winter.

He pressed down on his arms to take his weight as he separated from her and rolled over her leg to his back. He looked up. Phillip was standing over them, staring down. A cut on his face and his raging eyes made him look like a wounded bear.

**

Martha

Martha felt angry. She looked at Diane and said, "You treated Phillip like that! You had a child with him! What were you thinking?" The hurt and betrayal Phillip must have felt seemed to her as if those feelings had just happened.

"Diane and Oota Dabun aren't the same person," Glen said. "They share a soul, but there are other factors."

"She didn't do anything wrong," Diane argued, apparently ignoring Glen's comment. "Phillip didn't own her."

"She and Phillip had a relationship," Martha said. "And their daughter was in the room with her and Chogan, which makes what they did even worse. No respect."

"They lived in wigwams, for God's sake. There was no privacy back then."

"Still..."

"Still nothing."

Martha didn't know what to say. They were arguing about something that had happened hundreds of years earlier and they were arguing with the priorities of two different generations. Diane was right about Phillip not owning Oota Dabun, but the Lenape woman shouldn't have hurt him. Diane knows that, Martha thought.

Glen stood. "This isn't helping. Phillip had a reason to be jealous and mad, no matter who was right or what their norms of privacy were. We have to watch him."

"Watch him? So now you're thinking Phillip's guilty of something?" she asked.

"I didn't say that."

"Maybe not in so many words, but you meant it. Regress me again, right now, so I can prove Phillip didn't hurt anyone. I'm not stressed and I don't want to wait until tomorrow."

Nobody said anything for a moment until Glen nodded, which seemed to give everyone permission to exhale. He said, "If you think you can relax into a session, then take your place and we'll try."

Chapter Thirteen
Phillip

Witnessing Oota Dabun and Chogan together was not a surprise. They had been growing closer for a time. The fact that Phillip was not from her village had once been an asset, but became a liability. And after the night of the canoe, it made sense she would choose the Lenape man over him. He needed to do something to salvage what he could of his life with her.

The only hope was in the lessons Phillip had learned from his mother.

He'd grown up in southern England near the Salisbury Plain, the only child of a woman who believed in the old gods. She kept her beliefs a secret, because the Celtic religion was associated with witches and the Christians were burning anyone suspected of witchcraft. His mother lost many friends to those trials, until one of those friends named her. The accusation caused Phillip to lose his mother, but not at the stake. She chose her own death. At the same time, he lost all of her possessions save one, the jewel in the handle of his sword.

Phillip was eighteen when his mother died, a young man. He was old enough to make his own way in the world and in need of a fresh start. He moved northeast to London, where he arranged to work his passage to America.

He glanced back at the wigwam he shared with Oota Dabun. He half expected she would follow him, to explain her choice, or even to apologize but still didn't understand the rules or the morals of the Lenape people. He was Kimi's father, yet he hadn't married Oota Dabun. Perhaps, among these savages, fidelity wasn't to be expected without commitment.

He needed his mother's magic, which meant he needed to find his sword. He was certain it was in Abooksigun's wigwam. The village wigwams were arranged in a U shape, with the open side facing the pond. There was no way to go through the entrance of any of them without being seen. Phillip had the freedom to move around the village, so getting into Abooksigun's home was no problem. Bringing the sword out was the issue.

Phillip circled the perimeter of the village, checking to be certain nobody was behind any of the huts. When he reached the back of Abooksigun's home, he walked between that wigwam and the one next to it, into the center of the village. He had been in this wigwam a few times. If he acted as if he belonged, he didn't believe he would attract unwanted attention. Once inside, he counted slowly to five hundred to be certain no one had followed him.

He found the sword wrapped in a raccoon blanket near the back of the hut, dirty but otherwise in good shape.

Phillip searched for an opening along the bottom of the wigwam's back wall wide enough to shove the sword through. The only openings he found would need to be torn larger, making them obvious. He had to cut a slice in the back wall in a clean way that wouldn't be noticed. Fortunately, the sword was sharp enough for that task. He passed it through the hole, then left the wigwam, circled around, and retrieved it. Nobody was in back by the woods and he didn't believe he'd raised any suspicions among the people inside the village. He stepped into the woods to get out of sight. When he was confident no one was following him, he headed to the place along the pond's shore, where he planned to perform his ritual.

He brought a knife with him, but not one of the metal blades he'd had back in England. They were gone. This was Oota Dabun's stone knife with a bone handle, used for cutting hides or, more accurately, tearing them. It didn't have much of a point, but would have to do. He needed to pry the stone in the sword handle out of its setting.

He poked and prodded until the jewel loosened enough for him to get his nails underneath. He wiggled it more until it fell into his hand, then placed it in a leather purse. When done, Phillip stuck the sword in the ground near the pond and sat cross-legged on the ground beside it.

He believed his mother had not been a witch, but her prayers had always worked. He was nurtured on her words and they were still as much a part of him as his heart and soul. He looked at the ripples in the water and spoke in a clear, careful voice, almost a chant.

"I plead for help from Boann, goddess of water. Your thirst for knowledge caused you to approach the well of Segais and, as a result, the River Boyne was created. You were the lover of the Dagda, a great protector. You and he made the sun stand still for nine months, to hide the birth of your son, Aengus, a god of love. I ask you now to use your knowledge, your strength, and your love to help me in my quest to win the heart of Oota Dabun."

Without rising, Phillip reached for the sword. He twirled it over his head three times, then let it fly out over the pond. It rose in an arc, then descended into the water, tip first.

"I offer my sword in your honor."

The image of a woman appeared in the pond. She was dressed in a burgundy gown with white trim. Phillip had expected the Boann he remembered from his childhood, the goddess his mother could conjure. She was a fair-skinned woman with strawberry-blond hair. Although he was certain this woman was the same goddess, she had the head and hair of Oota Dabun.

She looked at him, but said nothing, then disappeared. What did that mean?

Philip had been living with the Lenape long enough to understand aspects of their spirituality and could see similarities with their way of thinking and the Celtic way. His mother had expressed the Celtic belief of souls in every living thing: flowers, trees, fish, and insects. The Lenape approached life with a similar philosophy. Someone's spirit guide could be any animal from an ant to a bear. And the belief was true of plant life as well. People in the village would travel hundreds of miles to a specific sacred oak tree when they had problems requiring prayers. Could Boann's silence have meant there was something more important than his desire for Oota Dabun, something spiritual?

Phillip had to leave for a while. He had to think things over.

***

Martha

"What the hell was that about?" Martha asked, jumping up quickly, then standing and looking about like a wary heron.

"Don't get up so fast," Glen warned her. "Let your blood flow before you push yourself. You've been lying down for a while. Let your body adjust."

She sat down. "Tell me what that was about. Phillip was raised by a witch?"

"During the 16th and 17th centuries, the Celtic religion was still popular within certain groups," Glen explained. "The Christians didn't like it, which is why there were witch trials in Europe and in America."

"Do you believe this really happened?" Martha asked. "He called on a goddess and she showed up?"

"He had a vision. It could have been his mind playing tricks, especially since the woman he saw was Oota Dabun, not the goddess. But it seems to me, the answer to his prayer was that his love was misguided."

"I need to know what happened next," Martha told him. "Did he give up on her? And what about the jewel? How did it end up in the medieval forehead band passed from my ancestors?"

"A forehead band passed to you?" Ryan asked.

Diane leaned forward. "It's a long story."

"You've got to tell us these things," Glen said, shaking his head.

"I was planning to," Diane told him, "when the proper moment came along."

Diane was the one Glen was criticizing, but Martha knew this concerned her as well. Hopefully, they could understand the pull of her history. The forehead band had been handed down in her family for generations, with specific instructions to follow when the situation was right. The stories said nothing about sharing what she was called to do.

"What about Maya's vision?" Ryan asked. "And the way Oota Dabun came to me in my dreams? If her appearance was in Phillip's mind, does that mean our minds were playing tricks as well? When that happened I hadn't been through a regression, didn't even know what the word meant."

"Still, all those memories were buried in your mind and soul," Glen told him. "Dreams are a perfect outlet."

"Can you regress me now?" Diane asked. "We need to know what Oota Dabun was thinking when Phillip left."

"Not today. We're all tired and stressed. Think about the things we've discovered. Tomorrow we'll look back into her memories and Chogan's."

Martha wondered what Diane was thinking about Oota Dabun. It was clear the young Lenape woman was more than she seemed. But was she a goddess or a witch?

***

Heather

"I'm glad we're meeting here again." Heather looked around at the pink walls and noticed the framed degrees. She tried to read them, but only the first was close enough and all she could see were the names Kari Montero and Columbia University. She also looked at the aquarium and the largest fish, whose color matched the walls. She liked the tank. It relaxed her.

"As I said before, it was a timing issue," Kari told her. "Now you can sign up for an appointment without raising suspicion."

"Well, I like this. Have you got another assignment for me?"

Heather enjoyed the way Kari smiled while looking at her.

"One aspect of my project is to study the effect of death by drowning on the spiritual beliefs of the person left behind. It was easy to get Maya to think about an afterlife. But she's a child, so it will be more difficult with Diane. Do you know anything about her beliefs?"

There was something that might help. Heather had never told anyone about it, because it was personal. But if Kari could use it, Heather would go there.

"Diane and her mother were living with my father, living the lives we should have had. My mother hated the situation, but she didn't hate my dad. I went through her stuff after she died and found a journal she kept about him. He hadn't been around when I was young, so I learned most of what I know about him through the book. My mother didn't believe in God, but he did. I didn't inherit his religious side, but he was around Diane when she was growing up, so maybe he convinced her."

"It's a thought," Kari said. She seemed to be speaking more to herself than to Heather. "Do you know what her mother believed?"

"I know less about Lori than I know about Diane."

Kari didn't say anything. She seemed to be lost in thought, so Heather suggested, "I could do something to scare Diane. People get religion when they're scared. She's bound to be on edge after what we've put her through. It should be easy."

"I don't think that's a good idea," Kari told her. "I'll just talk to her about it. I could put something religious on my desk during her next appointment, a Bible or a cross perhaps, to help bring up the subject."

"Then you don't want me to do anything?"

"Not for now."

***

Glen

The following day, after Maya left for school, Glen gathered everyone in Ryan's living room. "Phillip finding Chogan and Oota Dabun together and his prayer to the Celtic goddess, Boann, are both critical events."

"What he didn't do is more important," Martha asserted. "He didn't hurt anyone."

"Elias and Noah seem suspicious to me," Diane said. "They're the ones who gave Oota Dabun the liquor. She couldn't have been set adrift if she hadn't been drunk."

"But Phillip didn't stop them," Ryan said.

Glen held up his hand to tell everyone to calm down. "Here's the plan. I regress Ryan to the moment after Phillip saw Chogan with Oota Dabun. We know Phillip's reaction. We need to know Chogan's as well."

When everyone agreed, Ryan took his place on the couch.

***

Chogan

Chogan reached for his breechcloth and started to dress.

"Where are you going?" Oota Dabun asked.

"I have to find him."

"I'll go with you. We'll take Kimi."

"No. You need to stay here to keep her safe."

"Who's going to keep you safe?"

"I suppose you'll have to trust me to do that for myself."

"I trust you, but be careful."

He left the wigwam, then walked around it and into the woods. He wasn't sure where to start, so he headed toward the pond.

Chogan moved quietly through the woods, trying to avoid dry leaves or sticks that might crack under his feet. He thought Phillip might either run or attack if he was pushed to act. Chogan believed he could handle Phillip's reaction no matter what. Still, the situation would be easier to handle if he didn't surprise the man. He stepped over a fallen tree trunk and around the same tree's branches. There was no path to follow in this section of the woods, but that was good. He didn't expect Phillip to be on a path.

Chogan heard a noise off to the side. He crouched down for a moment and looked around, to decide how to approach. There was a large rock with a tall oak growing next to it. It was perfect. If he got behind the tree, the rock would hide his body.

As he carefully moved into the hiding place, he heard a man and a woman's voices. If Phillip was there, he wasn't alone. Chogan kept to his plan and when he could see the people who were talking, he discovered they were Abooksigun and Pules. Had she been in the woods since he saw her earlier? Had she been waiting for the shaman the entire time? And why were they meeting in the middle of the forest?

"You were in the pond beside me," Pules told Abooksigun, "both of us face down. The three white-faces were on the shore throwing stones at us."

"How did you see this?"

"It was as if I was looking down from the sky, but I knew the woman in the water was me. I couldn't see my face and my hair was drenched, but I still knew. I just don't know how."

"It was a dream. The world is different in dreams. Still, those visions mean as much or more than what we see when we're awake. They can be predictions of something important. Looking down from the sky often means death, but it is difficult to know when, why, or who will be affected."

"You and I were the ones face down in the water."

"Looking into water is a sign of great sight. If we were alive in your vision, we could be the ones who will know whose death approaches. But if we were dead in your dream, we could be the ones to die in the waking world."

"All I know is, we were floating face down. Could the dream have been about Nuttah's death?"

"Dreams can predict or reflect, but I believe yours is about the white-faces. There is a reason they were the ones throwing stones. Your daughter is already dead. This dream of yours seems to say that if we don't act, these men will bring more death to the village."

Chogan heard a squirrel scurry through the branches of a tree. He turned and saw Phillip under the tree, with blood smeared on his face as if he'd cut himself. Like Chogan, he was hiding where he could listen. Chogan knew Phillip didn't understand their language, but thought the white man might be able to pick out a few words. Phillip noticed Chogan at the same time Chogan noticed him.

Neither man could react without drawing the attention of Pules and Abooksigun.

Phillip stared, then turned and went into the woods. Chogan had to do the same. Once he was a good distance from Pules and Abooksigun's meeting place, he tried, unsuccessfully, to pick up Phillip's trail. The white-face was gone.

Chogan returned to the village and went to the wigwam where Noah and Elias were staying. It was empty. He walked through the village looking for them, but didn't find them or any sign they'd been there.

Something happened while Chogan was trying to pick up Phillip's trail. It was possible they left, but he feared Abooksigun and Pules had taken action in response to her dream and had made it look as if the men had decided to go.

***

Glen

Chogan's relationship with Oota Dabun drove Phillip away. Noah and Elias were missing from the village. The Celtic connection, which had been hinted at through the sword, had become clear. So much was happening as the case came to a head. Glen knew they had to keep pushing forward to take advantage of the momentum. He asked Diane to take Ryan's place and in a few minutes they were again exploring Oota Dabun's memories.

***

Oota Dabun

After Chogan went into the woods in search of Phillip, Oota Dabun stayed beside her daughter. As she watched Kimi sleep, she worried the two men in her life might be hurting each other. Eventually, she decided she needed to see what was going on. She woke Kimi, bundled her into the cradleboard, and followed Chogan's path into the forest.

The trees had held on to the dark green leaves of late summer this year. Their canopy was thick enough that her eyes had to adjust when she left the village. She knew where Chogan had headed, but following him from this point was guesswork. Still, she stepped over a fallen tree and kept walking.

Oota Dabun grew up beside the forest. When she was a teenager, she explored the woods with her friends and accompanied her father on a few hunting trips, but since she became a woman and a mother, she rarely went into wooded areas. When she did go into the forest, she would go to specific, safe places to pick berries, mushrooms, or other wild plants.

After Oota Dabun walked deep into the woods, to a point where she could no longer see the village, she became afraid she had been too impulsive. It wasn't just her own safety she should have considered. Her need to find Chogan and Phillip had put her daughter, Kimi, at risk.

There was a rustling of branches behind her. Oota Dabun turned to see if it was Chogan or Phillip, but it wasn't. It was a black bear. The animal watched Oota Dabun with what at first seemed to be the look of a hunter. Her fear eased as the bear looked away, then got down on its stomach and began to lick its front feet. It must not be hungry, she thought. It's ignoring me.

The bear stopped licking, then stood up and began to circle. Perhaps it had just paused to scratch an itch. Now, it would try to eat, because bears are always hungry. It walked with a slow, lumbering step, but Oota Dabun knew the animal could outrun her easily if it chose to.

There was a loud thump of wood against wood. She kept her eye on the bear as it turned to look behind her. The loud noise was repeated a second and third time. The bear seemed to lose confidence. It turned again and lumbered away into the woods.

Oota Dabun looked for the source of the sound that had saved her and saw Phillip. He was holding a tree limb he had used to bang on the side of a fallen trunk. It was a threatening noise and the bear might have responded by attacking him, especially since he had blood on his face. Fortunately, the animal hadn't hurt him.

"You could have been killed," Oota Dabun shouted to him.

He replied in a softer voice. "You could have been killed if I did nothing—you and our child."

He was still, but his shaking could be seen from where she was standing.

"How did you cut yourself?" she asked. "I was scared when I saw the wound because the smell of your blood might have attracted that bear."

"It's nothing," he told her.

She walked to him and touched his shoulder. "Protecting me had to be hard after everything you've been through." She was talking about the bear attack, the one that almost killed him, but she knew she had also hurt him.

"That was your animal spirit guide," he said, "the bear, not me. And you didn't need whiskey to find it."

"I don't understand."

"I wasn't injured to become your guide, but I was still a part of your vision quest. When I was a boy in England, my mother followed an old religion. She believed, as your people do, there is a spirit in all things—in all animals and even in stones, especially precious stones. Artio was a goddess my mother spoke of often, the Celtic bear goddess, so it was natural that a bear killed my mother when I was fifteen, a bear from the baiting pits in London. I watched her die."

"That's horrible!"

"She arranged it, opened his cage when no one was near." He held up the leather purse with the jewel in it. "She believed if the bear spirit was with her when she died and while she was holding the jewel I have in this purse, she would see the future. I was there to hear what she said about her vision."

"What happened?"

"Before she died, she shouted to me to go to the colonies. That was all she could say, but I assumed it had something to do with my future. I had the jewel set in the handle of my sword, then crossed the ocean and ended up here. I grew tired of the life I had in the woods, so I decided to see the future as my mother had seen it. I tracked a bear, then held the stone while I approached him. You saw the result and I did not see a vision. But I believe you have some of Artio's spirit and I believe you are the reason my mother sent me here."

"The bear is a powerful spirit. I don't know if I am worthy."

"You are." He handed the purse to Oota Dabun. "There are two other items in this bag. The forehead band belonged to my mother. Set the stone in the pendant. It will remind you of me. The second item is a bear claw, which possesses the spirit of the bear it belonged to. If you hold it along with the jewel, the vision should work for you."

"But only if I die, right?"

"True, so don't use it now. But maybe years from now, when you've lived the life you deserve and it's time to die."

"Why didn't you ever learn our language?" Oota Dabun asked him, changing the subject. "Was it because you never wanted to live in our village?" He didn't answer, but she could see in his eyes a mixture of feelings. They stared at each other for a moment, then Phillip's gaze moved to Kimi, who started to stir and whimper.

"She's saying goodbye," Phillip told Oota Dabun. "She's a smart child. She knows when to speak and when to be quiet. The black bear might have attacked if she had cried out a few minutes ago."

"Goodbye? Then you *are* leaving."

"I have to. All hope for a good life has disappeared."

She looked down at the branch he had used to make the noise. "I'm sorry," she told him.

"No need. I will miss you and Kimi, but things are the way they were meant to be. I do have a favor to ask."

"Anything."

He touched the cut on his cheek. "Warn Elias and Noah. The village isn't safe and I can't get to them."

***

Martha

"That was a powerful session," Glen said.

Martha agreed. She thought how her soul had been redeemed when Phillip put his life on the line for Oota Dabun, proving himself to be a man of character. But she was certain Glen was thinking of the revelation about a way to see the future.

"Do you think Phillip was right?" Diane asked. "Was the bear Oota Dabun's true spirit guide?"

Martha held her hand up to quiet everyone in the room. "I'm descended from the Lenape people who lived in this area," she said, "Isn't there a chance that Oota Dabun is one of my ancestors? Perhaps down the line through Kimi. If Oota Dabun could see the future, that would explain how she knew enough to get the necklace to Diane by leaving it to her through me."

Diane smiled. "I love the idea you could be descended from the woman I was in the other life, but if what Phillip said was true, then Oota Dabun would have been able to see the future for only a brief instant as she died. How would that be long enough for her to learn so much? And to communicate it?"

"People can stay in the border between life and death for a long time," Glen suggested, standing as he spoke.

"You mean a coma?" Diane asked. "We have no proof or any idea how the Lenape people would deal with someone in that state."

"Maybe it wasn't a coma, maybe it was an illness or injury that left her hanging on for a day or two. That would be long enough. And maybe Kimi or another daughter was by her side to hear about the future. I don't know of a tradition of prophecy among the Lenape people, but the Celtic religion was rich with prophets and seers. So Phillip's background introduced the possibility. And since Diane was Oota Dabun in her former life, it seems to me she should be able to use the jewel to predict the future."

"Not without dying," Ryan said. "I hope everyone understands that."

Diane rolled her eyes. "I heard what Phillip said and I have no desire to die. You can trust me."

"I still worry."

"We all do," Martha said.

"But the memory of what Oota Dabun saw would probably be a memory Diane could recall," Glen suggested. "We could look at the future through the past."

Ryan said, "I don't see how it will help us solve the murders. We need to move forward with the original plan."

"Something in Oota Dabun's vision might give us what we're after," Glen said.

"What *we're* after or what *you're* after?" Ryan asked.

Things are getting tense, Martha thought. She looked at Glen to see how he would reply.

"We should sleep on it. Let's meet here tomorrow morning, same time. We'll decide what to do then."

Martha liked Glen's suggestion to wait and also liked his suggestion to see if Oota Dabun had a real vision at the end of her life. She had thought of Diane's other incarnation as fascinating since learning of her through the first regression. Now she believed the woman could be her own ancestor and was even more intrigued. A seventeenth century Lenape woman with a Celtic connection was spellbinding!

Chapter Fourteen
Diane

There was a threat of thunderstorms. Martha drove Diane's car back to Raccoon Island and left the canoe on her dock. Ryan offered to drive Diane home rather than having Martha drive out of her way. Diane didn't argue, since she wanted alone time with Ryan. There was something she had been meaning to say as soon as the time was right.

"I was glad Oota Dabun and Chogan made love," she told Ryan as they walked toward her door. Diane was shuffling her feet and moving slowly, enjoying being beside him. "It felt right."

"As if our souls needed to complete a circle for that lifetime," Ryan replied.

Diane stopped suddenly and looked toward the door. "The closer I get to my house, the less I want to go inside."

"You don't have to. You know you can stay with me, if you like."

"Thank you, but I don't want to be forced out of my own home. I'd feel like a coward."

"You're not a coward. You know what I've been saying. I don't want you staying alone until we find out who drugged you."

Diane was shaking. She hoped Ryan didn't notice.

"Could you stay with me?" she asked.

"I can't, because of Maya. But I want you to come back and spend the night at our house."

Diane took hold of his arm. "Thanks. I'll do that." She pulled him back toward his car without even entering the house to get her toothbrush or a change of clothes.

***

Ryan

Ryan had brought Diane to his house and explained the situation to Glen, who was glad they had taken the safe course. He said it was reckless for Diane to consider staying at her house alone after the canoe incident.

When Maya came home from school, she was so happy she told Diane she should move in for good. Ryan laughed over that suggestion and winked at Diane. Maya said she could share her room for as long as she wanted, but Ryan explained that Diane would have his room and he would sleep on the couch.

After Ryan explained the sleeping arrangements, Diane told him she wouldn't stay if it meant he had to give up his room. She claimed she would be happy on the couch. But she couldn't have been too happy down there, because at 1:00 in the morning he woke up, feeling as if someone was in the room. He opened his eyes to see Diane standing next to his bed, lit by moonlight from his open window, dressed in her green T-shirt and white panties. He stared at her eyes as she looked back, then, without speaking a word, she slid into the bed beside him.

She was on her back, but when he wrapped his arm around her waist, she turned, curling into the spoon position. He slid beside her, touching her body with his own in as many places as possible. He pushed her hair away from her neck so he could kiss her there. Her body shook, rubbing against his in a way that made the room swirl. He lifted himself up and spun her so he could kiss her lips.

They had to be quiet because Maya and Glen were down the hall, but having to hold back intensified his desire. He reached up her shirt and touched one of her breasts. He found her nipple and drew little circles around it. She gasped slightly, then pulled back and sat up to take her shirt off. She started to lie down facing him, but he tugged on her panties, so she rolled to her back and, still without saying a word, pulled her underwear off. She was naked, but he wasn't. He took off what he was wearing, dropping his T-shirt and boxers beside the bed on her clothes.

Ryan kissed her again as they lay on their sides. Then he wrapped his arms around her and rolled so she ended up on top, straddling him. The move made noise, but hopefully it wasn't too much. Diane leaned forward and kissed him as he caressed her.

She sat up and he followed, hugging his face into her chest and kissing the soft skin under her breasts. She wrapped her hands around his head, squeezing him into her heart. He pulled back to look in her eyes and felt Oota Dabun's gaze crossing the centuries, as if his soul was connected with both women through the mixture of Chogan's memories and his own. It was as if all four people had melded. He blinked a couple of times and Diane was again the woman above him. She squirmed, then guided him into her body and gently rolled, as if they were dancing on waves. He felt her body grow tense, then release at the same moment as his own. She leaned forward and held him, burying her face in his neck, and squeezing him with her arms and her legs. He held her just as tight, until she pulled away and rolled off.

She got dressed and turned to leave. Ryan grabbed her shirt and pulled her back for one more kiss before letting her leave, still without a word between them. The experience had been physical and spiritual, but it hadn't been vocal. There had been no need for words. They were one spirit, together eternally through love.

***

Maya

"Lucas says he's part Indian," Maya announced at breakfast.

"You should say Native American," Ryan said, "not Indian. Indians are from India."

"Lenape?" Martha asked Maya.

Maya knew the woman with the bear claw would be interested. "I think so. He said his mom's dad was one and he told me something weird. He says the Ind... I mean Native Americans believe the world grew on a giant turtle. Do they really think that?"

"It's a Lenape legend. The tree of life sprouted on the back of a turtle."

"Really?" Ryan asked Martha. "On a turtle?"

"It shows the Lenape thought with their hearts and souls as well as their brains and it's no more or less believable than a story about a man building a giant boat and loading it with two of each species. The Lenape respected turtles because they live in water and on land."

"Like muskrats?" Maya asked.

"Exactly, like muskrats," Martha told her. "The Lenape legend honors the importance of water. Unlike the Christian story of Noah where water is a symbol of destruction, the Lenape see water as a symbol of life."

"When astronomers look for life on other worlds, they first look for planets with water," Glen said, "because all living things need water. So, in a way, our scientists have accepted the Lenape belief in the importance of water."

Maya wondered about muskrats, turtles, and her mom. What Miss Martha had said about the turtle seemed to mean the tree of life grew in the border between under the water and above, just like Dr. Kari said. And if her mom was in that border where the tree was, maybe she didn't have to be dead. Maya needed to find out more about turtles and muskrats. She would speak with Lucas at school.

***

Ryan

After Maya left for school, everyone gathered in Ryan's living room and listened as Glen admitted he'd decided Ryan was right. He'd thought through the discussion overnight and concluded there was a possibility Oota Dabun had used the jewel to glimpse the future, but the chance that her vision might help their cause was slight. Glen said he was intrigued with the unique opportunity, but willing to wait.

"You're saying you'll regress me next?" Ryan asked.

"Yes. Chogan might know something about Phillip's warning that Elias and Noah were in danger. We need to focus there."

***

Chogan

Although Chogan would have been content to spend the rest of his life lying on a pallet beside Oota Dabun, he knew he couldn't. They had to refrain from sexual relations for the next week, which would be impossible if they slept side by side. Everyone who attended Gamwing needed to be pure and neither of them wanted to miss the celebration. This year, Gamwing was to be held in their village longhouse. Hundreds of people from other Lenape villages would be arriving to honor the spirit Meesinghawleekum and to celebrate the harvest. Chogan planned to hunt deer, to make his contribution and also to have extra to give to

Oota Dabun. She was still breast-feeding Kimi and needed plenty to eat. The entire village was willing to share whatever they had, but Chogan wanted to be a good provider.

He would also have to clean and dry the meat he caught. The venison had to last for the length of Gamwing, which was generally 10 to 12 days and Chogan wanted whatever he caught for Oota Dabun to last a moon cycle or more.

Chogan knew the perfect place to wait for the animals, beside a path that led down to the pond. The deer had stomped the walkway clear by using it repeatedly. It was the easiest trail to the pond where they liked to drink. He would cover himself with a deerskin. Other hunters used wolf skins, so the power of the animal hunting spirit could drift into them. But Chogan had better luck with buckskin. When the deer thought he was a wolf, they ran as fast as they did from a man.

A few of the Maple trees had begun to change colors, but most of the forest was still thick and green. The mornings were cooler now, but this day was starting to grow warmer already. He glanced to his left and saw the great pond through the forest. He was headed closer to the water than he liked to be, so he turned slightly to his right and kept walking.

He was nearing his hunting spot when he saw someone he wasn't expecting, Etchemin the canoe builder. Everyone was allowed to hunt, but Etchemin was too good with fire and an adze to bother trying. He traded boats for food and other supplies. He had all he needed, especially since he had no family. Chogan thought the man might be looking for trees, long and straight enough to make his dugout boats. But there were plenty of trees closer to the village.

Etchemin leaned over and started to shuffle through piles of old leaves, searching for something. Chogan wondered what was hidden there. He watched as Etchemin moved through the area in a methodical manner, but without finding what he was after. Etchemin moved further away from where Chogan was standing and began looking through another pile, pushing through it with his feet.

Chogan decided to follow. He slipped the deerskin over his back and head because he was still hunting, even if his goal had changed. He circled around Etchemin at a distance until he reached a thickly wooded area, then moved stealthily from tree to tree until he was close enough to see whatever Etchemin might find. The canoe builder's lack of hunting experience helped Chogan stay hidden.

Etchemin bent over after he appeared to touch something with his foot. He picked up a glass bottle, held it up to the light, then set it down and picked up another and another. Chogan had never seen or heard of glass before the white-faced men brought their whiskey and now there were six bottles on the ground beside Etchemin. If what Chogan had learned about those bottles from Oota Dabun was true, they were filled with fire-water of the highest quality just in time for Gamwing.

Deer hunting could wait. Chogan needed to find out what the canoe builder was planning. He watched as Etchemin placed the bottles into two bags, both of which appeared to be medicine bags belonging to Abooksigun. Etchemin began to walk and Chogan followed until they were back at the village.

It did not take long for Chogan to discover how Etchemin intended to use the whiskey he'd dug out of the piles of leaves in the woods. The canoe builder went to the village then to his own wigwam, which was the place where Elias and Noah were staying. He entered for a brief time, then came out of the hut carrying the two medicine bags, now empty, and an iron carpenter's axe.

So much for the Gamwing theory. Elias and Noah were white, which meant they were impure and could not attend the celebration. Etchemin had traded the fire-water for a tool he could use in his daily work. But six bottles for one tool? And Etchemin was so good with a stone adze it hardly made sense.

Elias and Noah drank a lot, which meant they'd probably gone through most of their fire-water. They would need more. But who had been hiding these bottles for Etchemin? It could only have been someone with access to other whites. Abooksigun sometimes traveled and traded with white-faces along the way, but why would he hide the bottles?

Chogan had to think this through and talk it over with Oota Dabun.

***

Diane

Ryan opened his eyes, but stayed motionless long enough for Diane to wonder why. She was about to move closer to him, to be certain he wasn't hurt, when he sat up, looked at Glen, and said, "I think I know that man."

"Are you talking about Etchemin?"

Ryan nodded. "When he stepped out of the wigwam, holding that cast iron tool, I thought of a carpenter who works for me, Martin Malek. He's an excellent woodworker, doesn't have a family, and is always pushing me to buy new tools. He would trade a month's wages for a better table saw. Who could be more like Etchemin?"

Diane thought the men sounded too alike. Hadn't Glen said that genetics and environment affect who we are as much as our souls?

Glen said, "It will be nice if that's true, because Etchemin might have had something to do with the threat to

Elias and Noah. His idea could have been to use the liquor to incapacitate them prior to doing whatever they planned to do. If that led to murder, then it could indicate that this carpenter was connected somehow with Lori and Beth's deaths."

"Seems as if you're assuming a few things," Diane said. "First of all, Etchemin might have made the trade because he wanted the axe, not because he wanted to get Elias and Noah drunk. Secondly, nobody in our group knows this carpenter other than Ryan and he doesn't know him well."

"I don't know him," Martha said, shaking her head.

Diane nodded. Although Ryan looked as if he was about to say something, she continued to speak to Glen. "Aren't we looking for someone who is a full part of our spiritual family, not just someone watching from the outside?"

"Martin's connected to us through Heather," Ryan said. "She introduced him to me."

Diane didn't like that at all, but she stayed quiet.

"Clearly we don't have perfect evidence," Glen said, raising his eyebrows. "But these are good clues."

Glen explained his reasoning as Diane leaned back in her chair. "Etchemin had been using stone tools successfully for his entire life. He wouldn't have given up six bottles to get a single cast iron axe unless there was another reason. And the fact that someone had hidden the bottles adds to the suspicious nature of what he was up to. We also don't have proof that the carpenter has Etchemin's soul, but shared traits are what we're looking for. Like I said, good clues. We need to keep looking and that means it's your turn. We need to see this through Oota Dabun's eyes."

***

Oota Dabun

It had been a week since Chogan had told Oota Dabun about the fire-water in the woods and longer than that since Phillip's request to watch over Elias and Noah. The village was filled with people they hadn't seen since the previous year, here for the celebration. But Oota Dabun and Chogan had managed to keep an eye on the white traders. So far, nothing had happened.

"The fire-water I drank left me weak and vulnerable," Oota Dabun had told Chogan earlier in the day, when she was working on her outfit for the butterfly dance. "It could do the same to them."

"They know what it does."

"But what if someone hurts them when they can't defend themselves, when we're in the longhouse?" That had been hours earlier. Now Gamwing had arrived and the first celebration was about to begin.

The two white men had the new bottles of fire-water for a week, yet neither she nor Chogan had seen any signs they'd used the drink. Phillip's request still loomed in her heart, so she intended to look out for them as well as she could. Chogan had agreed to help.

Oota Dabun was dressed in an elaborate buckskin skirt with a matching top. There were five rows of soft leather tassels around her clothes as well as beads shaped like stars on her shoulders and around her waist. She also wore a beaded headband and soft moccasins. The final addition was a shawl, decorated with tassels and beads matching the ones on her outfit. The shawl was important because when the dance began, it would become the butterfly wings.

Once everyone was inside the longhouse, Noshi, the village chief, said a few words of welcome. After the introduction, it was time for The Butterfly Dance.

Dancing was like walking to Oota Dabun, so she wasn't nervous about the steps. She was, however, worried about Elias and Noah, who hadn't been invited to the celebration because they were white. Her fear grew when, as the drums and singing began, she saw Etchemin leave the building. But she had to finish the dance. She lifted her arms, dipped her right shoulder, and took her first step.

Oota Dabun glanced in Chogan's direction when she turned his way. He was staring at her as if he was expecting her to rise up on her butterfly wings and take flight. He hadn't noticed Etchemin. She could tell he couldn't see anyone in the longhouse other than her. She wanted to signal to him, to ask him to check on the white-faces, but she couldn't interrupt the performance, not in front of so many people from so many homes.

When the dance was over, Chogan rushed toward Oota Dabun. Before he could compliment her, she told him about Etchemin and started running toward the exit. He followed her to the pond, near Etchemin's canoes where they found Elias and Noah floating face down in the pond. When they pulled their bodies out, Oota Dabun could smell the fire-water. She thought about Phillip and how she'd let him down.

***

Martha

When Diane had recovered enough from the regression to sit up, Martha looked at her swollen eyes and could tell she'd been crying. Tears from the memories of what she'd experienced as Oota Dabun. Martha wondered if it was the deaths alone she had reacted to or if it was the fact that Oota Dabun had not been able to accomplish what Phillip had requested. She hoped it wasn't the latter.

Oota Dabun hadn't been close to either Elias or Noah. The canoe incident began with them giving her more liquor than she could handle, which meant she probably didn't trust them. Yet, the way Martha figured, one of those two men had been an incarnation of Lori. Diane must have felt a connection with the man's soul.

"This regression showed us we were right," Glen said. "Elias and Noah were the two murder victims from that incarnation."

"Did they drown because they were drunk?" Ryan asked. "Or were they held under water by the person or persons who killed them?"

"There was no indication of a struggle," Diane told him.

"There wouldn't be if they were unconscious," Glen said. "All we know is Etchemin gave Elias and Noah the liquor and they drowned. Everything else is speculation."

"Send me back," Martha suggested.

"But you were Phillip and he's gone," Ryan said.

"There had to be a reason he asked Oota Dabun to watch out for the two Europeans. Send me to an earlier time, before he left. Maybe we can find the reason if we listen to their conversations."

"Maybe so," Glen said, as Diane and Ryan nodded.

***

Phillip

Elias rolled his eyes and spoke to Phillip, his voice sounding bitter. "We were hoping we could talk to their leaders through you, hoping to establish a trading partner. But after all your time here, you don't know the language any more than we do. So all we've got is that girl of yours and she blames us for the canoe night. She hasn't translated for me once since then."

"Most of the savages don't like us much," Noah added. "I tell you, the witch doctor is scary. I think he put a curse on us."

"Maybe so," Phillip said. "Supposedly, he helped Oota Dabun patch me up after she found me in the forest. But since I woke up, he's been nothing but trouble."

"Are there any people here we can trust, other than the girl?" Elias asked.

"They fed you and gave you shelter since you arrived," Phillip told them. "I think you can trust most everybody here. Just be careful around the medicine man."

The flap on the front of the wigwam was open. Noah looked out, pointed, and said, "What about the two who are always with him?"

Phillip turned to see Abooksigun with Pules and Etchemin. They were standing in front of Abooksigun's wigwam. Pules was doing most of the talking, her arms waving like branches in a storm.

Noah had surprised Phillip by saying *always*. He knew Pules' hated him and was convinced her hatred had spread to Abooksigun. If her anger had spread to a third person, it was getting dangerous.

"When did Etchemin start keeping company with those two?" Phillip asked.

Elias said, "We were hoping you could tell us that. You have more freedom here than we do and more chances to see what's happening."

What Elias said was true, but Phillip had wasted his freedom by not opening his eyes. He needed to find out if there was a plot underway. Talking to Oota Dabun was his best chance to find the truth.

He left Elias and Noah to go to Chogan's wigwam, hoping to find Oota Dabun there, alone. He got his wish, but before he could ask her about Pules and her friends, he saw a bottle of whiskey near the far wall. It was glass, not clay, which meant it was expensive.

"What is that?" Phillip asked, nodding toward the bottle.

"It is not your concern."

"I care for you."

"You care for fire-water, not me."

"So does Chogan, apparently."

"It is not his. It's mine. I got it from Abooksigun." She picked up the bottle and sat on her sleeping pallet. "I did things wrong the last time. I had a vision quest, but I don't remember it. I will use less when I try again."

"I'll sit with you without drinking, to make sure you don't end up on the pond again."

"No you won't. You were with me the last time, which wasn't good. A person should be alone during a vision quest—another thing I did wrong."

Phillip knew Oota Dabun well enough to know he couldn't change her mind when she made a decision. "Drink slowly," he said, "and eat something first."

He hoped she would listen to his advice, but he doubted she would. Most young Lenape men have very little food during their vision quests. This was different, but getting her to believe so would be impossible. He would watch Chogan's wigwam from a distance. That was all he could do.

***

Glen

"So it was Abooksigun who supplied the liquor," Diane said, while Glen, Ryan, and she watched Martha shift on the couch.

"Well—we know what Oota Dabun said," Glen told her, "but she could have gotten it somewhere else or the whiskey might have belonged to Chogan."

"I would have known if Oota Dabun lied," Diane said.

"You would have if it was your regression," Glen argued, "but you heard the story through Martha. You don't know any more than the rest of us."

Ryan stepped between Diane and Glen with his hands up. "Relax, you two. There's almost no chance that Oota Dabun lied, so let's assume Abooksigun supplied the whiskey."

"Phillip thought she was telling the truth," Martha said, easing Glen's doubts somewhat.

"And given that," Ryan continued. "I believe it's a good assumption that Abooksigun, Pules, and Etchemin acted together to murder Elias and Noah. I also believe it's a good assumption that Beth and Diane's mom were the two European men in that lifetime. The question now is— what do we do with this lead?"

Glen agreed, but there were complications he hadn't discussed with anyone. "We seem to have a case of what I call circularity, meaning the same event has happened to those two souls in other incarnations."

"You mean they've been murdered over and over?" Martha asked.

"Exactly. And we have to break that cycle."

"Oh God," Diane said softly. "I didn't think of that."

"I was looking for it. You weren't," Glen told her. Of course, Ryan's question hadn't been answered yet. What should they do next?

Chapter Fifteen
Maya

When Maya arrived home from school, she found her dad and his friends sitting on lawn chairs by the waterfront. None of them noticed her, because they all seemed to be talking at once. It was loud, almost as loud as her dad's boat at full speed.

She wished the people weren't there, because she wanted to speak with her dad alone. Lucas had told her more about muskrats and, although he had no clue about why she was interested, he had said a few things she hoped might help her find the border place where Dr. Kari had said her mother might be.

The people in her father's group stopped talking when Maya joined them. When her dad asked her about her day at school, Maya told them all about muskrats.

***

Ryan

When Maya was done talking about muskrats, she carried her backpack to her bedroom and Glen spoke in a quiet voice. "One of those muskrat traits Maya just mentioned gave me an idea."

Ryan wondered which one. Lucas had told her five facts he must have found on the internet, ranging from how they live in family groups to how they can hold their breath under water for fifteen minutes. But Glen was interested only that they rarely fight unless there isn't enough food.

"That's what we have to do," Glen told Ryan. "Heather and Martin are our best suspects. We need to give them a reason to fight. We need to play one against the other and see where it leads."

"You want to take away their food?" Ryan asked.

"Not exactly, but they work for you. There ought to be a way to upset them."

***

Diane

Glen spoke to Diane as she and Martha started to leave Ryan's. She was still scared to be home alone and planned to stay at Martha's that night. Even though she would miss Ryan, she didn't want him to get tired of seeing her.

"Would you consider the suggestion I made yesterday," Glen said, "to recall the day Oota Dabun died? It might help you understand the jewel."

It probably wouldn't help them find the people who killed her mother and Beth, but she contemplated the interesting aspects of Glen's suggestion as Martha walked toward the car. If there was a time when Oota Dabun was aware her life was almost over, she might have used the jewel to look forward to an important moment in Diane's life. As Martha had suggested, this theory would explain the story that had been passed from generation to generation along with the jewel.

"Exactly what are you suggesting?" Diane asked.

"Ryan plans to bring Martin to Martha's house tomorrow, under the pretense that she wants her kitchen remodeled. While they're talking, we'll have free time. I thought this might be an interesting way to occupy ourselves. And, who knows, it could be productive."

Diane was as intrigued as Glen, probably more so, but she was scared. She had been Oota Dabun in that other life, so it would be her own death she'd be witnessing. If Oota Dabun had looked forward to an event in Diane's current life, as Glen suspected, there was a good chance the event hadn't occurred yet, an opportunity to see her own future. In the end, her curiosity overwhelmed her fear. Diane decided to go for it.

"All right," Diane told him. "I'll come by here tomorrow morning."

***

The next day, Diane felt strange, because she was used to having Ryan and Martha near her when she was regressed. She expressed her fear that something might happen to her if the memory of a previous death was brought out.

"Some of the people I've regressed over the years remembered the events leading up to their deaths," Glen told her. "They didn't have any negative experiences. I don't know of any reason why you'd be different."

"What did they see?"

"Nothing. Many of them came out of their regressions early. Others slipped into memories from different past lives. But either way, the process didn't cause any harm."

OK," Diane said, as she stared again at the focal point she'd used before. And the process of drifting back into her past life memories went as smoothly as it had with her other sessions.

***

Oota Dabun

"It's time," Oota Dabun said. Her voice was weak, little more than a whisper. But her daughters were by her side. They were both grown women now, evidence that her life had been a good one.

Phillip's daughter, Kimi, had studied with Abooksigun and after his passing had become the village medicine woman. Chogan's daughter, Chepi, had two children of her own, a daughter, Hurit, and a son, Machk. Machk's name meant bear, which added another level of meaning to the task Oota Dabun had asked Kimi and Chepi to undertake.

Oota Dabun had fallen while berry picking. She walked too close to the great pond and slipped on a wet rock. It happened because her old body wasn't as agile as it had once been. The cut on her calf was less than the length of her middle finger. She had thought it would heal, but it hadn't and now her leg was red and tender. She felt weak and hot.

She was having trouble thinking, but she had considered her plans for years, ran Phillip's description of his mother's death over and over in her mind. The jewel was set into the forehead band and the bear claw attached to a leather thong. She had held both items since she was injured, only setting them down to eat and sleep. Both her daughters had instructions to wake her if it appeared she would not make it through a night. They watched over her in shifts, but this day they were both with her because Oota Dabun told them she would cross over soon.

"This may be the most important part of my long life," she told her daughters. "You both know it is true, especially you, Kimi." Her medicine woman daughter nodded, but didn't speak. Chepi and Kimi held on to each other as if their grief prevented them from standing on their own. "You both need to watch and listen. I'll tell you what I see when I see it." It was a struggle to speak, but Oota Dabun knew what to say and her words were coming as she had practiced them.

The sun could be seen through the opening of the wigwam. It was near the horizon. This seemed appropriate to Oota Dabun since her life was also setting. She lay still on the ground as it became harder to breathe. She held the jewel and the claw close to her heart and waited. She nodded off a couple of times, but shook her head to wake and somehow found the strength to shout to her daughters.

"I'm floating over my body, but I'm not staying here. A force is pulling me up toward the clouds. I see two white women, both with golden hair. The younger one is wrapped in white clothing, with a skirt so long it drags on the floor. I'm starting to see through the eyes of the older one and feel her emotions. It's a strange world. We're inside, but there is plenty of light, coming from what appears to be little suns in the roof. I'm sitting on a seat in front of a magic wall that reflects like the surface of the pond when it is still, only the wall is clearer. This place is amazing, but the older woman only notices the younger woman in her bright, white dress."

***

Diane

"Why have you never let me call you Mom?" Maya asked.

That is Maya's question? Diane knew her stepdaughter wouldn't have any questions about sex. She was twenty-eight and had been dating Lucas since they were old enough to allow their friendship to become something greater. Still, there was more to a successful marriage than just physical intimacy. Asking Maya if she had any questions seemed an appropriate thing to do on her wedding day.

"I love you, Maya," Diane told her, "as much as any mother can love a daughter. I hope you know that."

"I do."

"That's what's most important." Diane paused while she took a breath. "When I married your father, I took on the role and responsibilities of your mother, but I wanted my place in your heart to be separate from hers. We learned so much the year we solved the murders, but the most important lesson was that no one truly dies. That knowledge has been a comfort for me and I hope it has been for you as well."

"It has, but you've been here for Dad and me for years. Mom is a title you deserve."

She knew every word Maya was about to say. It had been eighteen years since Diane had first heard their conversation through the regression. Over the years, she'd considered changing the way it played out, just to see if she could. But now the day had arrived and she decided not to mess with the powers of the universe.

"I need to remind you of something we haven't talked about in a while."

"I know what you're going to say and I know about the notes you wrote. I know what's in them and I know where they're kept. I could never forget that."

"Good. Years ago, I had a glimpse of this day, so I knew it was coming. But I don't have a clue about what happens after today, which means I have to speak clearly now. After I die, the notes belong to you. They list steps you can take to break the cycle of murders. If you see the signs, you are to use them. If you don't, you will need to pass them on to your own daughter so the chain isn't broken."

"My daughter? That part you never told me."

"You'll have a child someday, someone you will love and trust."

Diane took one of Maya's hands in her own.

"We've talked about this many times before. My notes just put it all in writing. Two murders will keep occurring in other lifetimes unless someone stops them. I've tried to explain what to look for."

"You mean a carpenter, a half-sister, and a psychiatrist?"

"They probably won't have the same occupations, not exactly. Look for their general characteristics..."

***

$\mathcal{D}$iane's words were cut off as she spun back to her place on Ryan's couch. She looked up at Glen who said, "Wow!"

She was having trouble processing everything she'd just experienced. Oota Dabun lived hundreds of years before Diane. The scene from her future could have been part of the life Diane had already lived, but it didn't turn out that way. Diane had a glimpse of a life that included marriage to Ryan and raising Maya. And, thank God, she and her stepdaughter seemed happy and blessed. Hopefully, Ryan was as well.

"You realize what this means?" Glen asked.

Diane was too overwhelmed to answer, but she knew. For one thing, it meant this Celtic stone was damn powerful.

"What we did up to this point was just recalling memories," Glen told her. "But people can't remember events that haven't happened. So this has to mean the quantum physicists are right, time is just another dimension. We can look backward or forward."

"I'm not sure about that, but we now know the three people we're looking for—a carpenter, my half-sister, and a psychiatrist. They have to be Martin, Heather, and Dr. Montero. Ryan was right about the first two and he'll be excited to learn the third. We're on our way to solving this crime."

"That we are," Glen told her. "That we are."

***

Martha

$\mathcal{W}$hen she heard a knock at the back door, Martha went through the kitchen to let the two men in. Ryan introduced her to Martin, whom she hadn't met previously. He looked fifty, maybe younger. His hair was gray, but thick, and cut so the sides didn't touch his ears. He had a tiny, white, soul-patch beard, which looked attractive. He was the type of man she would have wanted to get to know, if she wasn't aware he was a killer.

"You can see my kitchen's small. I was hoping you might have ideas to increase the counter space."

"Like hanging the microwave over the stove?" Ryan asked.

"Exactly. I want everything replaced, so there should be plenty of opportunities to be creative."

Martha wondered what would drive a man to kill two women. Did he know Lori or Beth? Did he have an affair with one of them or a secret business deal that went wrong? Or could he have just felt a thrill in the act of murder regardless of the victims' identities? Of course, if Martin is the current incarnation of Etchemin, which seems logical, he might have been an accessory to murder rather than the actual killer. In that case, the reasons may not have been his own.

Martin looked around the room. "There are a number of options to get the most out of a small space: cabinets with fold out shelves, Lazy Susans in the corners, or a peninsula with a fold out counter."

"I told you he's good," Ryan said.

Martha signaled for the men to follow her, then led them through her living room and porch to the lawn in front of the house. As they walked toward her dock, she said, "There's another project I'd like you to do while you're here for the kitchen."

When they were all on the dock, Martha pointed across the lake. "My best friend was killed over there, on her own dock. You might have heard of her, Lori Larimer. Her body was dumped in the lake and washed up here. I want to build a memorial for her, like the crosses people put up at the scenes of fatal highway accidents."

"We do kitchens," Martin told her. "Only kitchens."

"Martha's a friend," Ryan said. "I told her we'd do this for her."

"It'll be expensive," Martin said.

"I think I can give her a good price," Ryan said. "In fact, I told her we'd do it for free, but she insists on paying."

"It's your choice," Martin said, managing to sound as if he meant to say—*It's your funeral*.

"I know."

"This is where the real creativity comes," Martha said. "I want something large enough to be seen by passing boats and I want people to know it's a memorial. But I don't want a cross. Lori was a Christian, but not an active one and I have my own religion."

"I'm an atheist," Martin told her.

"I'm certain you're our man," Martha insisted. "Maybe if I tell you something personal about her, it will give you ideas. She was a wonderful woman."

Martin shrugged.

"Lori loved her house and loved this lake, like most of us who have been fortunate enough to live in this area. But while the rest of us were keeping our places to ourselves or sharing them with business clients who could return our favors, Lori signed up for *The Fresh Air Fund*, which meant she opened her home to inner city children from Newark. They were kids who had rarely been out of Newark and had never had a chance to go sailing or rowing or tubing behind a powerboat. She would have a child in her home for two weeks, then move on to another one. She taught at least five children to swim. I remember the first time one little girl stood on Lori's dock. The child pointed at ducks and shouted, 'Look at the chickens.' I laughed to myself when I heard her mistake, but then I cried tears of happiness. These things the rest of us had grown up with and had treasured for our entire lives were new to her, as fresh as morning rain. Lori had made something beautiful happen because she was a beautiful woman. Then someone killed her, some heartless fool whose own life is worthless."

"You don't know that," Martin said.

"We know more than you think," Ryan told him.

Martin reacted with a start, but Martha changed the subject back to the memorial. She suggested each of them come up with a concept, then present it to the others. They could pick one or choose the best features from each.

***

Diane

𝒟r. Montero did not have a receptionist, just an answering service to schedule appointments. At first, this seemed odd. The patients would sign in when they arrived, then would sit in the waiting room until she came out to take their insurance information and usher in the next one. When it was Diane's turn to sign, she discovered the sign-in sheet hadn't been changed in a week and Heather Cox had been to see the doctor a few days earlier. She made a mental note of the day and time.

Glen agreed with Diane's suggestion they not tell Ryan specifics about the conversation which would occur on Maya's future wedding day. But they told Ryan and Martha about how Oota Dabun's deathbed glimpse of the future had revealed how a psychiatrist was involved in the murders of Beth and Lori. Since Dr. Montero was the only psychiatrist close enough to their circle to be part of their spiritual family, they agreed she was the third person they were seeking. They believed she had been Abooksigun in the former life.

Ryan and Martha explained how they'd fed Martin just enough information to leave him feeling insecure. They wanted to do the same to Dr. Montero and, since Diane already had an appointment, she was the logical choice to do the deed.

"The last time we met we were talking about water," Dr. Montero said, after Diane took a seat on the couch across from the doctor's desk. "You were saying water can bring peace or fury and you choose peace. Would you care to continue that conversation? Have you thought more about your reaction?"

Diane sat up as straight as she could on the soft upholstery. Dr. Montero could be intimidating, especially in her office.

"If you were to drown, would you want your friends to skip the mourning period and move straight to inner peace?" the doctor asked.

"I will be mourning my mother for the rest of my life and I'm sure Maya will be mourning her mother for longer, given her age. But we owe them more than simple grief. We owe them justice."

Now it was the doctor who sat up straight. "Justice?"

"We have reason to believe their deaths were caused by three people, each with their own reasons."

"Three?" Dr. Montero asked. Her expression seemed to freeze and her skin turned a shade paler, but Diane wasn't certain if she was imagining her reactions. "I thought the police determined both deaths were accidental."

"I'd like to talk about Maya," Diane said.

"She's a patient of mine, so I can't speak freely."

"That's OK. I can."

Diane squinted as she stared into the doctor's eyes. "Nothing in my life was worse than losing my mother, even losing my father couldn't compare. Like childbirth, Mother-daughter relationships bring painful and frustrating moments, but they also have the greatest potential for joy and awe. I was twenty-seven when my mother died and living on my own, so she had been with me as I became a woman. She gave me advice about my boyfriends, helped me with my homework, and made sure I ate balanced meals, all the things I needed, no matter how mundane or difficult. She was my best friend when she was killed…"

Dr. Montero's eyes went wide for an instant before she seemed to regain control.

"…but by that time she had taught me how to live my life. Maya was nine when her mother was killed," (Diane used the same word, but saw no reaction this time), "which makes her situation a world apart from mine. Her mother will never talk to her about the ways her body changes as she grows, will never help her pick out her first prom dress, or hold her tight after her first heartbreak. Ryan's a wonderful father, but he can't be everything—nobody can."

Diane paused, but continued to stare at Dr. Montero. When it seemed the doctor was about to speak, Diane continued talking.

"I've been looking around with help from my friends. We've found someone who knows something, a carpenter of all things, someone who builds for a living, but destroys for fun. I believe this man will point us where we need to go."

"What if he lies?"

"All we need is enough to get the police to reopen the case. The truth will come out."

***

Ryan

After Martha's speech about a memorial for Lori Larimer, Ryan half-expected Martin would quit his job. He didn't, but Heather did. Since she'd been working for Ryan for over five years, her choice to leave was unexpected. It confirmed his suspicion that Martin and Heather had been exchanging notes. It also complicated things because

Heather was the last of the three suspects they planned to confront and Ryan could no longer approach her at his shop.

Diane suggested talking to Heather at Dr. Montero's.

"She had an appointment last Tuesday afternoon at 2:00. If she sees Dr. Montero regularly, she'll probably be there next Tuesday at the same time. We can catch her going in or coming out."

Ryan thought for a moment then said, "Or we can barge into their session and confront the two of them together."

Diane agreed his idea was possible. "There's no receptionist," she said, "and the doctor doesn't lock the door to her office." But Ryan could tell she was worried.

The following Tuesday, they arrived at Dr. Montero's office ten minutes after the hour. Heather's car was in the drive. They parked beside it and went inside. The office was in the doctor's residence in a small house along route 10. There were no other businesses in the building.

They found the waiting room empty, as they expected it would be. Diane had canceled all her future appointments and Ryan had done the same for Maya, so they had no excuse for being there. But excuses would be useless once they broke into the session.

Ryan was seeking justice for Beth, but Diane was in his head. It wasn't long ago when his daughter was the only reason he got up in the morning. All that had turned. He could now envision a future with something in it other than loneliness, a future that could happen once the killers were punished.

He stepped around the waiting room desk and looked at Diane. She looked back with wide eyes and gave him a nod. Ryan turned the doorknob, pushed, and stepped into Dr. Montero's office with Diane on his heels.

Heather and Dr. Montero turned simultaneously. Their expressions changed from surprise to shock then to two different reactions as Heather's eyes widened in fear and the doctor's narrowed in anger.

"This is a private session," Dr. Montero said. "You can't come in."

"We already are in," Diane told her.

Ryan looked at Heather. "I heard you were responsible for Beth's death and also for Diane's mother's. You quit work the day I heard what you'd done. So we're here to find the truth."

"It wasn't me."

Dr. Montero cut Heather off. "She means she doesn't know anything about murders."

"Let her speak for herself," Diane told the doctor.

Ryan said, "We heard the opposite."

"I worked for you for more than five years," Heather pleaded, her eyes starting to fill with tears, "yet you believe Martin over me."

"I didn't say who told me."

Dr. Montero stood and reached for her purse, but Diane grabbed it first. "You're not calling anyone until we're finished." After she spoke, she moved to the landline and pulled the chord out.

"I'm a doctor and she's my patient," Dr. Montero said. "Even if you force me to tell you something about her, it won't hold up. There's such a thing as doctor-patient privilege."

"Now there are two people pointing at you," Ryan told Heather.

"It was the doctor," Heather said.

"Don't tell him that!" Dr. Montero shouted.

"Why not? It's true. She's writing a paper, something that will make her seem real important. It's about the different ways adults and children react to trauma, specifically trauma involving water. She chose Diane and Maya as her subjects, then arranged for their mothers to drown."

"No I didn't! It was her!"

Heather ignored Dr. Montero's interruption and continued to speak. "Then she used her sessions with Maya to leave little hints and suggestions in the child's mind until she responded by going for her midnight swim. After that, it was easy to drug Diane and set her adrift on the lake. The good doctor used roofies from a former patient."

"You know she's lying. Maya didn't become my patient until after her mother was dead. And others will tell you I stayed at the restaurant on the night Diane was drugged long after you left. Heather hated Lori all her life because her father chose to stay with Lori rather than divorce and marry Heather's mom. And Beth was a part of this mess because she was Diane's other half-sister. Heather was angry, angry all the time."

Ryan didn't know if the recorder he had in his pocket would give them something that would be admissible in court, but it didn't matter. He had enough to convince the police to reopen the case. They would determine which one of the threesome did the killing and seek an appropriate penalty. Their part in solving this crime was done.

Chapter Sixteen
Glen

Ryan and Maya were having breakfast with Glen on the day he was supposed to head back to Vermont. He was planning to stay with a friend of his until another case came up. The friend was a woman whom he'd helped with a previous case. It was Saturday, so Maya was going to ride with them to Newark airport. But Glen had something else on his mind.

"I'd like to do one more regression before I leave," he told Ryan as he nodded toward Maya.

Ryan glanced at his daughter then back at Glen. "What do you want to accomplish?" he asked.

"We solved the crimes, but remember, that was just one of our goals. We need to stop the killings in future incarnations. It's tricky, because the last time they occurred was in the seventeenth century, so they don't happen in every lifetime. But even if Heather, Kari, and Martin are convicted for what they did, we need to set up a system to warn our future selves.

"The Lenape oral tradition worked for Martha. I believe something similar can work again and Oota Dabun's look at Diane's future seemed to confirm that. Maya is the key, because she's the next generation, but I want to be certain her soul was close to Oota Dabun's. Right now we don't even know if she is a part of the spiritual family."

Glen could tell by the way Ryan looked at his daughter, he still wasn't thrilled with the suggestion.

"I can guide her to a pleasant memory, to reduce the possibility of something upsetting."

"Reduce?" Ryan asked.

"You know what the process is like. I can set the odds in her favor." Glen glanced at Maya then back to her father. "She'll have considerably less chance of remembering a bad day than she has of living through one in her everyday life. And she'll learn from the experience, like you did."

"All right," Ryan told him. He took Maya's hand and squeezed it. She was smiling and seemed to be looking forward to what was about to happen.

Glen led them to the couch and Maya took the position Martha, Diane, and her father had all occupied. Glen told her to stare at a spot on the ceiling and to imagine herself swimming by the steps near her dock.

"Now you see a light," he said. "It's a short distance beyond the edge of your dock. You're drawn to it, so you swim in that direction. You swim underwater, but you can breathe as if you were above. The light pulls you closer and starts you spinning. You twist in a gentle, soothing motion, not so much that you grow dizzy, more like floating in a tube. As you get closer to the light, you start to see shapes and people. You are remembering the person you once were..."

***

Kimi

"I am taking Kimi to look for strength in animals," her mother told Chogan. "We would like you to come."

She hoped Chogan would come. Her mother told her stories of another man, a white-face who was her father, but Chogan was the man who lived with her and took care of her. She loved him and wanted him near her and her mother.

"I can lead you to a muskrat den in a cove not far from here," Chogan told them. "The stars will be out soon, so they should be looking for food."

They allowed Kimi to follow on her own. Since she couldn't walk as fast as they could, it was starting to get dark when they reached the place. They found a fallen tree near where Chogan said the burrow was and they settled there.

"They know we are here," Chogan said, "but if we stay still and quiet, they will learn we mean no harm. It will take time, so we must be patient." The last part he said directly to Kimi.

As the sun continued to set, small heads appeared in the water. Chogan pointed them out to Kimi. "I believe those two are one of the kits and the mother. The others should follow. When they are very young, the mother brings the food to them. After they grow, she must show them how to take care of themselves. It's no different than what your mother does for you."

Another head appeared to join the two swimmers, then the three muskrats entered a patch of weeds at the water's edge. The mother stepped out of the water to get better access to the plants and the little ones followed.

"Muskrats are at home on land and in the water like otters, my own spirit animal," Chogan told Kimi, "but they are different from each other in one important way: muskrats eat plants, while otters eat fish and other animals, even muskrats."

He moved his hand slowly, raising it up from his leg slightly so he could point. "Look at the mother. She's bringing food to their den. She must have kits in the burrow who are too tiny to get their own."

Kimi understood what Chogan was trying to say, mothers look out for their children. No one spoke as the muskrats made a few more trips to the plants beside the water and back to their den. The large one kept bringing food while the little ones seemed content to follow her. Kimi and her mother kept watching until Chogan signaled it was time to go back to the village.

Kimi was too tired to return to the camp under her own power. Her mother carried her on her hip and the three traveled like a family, just like the muskrats.

Chapter Seventeen
Maya

𝒟eath with dignity was the law of the land, so people no longer had to move to one of the assisted suicide states. But there were still plenty of bureaucratic rules designed to maintain the rights of the sick and elderly. Diane had a living will and a stack of notarized letters. She'd written one each year since she turned sixty, all clearly stating her wishes, most of them dated prior to her cancer diagnosis. Still, Maya and Lucas could get into legal trouble if things didn't go exactly the way they should. They brought in a doctor to administer the lethal dose, but the case could still be complicated, because Diane did not want to be put to sleep prior to her death. She needed to be conscious long enough for the jewel and claw to take over.

The idea had been to recreate the method Oota Dabun had used at the end of her life. She'd looked forward hundreds of years and had seen Maya and Diane on Maya's wedding day, a vision that had proven to be accurate and helpful. As long as Diane held the jewel and the claw, Maya expected her step-mom's vision would be similar.

"That's it," Maya told Diane. "You are certain you're ready?"

She nodded.

"Are you ready?" Lucas asked the doctor, then told Diane, "We are where we can see and hear even if your voice is soft."

"It won't be," Diane told him.

"I will stay here and hold your hand," Maya said.

Diane was on her back, lying on the bed she had shared with Ryan for fifty-six years before the heart attack took him from her. She reached for Maya's hand and squeezed it. "I'm ready to learn if the message we will pass down through Chloe and Sophia will work."

It would have been nice if Maya's daughter, Chloe, and granddaughter, Sophia, were with them to hear the last time Diane spoke their names, but Diane thought her suicide would upset them too much.

"Take the jewel and claw when this is over and pass them on with our message," Diane said. "My soul will be back and perhaps I'll have a chance for another vision quest. But if not, at least I'll have today. I will miss you, Maya, until your father and I meet you again."

Diane made a slight yelp before the light left her eyes, but that was all she said. If the jewel and claw had brought her a vision of the future, she didn't pass it on. Perhaps she'd had a vision and simply lost her ability to speak or maybe the vision was unrelated to the killings, something she didn't want to tell. But Maya believed Diane had died before the jewel could work.

They would never know for certain if the circle was broken, but the bear spirit was a powerful force. Maya would pass the jewel and claw on and with it their hope for a better future. Perhaps, at the end of her own life, Maya might glance the future long enough to pass on more specific instructions, but that time was still years away.

Maya would also pass on to her daughter and granddaughter the most important lessons she'd learned all those years ago, that everyone's soul is eternal and that we will all cross the most mysterious border of all, the one between life and death. But, like the muskrats, otters, and turtles that live their lives in both the world above the water's surface and the world below, we can cross back.

About Steve Lindahl

Steve Lindahl's first two novels, *Motherless Soul* and *White Horse Regressions*, were published in 2009 and 2014 by *All Things That Matter Press*. His short fiction has appeared in *Space and Time*, *The Alaska Quarterly*, *The Wisconsin Review*, *Eclipse*, *Ellipsis*, and *Red Wheelbarrow*. He served for five years as an associate editor on the staff of T*he Crescent Review*, a literary magazine he co-founded. He is currently the managing/fiction editor for *Flying South*, a literary magazine sponsored by *Winston-Salem Writers* and is also a board member of that organization.

His Theater Arts background has helped nurture a love for intricate characters in complex situations that is evident in his writing. Steve and his wife Toni live and work together outside of Greensboro, North Carolina. They have two adult children: Nicole and Erik. *Hopatcong Vision Quest* is Steve Lindahl's third novel, his first with *Solstice Publishing*.

Acknowledgments:

I would like to credit my wife, Toni, my daughter, Nicole, and my son, Erik. They give me constant encouragement and are the best critics any author could have. I also want to thank the writers in my critique group: Joni Carter, Robert Shar, and Ray Morrison, talented people who are fun to be around and have improved my work in ways too numerous to list.

Source Materials:

The Delaware Indians: a history, by Clinton Alfred Weslager, published by Rutgers University Press, 1972

The Delaware People, by Allison Lassieur, published by Capstone Press, 2002

The Indians of New Jersey: Dickon among the Indians, by Mark Harrington, published by Rutgers University Press, 1963 (twelfth printing edition)

Religion and Ceremonies of the Lenape, by Mark Harrington, published by Forgotten Books, 2015

The Celtic and Scandinavian religions by J.A. MacCulloch, published by Cosimo Classics, 2005

The Nanticoke Lenni-Lenape, An American Indian Tribe (website) http://www.nanticoke-lenape.info/history.htm

About the Lenapes (website) http://www.lenapelifeways.org/

Lenape Lifeways Videos
        Vision Quest –
https://www.youtube.com/watch?v=U5P1EgQZJHY
        The Lenape Culture - Home Building –
https://www.youtube.com/watch?v=B0jfdunGbFk
        The Lenape Culture – Gathering -
https://www.youtube.com/watch?v=4E01oDW5ssc
        The Lenape Culture – Hunting –
https://www.youtube.com/watch?v=MF_mSVX9JhE
        The Lenape Culture - Catching Fish –
https://www.youtube.com/watch?v=n4on0cNctpE

The Lenape Culture - Dugout Canoes –
https://www.youtube.com/watch?v=W4AckOUlFzs

Official website of the Delaware tribe of Indians –
http://delawaretribe.org/culture-and-language/

Male Native American Names (website)
http://www.20000-
names.com/male_native_american_names.htm

Female Native American Names (website)
http://www.20000-
names.com/female_native_american_names.htm

Sacred Water: The Spiritual Source of Life, by Nathaniel
Altman, published by Hiddenspring, 2002

List of Celtic Deities, (website)
https://en.wikipedia.org/wiki/List_of_Celtic_deities

Boann, (website) https://en.wikipedia.org/wiki/Boann

Water Goddess (website) http://www.goddess-
guide.com/water-goddess.html

Lake Hopatcong (website)
https://en.wikipedia.org/wiki/Lake_Hopatcong

Lake Hopatcong Historical Museum (website) –
http://www.lakehopatconghistory.com/

Lake Hopatcong Yacht Club – http://www.lhyc.com/

Historical Perspective of Lake Hopatcong –
http://www.lakehopatcong.org/history%20of%20Lake%20
Hopatcong.htm

Social Media Links:

Website: http://www.stevelindahl.com/

Blog: www.stevelindahl.blogspot.com

Facebook: https://www.facebook.com/steve.lindahl.3

Twitter: https://twitter.com/lindahlst @lindahlst

Amazon author page: http://www.amazon.com/Steve-Lindahl/e/B0031GLA5Y/ref=sr_ntt_srch_lnk_1?qid=1463052920&sr=1-1

Goodreads author page: https://www.goodreads.com/author/show/3117087.Steve_Lindahl

62614861R00138

Made in the USA
Charleston, SC
14 October 2016